TO HELL AND BACK

A Seven Families Novel

L.B. GILBERT

CREDITS

Cover Design: Covers by Christian
http://coversbychristian.com/

Logo Design: Juan Fernando Garcia
http://www.elblackbat.com/

Editor: Cynthia Shepp
http://www.cynthiashepp.com/

TITLES BY L.B. GILBERT

The Elementals Saga
Discordia, A Free Elementals Story
Fire
Air
Water
Earth

A Shifter's Claim
Kin Selection
Eat You Up
Tooth and Nail

Charmed Legacy Cursed Angel Watchtowers
Forsaken

Writing As Lucy Leroux

The Singular Obsession Series
Making Her His

Confiscating Charlie, A Singular Obsession Novelette
Calen's Captive
Stolen Angel
The Roman's Woman
Save Me, A Singular Obsession Novella
Take Me, A Singular Obsession Prequel Novella
Trick's Trap
Peyton's Price

The Spellbound Regency Series
The Hex, A Free Spellbound Regency Short
Cursed
Black Widow
Haunted

The Rogues and Rescuers Series
Codename Romeo
The Mercenary Next Door
Knight Takes Queen
The Millionaire's Mechanic
Burned Deep - Coming Soon

CHAPTER ONE

Valeria sucked in a breath, fighting through the painful stitch in her side. Blinking to clear her vision, she stumbled down the alley, nearly hitting a dumpster because she was too tired to move out of the way.

Find a place to hide. She had to find a bolt hole for a few hours so she could recover. But she was so tired. Her skin crawled, and Valeria knew she couldn't afford to stop. The hunters were too close.

She looked down at her hands, wincing when they trembled. Fighting them off wasn't going to be possible. Not today. She hadn't slept in over forty-eight hours. Her last meal had been yesterday, a quick fast-food burger. It had been cheap and dry, but she had choked it down because she couldn't wait long enough for them to fix a fresh one, although the guy behind the counter had offered.

Her stomach hurt, and her mouth was dry like sandpaper.

I need just one small safe place. A closet, a basement. Literally any place she could hole up for a few days. Hell, at this point, she'd take a couple of hours.

The alleyway abruptly spilled out onto a shop-lined street. Valeria swore under her breath as she took in the fashionable people milling around, shopping and having brunch. There were too many. Her days of melting into a crowd and disappearing were over.

These hunter *cabrones* had been on her trail for weeks. It was as if all the lessons her mother had taught her were meaningless. No matter what Valeria did or where she hid, they always found her. After weeks of relentless pursuit, she was running on empty, the very last dregs of her reserve gone.

A man in a tight V-neck t-shirt accidentally brushed against her. She jerked to the side to avoid touching his bare skin, then overcorrected so wildly that she almost fell. The stranger grunted and walked on, dismissing her as one of the city's many mentally ill derelicts.

Actually, he probably thought you were drunk.

But Valeria didn't care. Her caution was warranted. All it would take was one hunter knocking against her in a crowded street and they could stick her with a pin like a government spy taking down a target. Only this pin wouldn't be laced with radioactive poison. That would only kill her.

Her pursuers wanted her alive.

Skirting the crowd, she scanned the various storefronts for a decent hiding place. A small jewelry store—*no.* An empty gallery with seascapes on the walls—*also no.* A crowded café—a big *hell no.*

Valeria was almost at the end of the block when she saw a man wearing a white shirt and beige pants. The telltale glitter of a gold cross strung around his neck winked at her, a tiny warning that said she wasn't going to get out of this without a fight.

The stranger didn't stand out. Anyone else paying attention would only see an average middle-aged man, someone who fit in working at a bank or an insurance company. He didn't look like the type who sacrificed small animals in blood-laced rituals yet still wore his religion on his sleeve. But that was who and what he was. Valeria knew his face. He was one of the hunters and he was just across the street, scanning the crowd as intently as she was.

Acting on instinct, she ducked into the first doorway she saw. After the bright sunlight outside, it took a minute for her eyes to adjust.

The store was cramped and dusty. High wooden shelves were set out with narrow lanes in between, each covered with a random assortment of objects—porcelain plates, music boxes, small statuettes. The walking space was obstructed by end tables, planters, and the occasional oversized vase.

Most of the light in the store was provided by the high transom windows visible just over the jumble of furniture and crowded shelves. Heavier pieces were lined against the walls, including a tall grandfather clock and chest that obscured the storefront window.

If the hunter had seen her, she'd only have seconds before he spotted her again. Fighting the inevitable more out of habit than will, Valeria retreated further into the store, scanning the shelves for a passable weapon. She picked up a small statue, but put it back down in favor of an ornate fireplace poker she tripped over.

The ornate grip was uncomfortable, but Valeria felt a surge of renewed strength. It was false bravado, but she squeezed the handle anyway, crouching so the top of her head was below the highest shelf.

Minutes crawled by, but the jangly bell attached to the door remained silent. Her knees were aching when she finally relaxed enough to stand.

Catching a blur of movement out of the corner of her eye, she parted her lips to scream. Reacting with sluggish and shaky movements, she reached for her weapon before realizing she was staring at herself.

Stupid mirror. Her reflection had almost given her a heart attack. Giving herself a little shake, she slumped, lowering the poker. The oval, antique looking glass was hazy, her bedraggled reflection dark and streaky.

More than likely, it was backed with silver. *So, you will see your enemy, the vampire, and know who they are...* Her mother's voice was so clear in her mind it was almost as if she was in the same room.

Ravenna had taught her about magic and the metals that disrupted it. Platinum was the best but too expensive, so silver was the most common. Gold would also work in a pinch, but anything gold was as out of her reach as platinum.

No one backed mirrors in silver anymore, which must have been a relief to the vampire population.

Swaying, she reached out to steady herself by holding the frame. *Mierda.* She looked like death warmed over. Her hair was lanky and in greasy clumps, her cheeks sunken from too many missed meals. She could probably fit all her belongings in the bags under her eyes.

Valeria must have been more tired than she thought because the image in the mirror wavered. Eyes watering, she blinked to clear them, but the image only darkened, swirling as if there were a storm trapped inside. A shadow coalesced and a man appeared out of the depths, his dark eyes burning as if he were staring through her.

Whirling around, she raised the poker, ready to make a desperate last stand against this new assailant, but there was no one there. Her head snapped back to the mirror.

The man was still there in the reflection. *It's official. I've gone mad.*

Scrubbing her face, Valeria tried to make the apparition go away. But the stubborn hallucination stayed right where it was. Lips parting, she stepped closer to the darkened surface of the mirror. She wasn't reflected at all anymore. There was only the muscular, dark-haired stranger with those coal-colored eyes that seemed to glint with flecks of glowing red and orange.

Who had eyes like that?

Valeria stared at the warrior, mesmerized. And that was what he was—a fighter. It was in every line of his body, in the harshly carved lines of his face. The intensity of that ember-filled gaze made her shiver.

The man flickered suddenly. A swirl of wings and scales made her eyes water before fire flowed over the surface of the mirror. But it was gone before she was sure of it. The man snapped back into focus once more, his unyielding expression making her muscles tense in an instinctive fight-or-flight response.

If this man were real, Valeria knew she had to stay far away from him. He was no one she wanted to meet.

But then the warrior turned to stare directly at her. Blood draining from her face Valeria flinched, throwing her arms up into the air. But she didn't accidentally strike anyone. The mirror wasn't revealing a cloaked hunter. She was alone.

Was it some sort of video feed? Valeria waved a hand in front of her. The man in the mirror didn't react to the movement.

Okay, so this was a non-interactive hallucination. She could handle that. Eating her last energy bar might be enough to get rid of him. On that note, her stomach rumbled. Disregarding the extraordinary in favor of the mundane, she dug through her pockets for the high-calorie nutrition bar.

That act may have broken the spell. Between one blink and the next, the outlandish vision disappeared, leaving the overcrowded junk shop in its place.

CHAPTER TWO

Valeria chewed her energy bar thoughtfully, staring at the mirror. Could the piece be haunted? The stranger may have just been an afterimage of the previous owner. A fiery death could have explained the flames.

And what about the wings and scales?

Disregarding the bits of the vision that didn't fit with that neat explanation, Valeria turned her back on the mirror. She jerked her jacket closed, trying to shut away the memory of those eyes that seemed to strip away her soul.

"Hello," a voice called out. A lanky, long-limbed man came out of a door marked '*Office*'. Unkempt but clean, he was wearing a checkered sweater vest that had seen better days. The man looked harmless, but his presence rubbed her the wrong way, as if she'd bitten tinfoil.

Not completely human. Valeria backed up a step, surreptitiously checking the mirror, but the outlandish vision didn't reappear. The only thing behind her was the dusty interior of the shop.

"Hello," she murmured as the shopkeeper came to a stop a respectable distance away.

"Welcome to Charmed Antiques and Wicca Emporium," he said.

She thumbed at the sign painted on the glass partially obscured by a set of shelves. "I thought it was just antiques."

The shopkeeper gave her a determined smile. "We're under new management. I'm Viz—the new manager."

He gestured for her to follow him. One aisle over, the clutter thinned out, the wooden shelf replaced by a glass one. An assortment of crystals, vials, and dried herbs had been laid out into either neat circles or rows.

An alarm bell rang in the back of her mind. Had she known this was the shop of a non-human practitioner, she would have chosen some other place else to hide.

Stay calm. Just because you know what he is doesn't mean he knows what you are.

"Oh, um, thanks. But I'm just browsing," she murmured, schooling her features into passivity.

It was unlikely he was connected to the hunters. As long as she didn't tip her hand, she'd be able to hole up here long enough for her pursuers to move on.

"No problem," Viz said. "Let me know if there's anything you need. We have a lovely new assortment of rune stones just in. I haven't even had time to take them out of the box."

"Maybe next time," she murmured.

Valeria had around twenty dollars left to her name, and she needed it for food. Not that she would have ever wasted money on something as frivolous as rune stones, even during one of those brief lulls where she hadn't been chased and had been settled enough to work a regular job.

Waitressing had been hard on her feet, but it had paid for a cheap studio apartment once upon a time. Having spent more time in shelters and cut-rate hotels, her memories of the cramped studio were tinted in a rosy light, the memories precious to her. It had been the only place she'd lived that was totally her own, the memories of houses and apartments she shared with her mother too hazy to count.

"We also have a complete assortment of essential oils and diffusers if that is more your speed."

Valeria lifted a shoulder noncommittally. "I'll let you know."

She and Viz stared at each other for an awkward moment before he inclined his head, conceding a reluctant defeat. "All right then. If you change your mind, just holler."

His yellow teeth flashed before he retreated behind the counter.

Valeria ducked her head, then drifted back to the crowded section of the store. Keeping an eye on the grandfather clock—the only one of dozens of timepieces that actually kept the right time—she pretended to browse, picking up and discarding random objects.

She was about to pick up a pyramid-shaped paperweight with Celtic symbols on it when the taste of iron flooded her mouth. Snapping her hand back, Valeria wiped it on her pants.

Definitely don't touch that one.

Turning the corner, she peeked out of the bit of window visible behind a ramshackle chest. Only a small section of the street was visible, but she believed that crowd had thinned, the lunch hour had passed. However, there was no way of knowing if it was truly safe. She couldn't see the sidewalk in front of the door. For all she knew, the hunters could be lying in wait.

And she couldn't hide here forever. Valeria had eaten her last granola bar, but it had done little to ease the hunger pangs tearing strips out of her stomach. Salivating, she recalled there was a taco shop a few blocks from here with a two-for-one special. It was her least favorite chain, but beggars couldn't be choosers.

She headed to the door when a dull gleam caught her eye. Leaning forward, she spotted the blade in the wide-mouthed vase holding half-a-dozen letter openers. It was a dull, knock-off athame made of modern steel. But with a little sharpening, it would be a lethal last-minute surprise for any hunter stupid enough to lay his hands on her.

Valeria stumbled, catching herself on the shelf. A few things were rearranged in the process, and the athame fell into her backpack. She headed to the door, pausing only long enough to nod politely at Viz.

She wanted to run out the door, but she forced herself to walk. Running while wearing anything but workout gear was the best way to call attention to herself, something she needed to avoid at all costs.

The long wait in the antique store had failed. She felt the hunter's eyes on her before she saw him. Valeria didn't bother to search the crowd. Too weak to fight, she ran.

She ended up on the pier. Exhausted, starving, and out of options, she slipped over the edge into the icy water—and nearly drowned.

Something tight spiraled into a ball on her back, squeezing into a knot. The air left her lungs, and she sank completely under the surface, saltwater filling her mouth. The bonds of the knot twisted so hard that they broke, and she was suddenly free. Kicking to the surface, she gasped for air.

Of course. She was an idiot. Valeria had been marked. She didn't know when or how, but a hunter had somehow gotten close enough to put a tracking hex on her, giving the asshole enough time to gather reinforcements so they could overwhelm her with numbers.

Those spells were notoriously hard to get right, especially when used against a witch. Too weak—and the spell dissipated. Too much juice—and the hexee discovered and undid it. It was as easy as taking a dip in the ocean or rubbing table salt on her body in the shower. Water alone might have been enough, but add salt and the spell didn't stand a chance.

She knew this, but she hadn't even thought to check herself for a hex. Now she was freezing to death in the—wait... what ocean was this?

The Pacific. She was in Los Angeles. Okay, maybe she wouldn't freeze to death. It just felt that way because she was weak and hungry.

Valeria waited as long as she could before crawling up through the gently lapping surf to the beach above. Staying out of the lights, she walked up and down the beach until she was dry enough to blend in with the crowd. This time, no one followed her.

VIZ HOBBES WAITED until the little witch had left to burst around the counter. He locked the door and then half-ran, half-jumped to the mirror in the back.

He ran his hands over ornate metal studded with semiprecious stones, peering into the cloudy depths. Despite its age, the piece wasn't worth much. A couple of hundred dollars at most for the stones and metal, or so his appraiser had said.

But Henry, his uncle and the relative he'd inherited the store from, had refused to sell it for anything less than what he thought it was worth. That amount varied wildly—anything from a cool hundred G's up to a million dollars.

"It's the legend behind it," Henry had said more than once. "That is what makes it priceless."

However, no matter how hard Viz racked his brain, he couldn't remember what that legend was. But he hadn't imagined that huge, glowing eye that had appeared as the girl turned his way. It winked shut and disappeared a second later, but he *had* seen it. What was more, he could see it again thanks to his uncle's planning and foresight.

Rubbing his hands together, Viz went back to the manager's office, rewinding the security footage from the camera hidden in the pile of vintage cameras—a little joke his uncle had chortled about when he'd told Viz about it.

Almost jumping with excitement, he sat in front of the outdated computer and brought up the camera feed, rewinding until he got to the girl's departure. As suspected, she had stolen something. She had been very slick about it, and the camera hadn't caught the actual theft, but one of the letter openers was gone, so he knew it had happened.

She was rather good, too. Without the camera, he would never have realized.

But that isn't why you are looking through this, he reminded himself. Viz held his breath, rewinding it to the point where he appeared in front of the girl.

Holy shit, he was right. There was a huge eye in the mirror! A little more rewinding, and he sat back. The flame and that wing—*in those colors*. He shuddered.

Viz had been hoping to make some money on this. When an artifact as old as that mirror reacted, there was always *someone* willing to pay for the information. But that had been when he thought it would be one of the big seven he'd be dealing with, a dangerous enough proposition on its own.

But now he knew who the main party of interest would be, and he suddenly wasn't sure if it was worth it.

CHAPTER THREE

Rhys topped the rise and stopped, crossing his arms as he watched his men go through their training routine. They were too far to see him, so he let a small smile grace his features as Jerik slammed the heavier Tanik against the ground.

"He's coming along nicely," Naveen, his second, commented, coming to stand next to him.

Rhys murmured his agreement. Jerik was the youngest member of the clan, now over two dozen strong. But the strength of the Draconai Imperia had never lain in numbers. Each one of his dragons was a lethal disciplined warrior, capable of laying waste to an entire city. Not that they did that anymore. It would have violated the treaty they signed to stay in this world.

Visions of blood and war-ravaged landscapes flickered across his mind, but he ruthlessly shut them down. He did not allow the past to shackle him, as his predecessor had.

Rhys hadn't been the clan leader when his people came to Earth. That responsibility had belonged to Markus. But his mentor hadn't been able to adapt to life on Earth. Compared to their birthplace, this realm was lush and comfortable—too comfortable for warriors like them.

But they had to adapt. Markus had never understood that. His mind had been frozen in an unending war. Rhys' soul had lived in that place for a long time, too, but once they had won, he'd forced himself to let it go. Because winning the war had cost them everything.

Humans called it a pyrrhic victory when the price of triumph was so high it may as well have been defeat.

Victory had cost them their home. Now that Rhys was the head of the clan, he would not allow them to lose another. Ever vigilant, the remaining members of the Draconai Imperia trained for battle ceaselessly, sharpening their skills against each other and the few predators that escaped the nets of the Elementals, the female enforcers of supernatural order on this world. Not that they advertised this fact to that small band of women.

They probably know of the monsters we hunt anyway. The creature they called Mother, the creator and founder of this world, kept them wellinformed. It was of little consequence. As long his people abided by their rules, the two groups avoided each other, giving him the autonomy to govern his people as he saw fit.

Turning to Naveen, he got the bi-weekly report on internal clan matters. "Sanaa has invited the entire clan to her home the week after next for the celebration," his second informed him.

Rhys paused, his hard features softening a fraction. "How is she?"

"Quite well," his second informed him. "As are the babes according to the healer."

A skitter of nerves crawled up his spine. Sanaa, one of the few females of the clan, had taken a mate ten years ago. The male, an Earth-born bear shifter, was a quiet and careful man who'd won his trust—after a few years. Neither group was particularly fertile, so they took no precautions against conception. Many years had passed before Sanaa conceived, but, when she did, she was blessed with two babes.

It was one of the reasons they had chosen to stay on Earth as refugees, rather than searching out an uninhabited planet they could rule. If their species were to survive, they needed to breed. Their surviving numbers were not large enough to found a healthy population. But humans were abundant and as the old myths told them, they were biologically compatible.

More than one dragon had come to Earth to find their mate back when travel between realms had been possible. His kind had courted their women, taking the females back to their homeland after winning them. Humans still told stories about those females, but they twisted them into tales of horror. In those dark legends, the women ended up as food, instead of living out their lives as cosseted and treasured mates.

Rumor had it he had a human ancestor in his lineage, but it was so far back in his history as to be of no consequence.

Compared to a dragon's complex nature, human biology was quite simple. It was one of the curious details about them. The genes that governed growth, reproduction, and aging were basic and unspecialized. That primitiveness gave them plasticity. Humans and their magically adept derivatives, shifters like Tom, were almost a blank slate. That made them biologically compatible with any number of more complex lifeforms...namely his dragons.

It had been his intention for all his clan members to take a life mate, but few had chosen partners. Despite having access to a large population of compatible females, their possessive and inflexible natures would settle for nothing less than a true mating. Sanaa and a few others had gotten lucky. The rest were still waiting.

But not you. His chance had come and gone.

Rhys pushed away that thought, crushing it in an imaginary vice for good measure. "We will clear the schedule once the birthing starts," he announced.

The entire clan had been anticipating this since Sanaa's scent had changed, signaling her pregnancy. They would all want to be there. Releasing them from their training regimen was the least he could do.

"Actually, Sanaa wants to have us over beforehand."

"Before?" Rhys frowned.

Naveen shrugged. "According to Tom, it's traditional. He calls it a baby shower. We are to bring gifts."

Rhys sniffed. "What greater gift does he desire than our acceptance of him in our clan?"

"That's what I told him. He looked at me as if I were crazy." Naveen snickered. "I'm not sure he sees the value for the prize it is. He said as much—that he loves his mate and therefore 'puts up' with the rest of us."

Rhys was tempted to 'put up' a few things in Tom's orifices, but given the man was about to have his hands full corralling two baby dragon shifters, Rhys decided to let the insult slide.

"Anyway, Tom clarified," Naveen continued. "The gifts are for the babes—blankets, infant-sized clothing, and instruments of play. According to a website I read, these gifts are meant to help the parents get ready for the arrival of the infants."

"Oh." Rhys considered that. "A useful tradition."

"I thought so, too."

Dragons did give gifts after the birth of a babe—jewels or gold were customary. But this was a holdover from the old world, when a pregnant female was hidden away in an aerie, far from any other dragons that weren't of the father's bloodline. Non-family members couldn't see a babe until it could fly, usually once it was a few years old. Everything was going to be different now.

"What is the most expensive item they need?" Rhys asked.

"Tom mentioned a stroller with twin cabs to wheel the children about."

"That will be my gift," Rhys declared. "What will you buy?"

Naveen drew a notepad from his pocket. "Something called a diaper genie."

Rhys growled low in his throat, and Naveen looked up. "Not a real djinn of course. It's just a brand name."

Rhys grunted. How foolish of the human world to name a baby product after such deadly creatures. But then, the choices of what Naveen called 'the marketing machine' of this world never ceased to amaze him.

The first time he'd come across a store display of the beverage called 'Dr. Pepper' had been a moment of great confusion.

"Keep me updated on this event," he ordered, remembering the near-miss he'd had then, his honor demanding he smash the bottle of liquified physician before the locals imbibed the poor man. "We don't want Sanaa to overexert herself observing Tom's traditions."

Naveen straightened, inclining his head before departing. Rhys watched his wing, what the Drak's called a squadron, a bit longer before shifting. Bunching his muscles, he took to the sky, flying high over the sea of pines.

His clan had chosen the Canadian Rockies as their home, mainly because it echoed the savagely rocky vistas of their homeworld, albeit a much greener version. Also, the ruggedness of the terrain promised humans would keep their distance. This was becoming less true in this age of satellites and air jets. But after the pioneering efforts of Aldasoro and Wright brothers in flight, Rhys had seen the writing on the wall. He'd taken steps to protect their territory.

The members of the clan had lost most of their fortunes when they abandoned their world, so they had been forced to rebuild them on Earth.

However, if there was one thing dragons excelled at, it was hunting treasure. Their senses were attuned to the task. He could smell gold and taste the tang of precious stones in the air whenever he was near. After the financial markets were created, it was easy enough to invest what they had found. Making money was a gift. Buying their own satellites to protect their skies, occupying the only available orbital paths, had been simpler than shooting down all the others that passed overhead.

Rhys landed in front of his home. Made of massive redwood logs and beams he'd harvested at the turn of the century, he'd crafted a sprawling three-story lodge slash mansion.

It had started as a small one-room cabin, one that he'd built with his own two hands. Over the years, he'd added to it, a room at a time. Occasionally, he tore parts down to add a picture window and, more recently, a deck without rails that wrapped around the entire third story.

He landed there, angling his wings to sweep off the dry leaves and pine needles that had fallen on the wooden surface. *Better than a broom,* he thought as he shifted back to two legs. He crossed the freshly sealed wooden boards before throwing open the doors to his office.

The sunlit space sparkled as he moved. Rhys stroked one of the many dragons responsible for the glittering gleam.

The lavishly jeweled beasts graced every table and shelf in the room. Naveen had given him the first one as a joke, amused that so many human artists were enamored of their winged form.

But Rhys had taken a liking to the curiosities. His collection spread over three rooms with his favorite specimen, the obsidian with ruby eyes, sitting next to a massive four-poster bed in his private chambers.

Other treasures glinted in the light—a golden cross recovered from a sunken vessel, a ruby-encrusted goblet found in the basement of an abandoned castle, and a shelf of golden plates scavenged from the ruins of Pompeii.

He weaved in between the tables and shelves, dropping a fifty-nine-carat sapphire he'd been carrying around in his pocket into one of the open chests flanking his desk. Sitting in the custom-made leather chair, he booted the state-of-the-art computer Naveen had recently upgraded.

The clan made it a point to embrace human technology. They also owned a significant amount of property and businesses. According to the treaty they had signed, they had the right to invest in themselves so long as their activities didn't harm the humans they employed.

It was harder than it sounded, like constantly having to check he wasn't walking on ants. But he did it because money meant security for his people and being ethical meant avoiding scrutiny.

He threw himself into today's work, checking on the clan's investment concerns. Such an important task was divided among three of his people, but Rhys always double-checked their work and frequently made significant financial moves on his own.

However, today the usually enjoyable task felt monotonous, and he was glad for the distraction of an email alert from one of the junior clan members. At least until he opened it.

Rhys took one look and hissed, just barely avoiding melting the screen with a stream of liquid fire at the grainy camera still embedded in the text. Trembling violently, he pushed his chair away from the desk until it banged into the glass and wood wall behind him.

It can't be her.

How was this possible? Rhys closed his eyes, his heart pounding faster than it had in over three hundred years. The woman on the screen was not *her. She* had been in her grave for centuries. This female simply looked like her.

It's not the first time you've run across a woman who bore a resemblance strong enough to give you pause. But this one...she was uncanny.

Giving himself a hard shake, Rhys forced himself to take a second look. He sat down, then pulled the oversized computer monitor closer to him. He'd overlooked the small play icon in the middle. It was a video file.

Stiffening his jaw, he moved the cursor and pressed play. His breath shortened as the stranger moved through a crowded store with *her* grace and *her* facial expressions.

What the hell was this?

And then the woman stepped in front of a large oval mirror. Rhys saw the surface of the mirror flicker before his image appeared. He watched the rest of the video, muscles rigid, the same breath stuck in his chest for so long it started to burn.

When the movie was over, he replayed it over and over again. After the tenth replay, he saw the message Jerik had written at the bottom of the email.

CANAAN, one of our informants, heard about a Fae male attempting to reach out to all the dragon shifter groups on Earth, offering to barter some 'juicy information' in the hope of a reward. He contacted the merchant, who sent him a still of this video, where our clan colors were identified from your wings in the mirror. He contacted me, and I authorized a payment to obtain the rest of the file.

Once he saw it, our informant sought out the Fae and is currently sitting on him at his shop. As far as we know, our clan is the only one to receive the entire file, but Canaan can't guarantee that other interested parties hadn't intercepted it.

OTHER INTERESTED PARTIES?

Those final words jarred him out of his stasis. He stalked to the door, throwing open the double doors to yell at the top of his lungs, "Get me Jerik. *Now*."

CHAPTER FOUR

The thin Fae male was sweating so much that he could probably slide out of his restraints by now. Rhys kept his disgust off his face, intent on transmitting only threats and intimidation.

"You said the video was recorded how long ago?" he asked.

"It's been over a week—a-almost two," Viz, the owner, stammered.

He was holding his hat, twisting the ivy cap into a shapeless mess. The sweaty little Fae stared up at the trio of dragons from the small wooden chair in the back of the antique emporium as if expecting to be eaten at any moment. Every so often, he would cast a pleading glance at Canaan, the wolf shifter who'd brought them the information.

But Canaan propped against the wall, his face impassive. There would be no help from that quarter.

Crossing his thick arms, Rhys growled, bringing the nervous man's attention back to him. "Was she alone?" he asked.

"Yes, um, she was," Viz answered, his Adam's apple bobbing. He gestured to Canaan. "Although, as I mentioned to your almost-as-tall friend there, the witch kept watching the door as if she were waiting for someone."

Rhys blinked. "She was a witch? You're certain?"

The male nodded, sitting up a little straighter. "Yes. She just had that vibe. Also, I noticed something after I re-watched the security footage of her browsing. Everything she picked up was magically charged."

"What things?" Rhys' face must have darkened because Viz leaned back as if trying to get farther away from him.

"Nothing harmful," the Fae rushed to say. "Just a bunch of trinkets. They're mostly harmless. But rest assured, I keep all the truly dangerous items in the back. I've got a genuine Burgess hat pin if you're interested. It's got a diamond—"

"Viz," Canaan interrupted from the door, his tone a warning. "I suggest you focus."

The Fae man bobbed his head, swallowing heavily. "Sure, sure. Anyway, even though she picked up a lot of charged stuff, the only thing the girl left with was a harmless knife."

Rhys held up a hand. "Wait. She *stole* something?"

The sweaty stick man was mistaken. The girl he had known would never have done such a thing, not in a million years.

Who was this female who walked into a shop and *robbed it*? Because that wasn't the nature of the woman he'd loved, the one whose loss had destroyed him.

"But you're certain she was a witch?" Jerik asked, returning to the crux of the matter. H gestured to the crowded shelves beyond the doorway. "There are many mystically tainted objects out there. Her choices could have been simple chance."

"True." Viz's head bobbed up and down again. "However, there was the fact she saw the vision in the mirror at the start and stayed a fair amount of time afterward. A human would have run out of here."

"The sweaty stick man is correct," Naveen murmured, echoing Rhys' impression of the shopkeeper. "Normal humans reject the proof of the supernatural. Nine out of ten would have left right after."

As if on cue, they glanced behind the Fae man. Someone had removed the mirror from the showroom floor and placed it on a table against the wall.

"Bring it here," Rhys ordered.

Viz scrambled up to retrieve the looking glass. He appeared to struggle with its weight. Trying not to roll his eyes, Rhys plucked it out of his arms with one hand. It was heavier than it looked, indicating the frame was metal, but it was still light enough that any reasonably sized male—even this poor specimen—should have been able to carry it without effort.

"Tell me about this," he ordered.

"Oh, uh yes, I can do that," Viz said, straightening. "Well, I can tell you what I know. I searched for my uncle's logs after she left. He made an entry on every item in the store—the potentially valuable ones, anyway."

Viz twisted in his chair, the cheap polyester making a wrenching squeaking sound on the plastic-covered cushion. "It's in that one on the top, the page with the receipt as a bookmark."

Jerik handed him the book in question. Rhys opened it to the relevant page, unsure what to expect. "It's just a list of names."

Written two by two, the list extended down most of a single page.

"Yeah, I get it's not super informative," Viz apologized. "I don't recognize any. A few came up in Google, but there was nothing informative there. It could have been matching randomly to people with the same name."

Rhys and his men exchanged looks. Wordlessly, Jerik took the mirror and small book before leaving after a military-grade bow.

"You may go tend to your shop. We have some things to discuss," Rhys said, dismissing the shopkeeper, who scrambled up.

The moist man paused. "Er...about payment?

Rhys stared down at the man. Viz gulped, raising his arms. "Never mind. We can talk about it later," he said, bowing and backing away, retreating to the front of the store.

He turned to his second. "She has a two-week head start. Cut the patrol around our territory to three dragons. I want you to get everyone else down here. Start canvassing the local businesses. And check if this municipality has cameras installed here. Buy the footage if you have to. I want her found yesterday."

Naveen nodded once, then rushed to carry out his orders.

Rhys went back to the main part of the store, going over the spots where the woman had lingered, but there was no trace of her scent on anything.

It's not her, he told himself for the millionth time.

But that didn't stop him from joining his men in the search.

A FEW DAYS LATER, Rhys walked to the window on the twentieth floor of the Caislean Hotel, the most luxurious accommodation in the city of the Angels.

He snorted. Again, the absurdity of Earth's naming conventions struck him anew. He crossed his arms, staring down at the urban sprawl.

Was she down there somewhere? Or had the mysterious witch in the security footage moved on?

Naveen came up beside him. Despite the fact he had been walking the streets most of the night, his second was alert, his dark ascetic face showing no signs of fatigue.

"Sanaa has gone into labor."

Rhys groaned, letting himself bend forward to hit the glass with his forehead. It was a moment of weakness he would have never allowed in front of the junior members of his clan. But this was Naveen, his most trusted lieutenant.

"This is insanity." He raised his head. "We need to stop this point-less search and go back to our territory. I need to return before the birth."

Naveen reached out to grasp his upper arm. "Sanaa understands," he said. "After what happened all those years ago—"

"It's not Gabrielle," Rhys snapped.

Naveen's lips compressed.

He cleared his throat. "I apologize. I am losing sleep over this, and I feel like a fool. We've been turning this city over, yet there's no sign of this woman—a witch who is not Gabrielle."

Gabrielle was in her grave, and she had been for more years than days he'd known her.

Rhys used to visit that grave before he'd stopped punishing himself. He hadn't been there in hundreds of years.

And yet, a woman with a passing resemblance appeared and he lost his mind and forgot his duty to his clan.

A hint of amusement touched Naveen's face. "As Tom has repeat-edly mentioned, the only members of the clan who need to be at the birth are Sanaa, him, and the midwife. No one will begrudge your absence under the circumstances."

"And what if I'm chasing a ghost?"

Naveen held up a sheath of papers he hadn't noticed. "I don't think you are," he said, handing him the documents. "These are the results of the search Jerik had run on the names the former owner of the antique store had listed on the mirror's entry. It's all families that used to own the mirror. The piece has a long history."

"I assumed as much," Rhys said, looking over the list of names and the details noted beside each.

Naveen inclined his head. "Yes. Much still needs to be unearthed. But I found it interesting that Hobbes chose to list two names from each family—mostly married couples."

Cynicism twisted Rhys' face. "So, it is not enough that we have to entertain the possibility of reincarnation, but now we're supposed to accept that the looking glass has matchmaking properties?"

Wisely, Naveen simply shrugged.

"I'll just set these here," he said, dropping the papers on the suite's coffee table. With a bow, he departed, leaving Rhys alone.

He turned back to the window, wishing the vista were of the wild corner of land they'd claimed of their own. But despite what he'd said to Naveen, Rhys couldn't leave this city, not until he'd had some sign or discovered where the girl in the video had gone.

If it were Gabrielle reborn...

She had left him once. He would not allow it to happen a second time.

CHAPTER FIVE

Rhys inhaled deeply, stalking up the stairs of the condemned building as the lightest trace of jasmine and amber teased his nose. The moist fetidness in the air was making it difficult to pick out the girl's scent. The signature was unfamiliar, but he recognized it instinctively.

His quarry had been here mere hours ago.

The idea made him angry, not because he had missed her—*again*—but that she had been here at all. This was a place for the forgotten, a derelict building where humans squatted because they had nowhere else to go.

And the woman is one.

He could taste the fire in his mouth as his nose wrinkled at a particularly unpleasant scent. The flames wanted out, eager for him to burn something down in cathartic release. But Rhys tamped the impulse down. He couldn't afford to lose control, not when he was so close.

His people had scoured the city, asking shop owners for whatever security footage they had from the day she'd been spotted. Between the banks and traffic cameras Jerik was able to hack, Rhys now had dozens of photos and video snippets of his mystery woman.

He had studied the pictures from every angle, trying to find one where she didn't resemble the lost mate burned into his memory, but soon conceded defeat. Every feature, every line of her body, was the same. Rhys could find no flaw, at least not on camera. Which made him all the more determined to find her in real life. Surely the illusion would fall apart once he had the flesh-and-blood woman in front of him.

Her scent was different, he reminded himself.

Poring over the images had brought something else to his attention. He wasn't the only one looking for her.

A camera outside a gas station had caught the woman. Ten minutes later, two men had paused in the same spot, their manner and bearing that of hunters. The same pair were spotted a second time, following soon after the woman passed a bank ATM camera several miles from the gas station.

After he realized they weren't the only ones searching, his people went back over the footage, identifying at least four other individuals, three men and one woman, in pursuit of the same quarry. Each of the strangers made an effort to present a benign appearance, dressing to blend in with the mostly human populace of the area. But Rhys could recognize the hard edge and experience of the hunt in their gaze and movements.

Rhys could not allow them to find her, but he knew he might not have a chance to get there first. However, having his adversary's faces gave him another way to find the witch. He ordered his men to track the hunters, following them in case they stumbled on the girl before him. Meanwhile, he joined the search, taking the location of their most recent sighting as a starting point.

That had brought him here. The building was new by his standards, but cheaply constructed with rows of tiny rooms laid out in straight lines. From the uninspired layout, he assumed it was meant to be offices, but the lack of open spaces made it claustrophobic, even in his two-legged form.

The stair under him creaked ominously under his weight. Rhys shot it a disapproving glance.

The structure was a recent foreclosure, but he couldn't tell from the condition. Given the stained and moldy drywall, he'd have expected the building to have been abandoned for multiple decades instead of just one. The shoddy construction had accelerated the rate of disrepair.

He went from room to room, eliminating possibilities. Many of those cramped spaces were occupied, but one look at his large, muscled form, and even the more reckless vagrants held their ground or hid instead of attacking him.

Her room was on the second floor. Rhys walked inside and staggered, the concentration of her scent in one place a veritable bombardment to his olfactory sense.

Except for discarded fast-food wrappers, the room was empty. She had left nothing he could use to pass her scent to the others, but it didn't matter. Her perfume was burned into his brain now. And Rhys had never lost a target.

VALERIA LIMPED UP THE ROAD, aware the knife wound on her stomach had opened.

It's a scratch, she assured herself. Yes, it was long, but it was shallow. If she could get a hold of tape or super glue, she could fix it.

The trio of witches had ambushed her early this morning, right after she'd exited a convenience store with a day-old donut and a coffee she had microwaved after finding it ice cold.

Thinking on her feet, she had thrown the hot coffee in the face of the largest witch, elbowing the second one before tripping him. But the third had grabbed her from behind, knocking her head against the outer wall of the store before she could twist away and elbow the assailant in the throat.

She hadn't even been aware that the woman had slashed her until she was several blocks away. Valeria had found an out-of-the-way bench in a small park where she had rested most of the day, but sundown had forced her up to find someplace warmer.

Despite being chilled to the bone, Valeria slowed her steps. Moving too fast kept stretching the cut and would only accelerate the bleeding.

She walked east, away from the cold winds coming off the Pacific. Maybe she'd find a fast-food place, an old one that didn't have those keypads on their bathrooms. It would be warm, and she could patch herself up.

But Valeria hadn't found a safe haven. The constant prickles up her spine pushed her on until she stumbled with exhaustion, her vision darkening with every step.

Blinking, she stopped and rested against a dumpster as the world spun around her. At the mouth of the alley, a trio of blurred forms appeared, and her shoulders slumped in defeat. Even if she had the energy to run, the blood trail would lead them right to her.

Still can't give up. She had been fighting and running so long she didn't know how to stop, even when she had nothing left.

Valeria pushed her soles against the asphalt, forcing her heavy muscles to move. But it felt as if each of her limbs weighed a thousand pounds. Somehow, she made it to the middle of the alley.

Reaching inside, she tried desperately to spark her magic, but it was like trying to pull a tree branch through a lake of mud. It finally lit with a weak anemic flame, one that threatened to go out as she swayed on her feet.

The trio of assailants fanned out in front of her. She could feel their magic welling, bouncing around inside her. Pushing it down, she tried to taste it, but they were coming at her too quickly for her talent to decipher it, so she pushed out, trying to drive them back with raw, unfinished power.

It was a difficult draining move, but Valeria was out of options. She hit out blindly, managing to strike the middle assailant. He fell back, his face spurting blood. Someone screamed, and she fell as arms reached out, grabbing at the air where she had just been. But she'd forgotten about the third man. Between one blink and the next, she lost sight of him. However, he made his presence known with a brutal kick to her back that sent a wave of pain so intense over her that she momentarily blacked out.

Vision blinking in and out, she saw her attackers standing over her. The triumph mingled with rage twisted their innocuous, average-looking faces into monstrous masks.

The man with the cross was the closest. She struck out a second time, but the force of it was much weaker. Cross man staggered back, putting a hand to his face, but her other attacker shook it off. He pulled his leg back as if to kick her, but then he and his partner were gone, replaced by a wall of flame and a roar of sound so loud her ears shut down.

Squeezing her eyes closed, Valeria held her breath until the blistering heat dissipated. Cracking her eyelids open, she saw the night sky, the lights of the city masking all celestial bodies but the moon.

Muscles trembling, she sat up. The alley was empty. Her attackers were gone. In their place were two greasy streaks of soot, both smoking ominously. There was no sign of the third man, the one she'd hit.

The nape of her neck prickled. Someone was watching her. Pulling herself together with slow, painful movements, she turned around to face a mountain of a man with coal-black hair and eyes that burned with the fires of hell.

"Perfect," she mumbled. "Just freaking perfect."

This had happened once before when a small coven had chased her in the Appalachian foothills. She had been close to getting captured. Then, a bounty hunter working for someone else had stepped in and taken them out for her, only for him to break his leg in the rough terrain when he misjudged a jump. It had been sheer dumb luck that she'd gotten away, but Valeria still relived the moment in her dreams.

The corner of the man's lip turned up, and Valeria had to fight the urge to smack the smug smile off the stranger's brutally handsome face. Touching him at all would be a huge mistake. This wasn't a dumb shifter tracking her. She knew it instinctively.

"I didn't catch that," the newcomer said, his voice a rumble of bass with hints of spicy dark rum.

It sent a shiver down her spine, warning and enticement rolled into one. Nope, this bounty hunter wasn't going to go down like the one in Appalachia. Her senses screamed at her to get away.

Valeria forced herself to calm down, letting the stranger's magic lap around her.

It was the only passive aspect of her talent. If she were calm, she could sense the nature of another practitioner's magic....and this time, she felt the familiar tingle of fire.

That flames she'd seen earlier hadn't been a mirage fabricated by her exhausted brain. The man was pyrokinetic. She could work with that. But it would cost her.

Mentally, she reached down, grabbing the gleaming strands of energy only she had ever been able to see.

The man's dark face clouded further. "What are you doing?"

Okay, so maybe she wasn't the only one who could see the energy. The man was looking at her, following the mental motion as if he could see what she was doing.

"Er...have you ever heard the expression, '*out of the frying pan, into the fire?*" she asked.

The stranger scowled. "What?" he asked, before shaking his head. "Never mind."

He held up a large meaty hand. "You must come with me if you want to live."

Her brow went up, and she almost laughed. Did this guy think he was the Terminator?

"That's the cheesiest pick-up line I've ever heard," she said, retreating into snark even as she slumped over on the filthy ground.

From her prone position, Valeria looked the stranger up and down. There was a whole lot more up than down. He was at least six and a half feet tall. He might actually *be* a Terminator.

That thought shook her out of her stupor. Valeria reached down and gathered the fire energy, hurling it back at the man with all her strength.

Halfway through her thrust, Valeria realized her mistake—right when the man walked through the flames completely unscathed.

"*Stop*," he ordered, his expression thunderous.

Panicking, Valeria kept going, pushing out the energy she couldn't afford to lose. She was well beyond her endurance.

Valeria fell to her knees, her vision narrowing to pinpoint.

Distantly, she heard his voice again. "Little one, you must desist. Stop it now or you're going to hurt yourself."

"Nice try, cheese-master," she slurred, her mind unable to think of a better insult.

Valeria kept going until she fell over. She hadn't just used the magic that her talent reflected. She'd thrown her own at him, draining the well until it was empty.

Valeria landed on her back, but her head didn't strike the hard pavement. Instead, she felt arms pick her up. Her last recollection was the sound of wings and the bite of a sharply cold wind on her face.

CHAPTER SIX

The smell of tomato soup and freshly baked bread woke Valeria. Struggling to focus, she rolled, making the soft ground around her crinkle.

What the...? Testing the silver-colored surface underneath her with a hand, she frowned when it gave and crinkled again.

"You're awake."

Startled, Valeria blinked owlishly at the large blur standing a few feet away. The smeared vision slowly coalesced, the image sharpening until the blob became a hugely pregnant woman holding a tray that smelled amazing.

"Should you be holding something so heavy?" Valeria asked, her voice scratchy. Damn, her throat ached.

The woman laughed, inclining her head and setting the tray down on an odd-looking table. Valeria had never seen a bedside table made entirely of marble before.

"You sound remarkably like my mate," the woman informed her, putting a hand to her lower back. "But you would be more convincing at expressing concern if you'd put your hands down."

Belatedly, Valeria realized she had her arms up, fingers bunched in a classic channeling pose.

"Oh." She put her hands down, squinting at her surroundings. "Where am I?"

"In my home. My name is Sanaa."

"And I'm Tom," a voice called through the door. "Don't hurt my wife or I will eat you."

"*Thomas*," Sanaa said, her sweet voice sharpening a fraction. "You promised you would let me handle this."

There was a grumbled response Valeria didn't catch.

"He apologizes," Sanaa said with an impish grin. She patted her belly. "He's a little on edge since my last false alarm."

A grunt that was definite disagreement filtered through the door, but the pregnant woman ignored it with a placid expression.

The woman rubbed her swollen stomach before gesturing to the tray. "Please go ahead. It's tomato soup, and Tom made the bread. He learned to bake when Veda, our healer, told us I was with child."

"Um, congratulations," Valeria said, eyeing the soup and bread with distrust.

Sanaa tilted her head to the side. "I can assure you that we would never adulterate your food. Harming a guest would bring the greatest shame to my family and my clan."

"Uh-huh." Sanaa appeared sincere, but Valeria had been through too much to take anyone at their word, even an innocent-looking pregnant woman.

Except...she was starving. *Bread is difficult to poison, right?*

Reaching out, she took the small loaf. Her body damn near melted when she found it was still warm. Valeria clamped her jaw shut to keep from shoving the whole thing into her mouth.

Sanaa poked her head out the door, murmuring something to the growly man outside. She returned a moment later with a sealed bottle of water and juice in each hand.

"Here you go," she said, replacing a cup on the tray with the bottles. "And I completely understand your mistrust. I have been in a similar position—waking up in a stranger's home, unsure if the person is a threat."

Valeria raised a brow. "You've been kidnapped before?"

Sanaa sat on a stool. "You haven't been kidnapped. And neither was I, although I had a moment or two of disquiet when I woke up after my accident to find Thomas looming over me. But that's a story for another time."

Trying not to appear as ravenous as she was, Valeria tore off a small piece of bread, nodding as if she was going to be around long enough to hear it.

Dear Lord, the bread tasted even better than it smelled. Giving up all semblance of decorum, she tore it apart, chewing it in big mouthfuls and washing it down with the juice when she began to choke on it in her eagerness.

There was no telltale dizziness or stomachache after the bread, so she decided to chance the soup.

"As interesting as that sounds, I'd rather hear more about this whole not-being-kidnapped thing," she said between bites.

Sanaa nodded obligingly. "As I said, you are a guest of our clan leader. He took you to our healer Veda. But after you woke up the first few times swinging, metaphorically speaking, it was decided we would move you here until your convalescence is over."

"Which it is now," the man behind the door called out.

Valeria's head was spinning. "That door is solid oak. How can he hear us? And why am I ...here?" she asked, turning to frown at the oddly appointed room.

She was resting on a bare mattress resting in a steel frame, but the cover of the mattress was that weird shiny silver material. In addition to the marble table, there was a granite-topped chest of drawers made of wrought iron.

Sanaa grinned at Valeria's perplexed perusal. "Thomas has very keen hearing. He decorated this room himself—for the twins."

She passed a hand over her swollen belly. "I keep telling him that it's not necessary. Our kind doesn't breathe fire right away, but since we don't live in a traditional home, he insisted."

"A traditional home?" Valeria echoed blankly. Sure, this place was weirdly furnished, but it had four walls.

"An aerie," Sanaa said helpfully. "Thomas is afraid of heights. It was one of the more interesting aspects of our courtship."

Belatedly, Valeria remembered the sound of wings. *Oh, mierda...* "Your clan isn't a coven of pyrokinetics, is it?"

Sanaa was almost apologetic. "I'm afraid not. I'm sorry if that's a disappointment. I can understand you'd be eager to meet others of your kind."

"My kind? Oh, yeah...because I'm a pyro," Valeria finished lamely.

It's good that she thinks that. The fewer people knew how her magic worked, the better.

"It's a rare talent among humans," Sanaa said approvingly. "But needless to say, it made hosting you a complicated matter. You set fire to Veda's spare room when you first roused. Fortunately for him, Thomas had this place ready to go. We just had to replace the cribs with an adult-sized mattress, but fashioning one was not a problem— we had plenty of leftover asbestos."

"Not lucky," the man behind the door chimed in loudly. "Not lucky at all."

Sanaa laughed as if delighted. "Don't mind him. Thomas is what your people call a grouchy Gus. More so than normal. I keep experiencing false labor, and it's making him tense. Also, he's concerned you'll burn our house down. Do you remember waking the first few times and setting everything in sight on fire?"

"Err, no. Sorry," Valeria said slowly.

There was a vague memory that involved a male voice, heat, and flames but none of the memories were clear. But this explained why she was here in Sanaa and Thomas' future fireproof nursery.

"Thank you," she added.

"No thanks are necessary. This is important to our leader and therefore to the entire clan."

Struggling to her feet, Sanaa rose and gestured for Valeria to follow her to a window.

Valeria hesitated, but her instinct told her the pregnant woman wasn't a threat. After so many years on the run, they were pretty finely honed.

At first, she saw nothing but a blue sky over a sea of pine trees visible because Sanaa's house was on a small hill. Then there was a shadow streaking over the tops of the trees.

"*Hijo de puta.*" Valeria pressed herself against the glass as the huge form passed in a streak of dark purple and gold. "I'm not hallucinating, am I? That's really a dragon?"

"Yes," Sanaa said in a chirpy voice. "We are the Draconai Imperia.

That is Rhys up there, our clan's leader. He's been circling the house since the healer brought you here."

Valeria had run into shifters before. A few had been paid to hunt her. Wolves and large cats in particular were a big concern.

With their enhanced senses, they made excellent bounty hunters, and the price on her head was sizable. The only reason one hadn't caught Valeria—because not all shifters were as careless as the one in Appalachia—was due to the fact shifters and witches considered each other mortal enemies.

However, there were exceptions to every rule, so Valeria made a point of avoiding all shifters whenever possible. But never in her life had she ever expected to run into a dragon shifter. Lions, tigers, bears...those were all within the realm of possibility. Valeria had even met a were-camel who waited tables in a kebab shop in Morocco once.

But a *dragon*? She'd heard the rumors, of course. She just hadn't believed them. Who would?

She'd always believed dragons were just misinterpreted dinosaur bones. Or so she'd always assumed.

Not that any of this weirdness explains your presence here.

"Rhys won't go away until you leave with him, so I hope you're feeling better," the man behind the door shouted.

'*Thomas.* Stop speaking. It's not helping," Sanaa snapped, then gave Valeria a beatific smile. "He will be very pleased to know you were not permanently damaged by your ordeal."

"Uh-huh." This conversation was making her dizzy. "And is Rhys that tall, dark, and fabulously terrifying man from the alley?"

Sanaa nodded, her eyes dancing with innocent humor.

Valeria rubbed her temples. "So let me get this straight. You are a dragon. Your husband is not, but he's concerned your twins will take after you, so he's made this asbestos-lined room. Your leader brought me here so I wouldn't burn *his* place down."

Sanaa rubbed her hands together. "Technically, you set the healer's home on fire, but the basics are correct. Also, I volunteered to be your host."

Valeria sat on the bed, rubbing her aching head. "You did?"

Her host nodded. "I told Rhys you'd be more open to speaking to another woman. And most people hesitate to attack the pregnant. That was a gamble on my part of course—"

"One I did not agree with," Thomas called.

"I think she understands that, Thomas," Sanaa said with a loud sigh. She reached out to pat Valeria's arm. "I am very pleased to do this for my clan leader. Also, it's nice to make new friends!"

She said the last with such genuine enthusiasm that Valeria took a step back, her eyes wide.

"That's, um, real nice. Thanks," she said, attempting a smile and failing miserably. "I don't suppose you'd like to clue me in on what your clan leader's reasons might be? Why I'm here?"

Sanaa gave her a sunny grin. "I'm afraid I don't know the exact details. It was from before my time. But I'm sure Rhys would be happy to enlighten you. He's been circling the house since dawn, waiting for you to wake."

"Please leave so he'll stop," Thomas called from behind the door.

"*Thomas*," Sanaa chided before her face transformed. "Oh dear, I have to urinate again. Excuse me."

She opened the door and waddled out, revealing a tall and burly man glowering in the hallway.

A bear shifter. Of course Thomas would be a bear shifter.

He and Valeria stared at each other. Then he looked behind her at her empty tray and huffed. "Are you still hungry?"

The growl in his voice was so on brand, Valeria had to suppress a spontaneous grin. She cleared her throat. "Yes, please."

Valeria followed him into the kitchen, checking out the house along the way. It was a very modern take on rustic, with exposed brick and heavy wooden beams that were in the same color family as the hardwood floors.

The kitchen and living were one expansive room, separated by a long marble-top bar. The living room area had two plush couches facing a large screen tv.

A small table with two chairs lay between them and the bar. Off to one side were a pair of unfinished wooden highchairs. A few pieces of used sandpaper rested on their trays.

"Did you make those?"

"Yes." Thomas' response was clipped. He moved behind the

counter. A row of cooling loaves rested on little wire racks. He sliced some brie, spread some cranberry sauce from a little jar on it, and popped it into a toaster oven on the other side of the kitchen.

"Do you always cook like this or are you nesting?"

He shot her some premium grade-A side-eye before the toaster oven pinged.

"The baking is new, but I've always cooked for myself, long before I met Sanaa. She's not much of a cook. The woman would live off berries and dandelions if I left her to her own devices."

He took out the tray with a shiny fish-shaped potholder Valeria assumed Sanaa had purchased. Turning, Thomas pointed at her aggressively. "This is why I'm in charge of feeding the twins when they finally get here."

Bemused, Valeria nodded. "Probably for the best."

Mollified at her agreement, Thomas took a saran-wrapped plate of sliced turkey out of the fridge. He placed a generous amount over the melted brie before replacing the top of the loaf and pushing it to her. "Eat."

Starving, she dove in eagerly, twisting her head to the right when a door opened deeper in the house only for it to promptly open and close again.

"Sometimes, Sanaa thinks she's done, but then she has to turn right around and go back," Thomas informed her with a shrug. "Twins."

Valeria murmured noncommittally, still trying to inhale the decadent sandwich without choking. She gave it her best effort, but her days of too little food caught up with her and she stopped halfway through. Wrapping the sandwich in the paper towel that had accompanied it, she tucked it into the front pocket of her sweatshirt. Life had taught her early on never to waste food.

There was a whooshing sound from outside. Thomas tilted his head at the ceiling and glared.

"Is he still out there?" she asked, her forehead creasing in consternation.

"Yeah," Thomas grunted, returning to his kitchen tasks.

"I don't suppose you know what he wants?"

The bear set down a bowl with a thud. "I thought that was obvious —he wants you."

CHAPTER SEVEN

Valeria blinked as Thomas pressed a paper bag into her arms as she stepped outside the back door of his home. She glanced down in confusion.

"More sandwiches," he growled. "For the road."

"Oh," she murmured. "Thanks."

Despite Sanaa's repeated invitations to stay, Valeria decided to leave with Rhys after Thomas made it clear she wouldn't be able to avoid him for long.

"Unfortunately, asking him to go away won't work," Thomas had told her, kneading another ball of bread dough aggressively. "Otherwise, he and the rest of the lot would never darken our door."

He'd said this last with the longing of a man who knew his dearest wish would never be granted.

Resigned to the endless shitstorm that was her life, Valeria decided to deal with her dragon problem head-on. Hiding in Thomas and Sanaa's home would only postpone the inevitable confrontation. And Valeria needed to find out what the hell these people—or more specifically this Rhys person—wanted from her.

You can handle this, she told herself as they walked farther from the house, presumably so the dragon could land without wrecking the structure.

A shadow streaked over them, blotting out the sun as it passed overhead. A sudden sharp wind whipped across her face. Dust rose in the air as a massive creature landed twenty yards away.

Okay, I can't handle this, Valeria thought, stifling a gasp.

The sheer size of the creature that landed in front of them was impossible. The dragon was the size of a truck. An exceptionally large *monster* truck. Or perhaps two put together.

Valeria stood frozen to the spot, all her fight-or-flight switches flipped to flight. Trying to calm her racing heart, Valeria clutched the doggie bag full of sandwiches to her chest, no doubt smashing them. But that didn't matter. What mattered was physics or the lack of it.

You're a witch. She did things that violated the laws of physics, as humans understood them, nearly every day. And yet, somehow, that was precious little comfort in the face of a thirty-foot dragon.

Steady, V, she scolded. *It's just a dragon. A magenta one.* Well, it was more of a deep purple with a big patch of gold on the belly. There were also touches of dark emerald green on his legs, close to the feet. The sharply *clawed* feet.

And there went what little equanimity she'd managed to hold onto. Valeria was seconds from turning on her heel and running away when there was a light show, a sparkly swirl of purple and gold. When she blinked, the dragon was gone as if it had been sucked into a black hole. In its place was a mountain of a man, almost six and a half feet tall with a frame so defined and muscular that he was almost more threatening than the dragon had been.

Staring at his boot-clad feet—and he'd appeared fully dressed—she moved her gaze up his body to finally settle on his face.

All the puzzle pieces clicked together. That dusty antique shop and the mirror, followed by the scene in the alley. Aw shit, the *alley*.

The universe had a perverse sense of humor. *I specifically said I did not want to meet this man in a dark alley. Thanks a lot, universe.*

The man began to walk toward them. Making an involuntary squeaking sound in her throat, she took a sharp step back.

Next to her, Thomas sighed, giving her a pitying glance. "You're welcome to stay here instead of going to his place."

The man stopped a few yards short, his face as dark as a thundercloud.

"No, thank you, Thomas," Rhys snapped.

Valeria stared at him, worried for the bear.

"But we appreciate your offer of hospitality," Rhys added grudgingly in a softer tone.

We?

Thomas groaned. "Little tip. Women don't like it when you speak for them."

The dragon raised one dark eyebrow, his eyes telling Thomas to butt out.

"Just saying," the bear muttered. "There's this thing called charm. Look it up."

For a second, she thought they would come to blows, but the appearance of the pregnant woman helped break the tension.

"Hello," Sanaa said in a chipper singsong voice. "What did I miss?"

The dark man's face softened further, and he inclined his head. "I was introducing myself to our guest."

The imposing dark-haired man turned to her, then bowed at the waist. "I am Rhys."

Valeria blinked, leaning away from the sheer force of him. "Uh...hello?"

He nodded approvingly, almost smiling but not quite, as if the gesture were too unfamiliar for him to get right. Waving a commanding arm at the bear, he announced. "We will go now. Please have one of the vehicles brought around."

Thomas sniffed. "Only because it means you'll be leaving," he said before stalking away.

Sanaa laughed, making cheery small talk until the Were-Bear pulled up in a four-wheel-drive Range Rover in hunter green. He got out of the driver's seat, then held the door open with an exaggerated flourish. "If Your Highness pleases."

Valeria tensed, expecting the oversized man to start breathing fire, but Rhys just held his hand out for the keys.

Sanaa reached for her arm. "Fortunately for my mate, many of our kind have trouble with sarcasm," she whispered. "But Thomas has been teaching me all about it," she added in the tone of one sharing a deeply held confidence.

Managing a half-hearted smile, Valeria nodded. "Thanks for the sandwiches," she told the bear.

Thomas grunted. He gave her an awkward pat on the head. "See you soon—far too soon if this one has his way."

Rhys raised one supercilious eyebrow, but he did not comment.

Sanaa stepped back, taking Valeria's hands in both of hers. "I might not see you again before the delivery, but you shouldn't worry. You will be safe and well cared for in Rhys' home. And you can call us should you have any questions. I'm fourth on the office speed-dial."

Valeria murmured her thanks again while Rhys crossed to the passenger-side door, opening it for her without the flourish Thomas had made, but still managing to make the gesture formal.

Feeling as if she were walking to the guillotine, Valeria ducked her head to avoid those intense black eyes following her every move. She climbed into the plush leather seat, almost jumping when she nearly burned her tush.

"My apologies." Rhys leaned over her, making her heart stop. But he just pressed some buttons, lowering the temperature of the heated seat before stepping back. "Our kind is more heat tolerant—for obvious reasons. The bear also runs hot. We forget most people don't enjoy that type of heat, even if they can wield fire."

He seemed to require an answer. "I see," she said, again silently confirming that she was pyrokinetic. It was safer.

Rhys gave her another one of those approving nods before shutting the door.

As he walked around to the driver's seat, she caught Thomas' eye. He gave her a commiserating glance over Sanaa's dark head, but it wasn't a warning. More like *'poor you'*.

Rhys paused to have a word with Sanaa, who'd waddled over with him to the front door. Valeria couldn't hear what he said, but Sanaa took obvious pleasure in his words, enough that Thomas stopped rolling his eyes. The bear looked at his mate with a wordless but tangible devotion he didn't bother to hide.

A small, shriveled part of Valeria's soul started to ache. Blinking, she turned away, holding her sandwiches with a tired, defeated sigh.

Rhys climbed into the vehicle a minute later.

"Thank you," he said.

She frowned. "For what?"

"For coming with me," he said, his dark voice the verbal equivalent of smoldering charcoal. "This action requires trust on your part. You have my word—the word of a Draconis—that I will be worthy of it."

His words rang throughout the cabin of the SUV with a preternatural verve that was more powerful than a shout.

Startled, she just stared at him. Outside the car, Thomas slapped a hand to his forehead as Sanaa waved goodbye with the enthusiasm of a child.

CHAPTER EIGHT

Rhys started the Rover, driving the vehicle around to the front of the house where the rough driveway connected to the dirt road leading up the mountain to his home.

The girl sat in her seat as if she were trying not to touch it with her skin. She pulled her braided hair forward, keeping her hands in her lap. Her posture was tense, but her heart had slowed to a steady rate. For a human.

"I had a bag with me," she said after they'd wound a little higher up the mountain.

"It's in the back." He gestured with his thumb, opting not to take his eyes off the road.

He and his people had carved the track—that fact was obvious given the precision it had been cut with. But he was starting to realize they had made a mistake by not paving it.

The rain and the snow had degraded the surface, cutting ruts and dips deep enough to rattle his teeth. When a particular deep furrow knocked the girl into the door, he slowed down.

"My apologies. I had no idea this drive was in such poor condition. I will task one of my people with its repair immediately."

The girl twisted, retrieving the bag she'd dropped in the alley from the backseat.

"I guess you don't have many occasions to drive this road, given that you can fly."

He nodded in confirmation. "That is correct. Most of us don't use vehicles unless we have to leave our territory."

"Oh..." She took a moment to process that. "Geographically speaking, where is that?"

"We are in Canada, the Rockies," Rhys supplied." The closest cities are Calgary and Edmonton, but they're not very close at all, which is how we like it."

She shifted in her seat uncomfortably. "Isn't this Columbia Basin Pack territory?"

"No. Our territory is north of theirs, although there is an area of overlap with a small Alaskan homestead under their purview. But Rafe Hawkins, the local alpha, knows better than to trespass farther than their precisely defined border." He glanced at her. "I take it shifters make you uncomfortable?"

The girl slumped down in her seat. "I haven't had the best of luck with them," she said in a tired voice.

"Is your aversion restricted to wolves or does it extend to all kinds of shifters?"

She took a deep breath. "I'm not too fond of big cats either."

"Why?" he asked with genuine curiosity.

"Because they make good bounty hunters."

"I see." That was a worrisome detail, rather casually shared. "And how do you feel about dragons?"

Her head drew back slightly. "The jury is still out. Can I ask something?"

"Go ahead."

She gave him a fixed look. "Are you planning on handing me over to the cross coven?"

"The what?"

"The latest group after me—all wear crosses. Or they have tattoos of crosses. They're not the only group after me, I think, but they've been the most relentless for the past year."

"Catholic witches?" he asked, his nose wrinkling.

She lifted a shoulder. "So, you're not with them?"

Rhys drew his head back. "Of course not."

"Are you going to barter for my blood?"

"What? *No.*"

"Not even an ounce?"

"Not even a drop."

"Uh-huh. And you're not going to wait until I'm asleep to cut my hair or fingernails off to use in secret spells you conduct in the bathroom, right?"

He twisted to stare at her, incredulous. "Did someone do that?"

"More than once," she announced with that same maddening equanimity. "Will you expect me to share a bed with you?"

Rhys almost drove the Ranger Rover off the road. When he finally found his voice, it was hoarse. "I would never presume."

He thought he detected hints of amusement on her face, but it was difficult to say because the road was poor again and he had to pay attention to his driving.

"So, you don't have a sex dungeon *a la Christian Grey* waiting for me at the end of this drive?"

It was a good thing he'd slowed down because he was in danger of driving off the road again. "I have no dungeon in my home, for sex or any other purpose."

She sat deeper in her seat. "Well, that's some comfort, I guess."

There was a long silence while he tried to digest all that he'd learned about this woman in such a short time.

"It's nice that Thomas lets you borrow his car," she said after a beat.

"It's not his," Rhys clarified. "This vehicle belongs to the clan. We maintain a fleet for communal use, at least two of which are stationed at Thomas and Sanaa's home at all times—three if we can get away with it."

"Get away with it?"

He moved his hand. "Thomas is still irritated that we replaced his dilapidated vehicle—an ancient Jeep. But having reliable transport is important when a mate is pregnant, especially when the progeny are too small to fly properly, which they will be for the first year or so. The best they will be able to achieve is a short hover or a moderate glide."

"Err...okay. Then, I suppose that makes sense." She appeared to search for something to say. "So, it's Rhys what?"

He glanced at her. "What?" he repeated.

"I'm asking if you have a last name," she explained.

"I don't. It's just Rhys."

"Like Cher or Retta?" she said.

This was a very perplexing conversation. "Are those friends of yours?" he asked with a frown.

"Never mind," she said shaking her head. "My name is Valeria."

"*Va-le-ria*," he said, sounding it out. "It's lovely. And the last name?"

She shrugged. "It's not important."

"So, you are also like your friend Cher?"

"In a way." Valeria studied the passing scenery outside. "I change it a lot. I'm not sure what the original was anymore."

The light dawned. "Because of the hunters."

"Yeah." She gave him another one of those piercing looks. "So, are you going to tell me what it is that your clan wants from me?"

Where did he begin? Somehow, he did not think telling her she was the spitting image of his true love, dead for over two centuries, was the appropriate course of action.

He settled on, "I believe it would be easier to show you. It won't be much longer." The trees were beginning to thin, marking the start of his personal property.

When he glanced over, she was watching him with slightly narrowed eyes. "Thomas warned me you'd beat about the bush."

"Pardon? I'm not familiar with this expression, but I suggest you not take all Thomas' opinions at face value. He is..."

"A grumpy bear?" she supplied.

An unfamiliar feeling that might have been humor bubbled up, but he suppressed it, choosing to nod instead. "Yes, exactly."

"And here I thought it was all the flyovers that had annoyed him."

"He'll live."

Her mouth twisted. "If you say, 'I'll be back,' in an Austrian accent, I'm getting out of this SUV."

This was shaping up to be the most confusing conversation of this life. He pulled up his drive, parking the vehicle under the eave he'd extended into a carport. "I'm sorry, but I don't follow."

Valeria didn't answer. She was busy gaping at the house.

He reached out to touch her arm, a move that made her edge out of the way with abrupt suddenness. Confused and slightly stung, Rhys withdrew his hand.

"Why don't you follow me and I'll show you the house?" he said.

"Sure," she murmured, clutching the bag to her chest with a tightness that betrayed her anxiety. But she followed him inside without further comment.

CHAPTER NINE

Valeria walked through the threshold of the massive log mansion and tripped. *Wow.* This guy lived here?

The multistory building was a modern take on a Frank Lloyd Wright, built entirely out of big redwood logs. The entranceway was a long but narrow foyer with a few tables and rows of hooks bolted into the wall on either side. An array of coats and hats hung on them. Just beyond this reception area, the space opened into a living area nearly two stories tall with a doorless threshold made from huge wooden beams.

Feeling as if she'd stepped into a dream, she followed Rhys inside. Spinning on her heel, she darted her gaze everywhere, trying to take it all in.

Valeria was with a dragon who could, in fact, be the Terminator—he was certainly built like one—but he had a damn fine house.

Sunshine poured in through massive glass windows on three sides of the concert hall-sized room. The result was a space that glowed with light, the better to showcase the handmade furniture and precious object scattered over every flat surface.

In the center of the room, the tables gave way to curved couches that formed a ring of concentric circles, with space in between so people could walk to the center, which featured a raised circular fire pit. A sparkly white stone that might have been quartz ringed the pit. But it wasn't pure white. It had veins of gold worked through it. Above it, a huge brass hood came down from the ceiling like the proverbial hand of God.

However, it wasn't the most prominent feature in the room. That honor went to the grand staircase against the far wall. Made of oversized boards cut into thick rectangular blocks, the individual steps were suspended from light metal beams that blended into the background. The effect was startling. It looked almost as if each polished step was levitating in the open air before they split, sweeping to opposite ends of the room and disappearing with a twist into the second story of the house.

Rhys pointed out that doors that led to the kitchens and what he called the 'crash rooms,' extra bedrooms that were available to the various clan members to use whenever they wished.

"The second floor mostly consists of spare bedchambers as well as a theater and a library in addition to a few multipurpose rooms—conference rooms, parlors, and a salon. There is also a cellar with a gymnasium as well as wine and ale caves below to supplement this drinking wall," he said, pointing to a section of the wall just beyond the couches. The semicircular mahogany bar had shelves of expensive alcohol bottles that stretched almost to the ceiling.

"That's it?" She laughed. "No swimming pool? No stables for your stallions?"

"Oh. No." Rhys appeared dismayed. "Unfortunately, those creatures don't tolerate my kind very well. They tend to panic in our presence. Do you enjoy the company of those beasts?

She shook her head. "No. I've never been around horses. I was joking."

"Ah, I see." Rhys scratched his chin. "Well, there aren't stables, but there is a conservatory attached to the kitchens. It houses several vegetable patches and fruit trees. The cook enjoys spending her free time in there in winter."

"You have a cook?"

"Yes. Aggie is the only other permanent resident of this home. She also functions as my majordomo."

"And she's also a dragon?"

"No. She's Fae. A brownie."

"Oh." *And I thought I was dizzy before.* At least the man appeared open to interacting with other species. She'd gotten a different impression from Thomas.

"My chambers and private study are on the third floor," Rhys continued.

"There's *another* floor?" she squeaked in disbelief. That, in addition to the basement that made four stories and he lived here alone with just a cook-slash-majordomo? Valeria assumed that was dragon speak for a butler.

"Yes," Rhys said in a matter-of-fact tone, completely oblivious to her stunned amazement. "There is a sun deck on the top floor. I believe there is enough room for a pool."

She blinked. "Do you swim?"

"Yes. But I use the lake at the bottom of the mountain." He paused, frowning. "It would be too cold for a human at this time of the year. I will inquire with my people about getting you a pool."

"Wait..." She held up her hands. "That's not necessary. I was just joking, remember?"

He shrugged nonchalantly. "It would be no trouble. We can add it to the deck. The structure is sufficiently strong enough to bear the extra weight."

Was he serious? Yes. Yes, he was.

"Okay, dragon dude—listen up," she said, putting her hands on her hips. "You need to slow your roll. I don't even know why I'm here or how long I'll be staying. And I wasn't asking for a pool. I was making a sarcastic comment on your huge stonking mansion. Which is lovely by the way."

That last was said with a snappish edge, which might have negated the compliment she was trying to make, but Valeria was stressed out. She had been since waking up on an asbestos mattress.

One of Rhys' dark brows reached for the sky. A trace of a smirk flitted across his face, but it was gone before she could call him on it.

"I see. I'm glad you appreciate the house. I have put a lot of work into it over the years. As for the reason you're here, I did promise to show you once we arrived. Please accompany me to my study."

He turned his back, gesturing for her to follow him up the floating staircase. A little annoyed at the weird mix of generosity and high-handedness, Valeria trailed after him.

By the time they reached the third floor, she was panting lightly, covered in a light sheen of sweat. The winding steps had ended at the midpoint of a wide corridor. At each end was a giant wooden door. Rhys moved to the one on the left.

Valeria hesitated at the threshold. The door was so thick that it had to weigh a ton. Clearly, dragons had super-strength. She didn't think the brownie would have sufficient muscle power to open it.

Rhys turned back when she didn't immediately step inside after him. "The answer lies within," he said, beckoning.

Valeria stayed put, suddenly very aware of the man's appeal. Rhys' features were strong but handsome in a rough granite-hewn sort of way. His tall body was densely corded with muscle with big hands and feet in proportion with his frame.

Taken altogether, Rhys was too masculine to be a normal man.

She gave herself a little shake. "Don't do that."

His expression clouded. "Do what?"

"Stop looking like that," she said, gesturing to encompass his whole body. "As if you're trying to lure me into the back of your van with candy."

Rhys stared for a moment before sighing quietly. He stepped away from the threshold.

Aware that the last dig may have been one step too far, Valeria finally entered the room.

The first thing she saw was the big mirror from the antique shop. Freezing to the spot, she weighed how far she'd get if she bolted.

Rhys must have noticed her expression of dismay. "Please be at ease. This is not a trap."

"Really?" she asked skeptically. "Because it looks like one."

He took a step toward her, but he checked his progress when she backed away.

"Let me explain," he said, putting his hands behind his back. "As you've probably realized, we like to maintain our anonymity here. We monitor certain communities for threats preemptively. One of our contacts was approached by the antique shop owner. He was reaching out to all the dragon shifter communities in an attempt to sell the information."

The fact that there was more than one dragon community in the world was lost in the face of the other news. Blood draining from her face, she leaned against the doorjamb. "He sold what exactly?"

"There was a security camera covering the interior of Charmed Antiques. Your interaction with this object was captured on it," he said gesturing to the mirror.

Her heart sank. "So how many people know about it?" she asked weakly.

Unlike so many other things that sailed over his head, Rhys immediately understood she was concerned about being recognized. "The Fae male said we were the only ones to pursue the information, but the original inquiry included a screenshot of the back of your head."

"*Oh*." She slumped against the wall in relief.

"I don't believe you're in any more danger than you already were. Very few people would recognize you from behind, especially in a grainy image. The shopkeeper assures us no one else approached him for more information."

"No one besides you?" she said with a wry twist of her lips.

"That is correct," he said with a nod. "And I don't think he would lie. That would be...unwise."

"I bet," she murmured, eyeing the muscles of his exposed arms. The veins stood out like someone had carved them out with a chisel.

Rhys gave her a long, considering look. "Even if the people who were searching for you somehow came across the information and positively identified you, I sincerely doubt they would breach our borders to come after you. The Draconai Imperia has a certain reputation..."

That was all well and good, but Valeria couldn't help but point out the obvious. "Except for the fact you like to remain anonymous."

Rhys smiled slowly. "Those unwise enough to enter a dragon's lair without doing their due diligence soon see the error of their ways. It's a lesson we enjoy teaching."

All right then. "Well, I guess you have to get your kicks in somehow," she murmured.

"It passes the time," he said.

Valeria eyed him suspiciously. There was not so much a blink or twinkle to indicate he was joking.

They stood there staring at each other for a moment.

"We secured the mirror a few days ago, but have not yet discovered the meaning behind it or the vision you saw."

"And this mystery is why I'm here?" she asked, not expecting an answer. But of course, he gave her one—a rather philosophical one at that.

Rhys turned to the mirror. "There are fewer mysteries in life than one would think. I would like to solve this one. Given your current circumstances of being hunted, I would like to offer you sanctuary so we can explore this little puzzle."

She pursed her lips, pretending to think about it. In reality, there was no choice. "Okay. Sounds like a plan."

"Would you like to look into it again?" he said, inviting her with a sweep of his arm.

"No, thank you," she said with a shake of her head.

For the first time, the dragon appeared taken aback. "It won't hurt you," he assured her.

"I'm not a child. I know it won't hurt." She crossed her arms in exasperation. "But the last time I looked into that thing a fire-breathing dragon showed up and disintegrated three people. Who knows what I'll see if I look into that thing again? Maybe a ninja were-mongoose will show up to sell me car insurance."

His thick lashes fluttered. "A were-mongoose?"

She threw up her hands. "I couldn't think of anything bigger and scarier than a dragon, so I went the other way."

"I see," he said. Valeria couldn't tell if he was amused or not.

"What happens if you look into it?" she asked after he was quiet too long.

"Nothing." He shrugged his big shoulders. "It must be keyed to your species."

They both stared at the mirror, frustrated with it for different reasons.

"I don't suppose you'll reconsider," he said in what she assumed was a tone meant to coax.

In Valeria's mind, the mirror began to glow a radioactive green. "Is your offer of sanctuary contingent on me looking in the mirror?"

"Of course not."

She gave the mirror a narrow-eyed glance. "Then maybe later," she muttered, aware she was being difficult.

If this offer of sanctuary, as Rhys called it, was genuine, jeopardizing it was self-defeating. On the other hand, getting anywhere near that magical artifact on purpose seemed incredibly stupid, and her mama hadn't raised a fool.

After an awkward pause, Rhys shrugged off the spoke she'd thrown in his wheel.

"Just so you are sure," he began, "this offer of sanctuary has no conditions. You are welcome to stay for as long as you like. I will not require your blood or strands of your hair at any time. Depending on how long you stay, you will be asked to contribute in some way. It is a point of pride that every member of the clan is productive, but this takes many forms. We have people in fields as diverse as engineering to full-time artists. Rest assured I will never ask you to perform any task that makes you uncomfortable."

"So, I won't be working in your diamond mine," she said, trying to sound enthusiastic. "Cool."

"Unless you would like to," he informed. Again, he didn't appear to be joking.

The realization sank in. "You own a diamond mine, don't you?"

He shrugged. "More than one. They belong to the clan. But our employees don't have very many complaints. We have very strict safety regulations and pay well."

She stared at him. "Uh-huh."

He moved closer to her. This time, she stood her ground. "I believe you are fatigued. Why don't I show you to your rooms?"

"That sounds like a good idea," she murmured, following him back down to the second floor.

He walked her to a door at the end of the long hall. "This is where you will stay," he said, gesturing to the door. "Rest. Be secure in the knowledge no enemy has ever breached the walls of a stronghold held by the Draconai Imperia."

With that, he left her alone.

CHAPTER TEN

She closed the door to her quarters, realizing Rhys hadn't misspoken when he said 'rooms' plural. He had given her a suite.

Wow. Valeria put down her bag on the floor, twisting her head this way and that to take it all in.

The first room was something between a sitting room and an office. At one end, there was a large desk and a bookshelf made out of some exotic-colored wood with hints of purple in it. Stroking the glossy surface, she wondered if anyone had ever used it. She didn't know anyone could bring themselves to write at it. It was too pretty. A plush leather couch and a large screen television set rested on the other side.

The bedroom lay just beyond, separated by a wide arched entrance that could be closed off by a pair of pocket doors tucked into the wall. A panel of glowing buttons on the wall next to the light switch controlled their opening and closing. After playing with them for longer than she wanted to admit, she took a running start and jumped on the bed.

When her body sank into the memory foam mattress, she moaned aloud in ecstasy. Rolling around on it, she giggled when she found another set of buttons above the bedside table. These made the lights overhead dim, then brighten dramatically.

Then she found another button that brought down lightproof panels suspended between two thick planes of glass that made up the windows. *I'm Kate Winslet in 'The Holiday'!*

Bouncing off the bed, she ran to the bathroom.

Yes! The tub was huge, and it had jets. An assortment of bath oils, bubble bath, and other toiletries lay in a basket on a small table next to it, just like a fancy hotel.

Valeria had turned the taps, stripped off her clothes, and was covered in bubbles before she realized she hadn't checked for hidden cameras. She'd stayed in some pretty sketchy places in the past, and unfortunately had a good reason to do this.

More unfortunate may have been the fact you continued to stay in that place after finding the cameras and confronting the manager. The little worm had offered to let her stay for free if she left them running. He'd offered an additional two hundred bucks because he'd been planning on uploading them to the internet.

Broke and exhausted, she'd conceded and taken the cash…followed by a quick break-in to sabotage the footage and *his* computer.

Still, the dragon might be on the up and up. He certainly read that way to her, with his formality and the reaction he'd had to her questions in the car. *But you will still check for cameras later,* she thought, lifting bubbles in her palms and blowing them away.

Leaning back in the tub, Valeria let herself relax. There hadn't been too many opportunities to slow down and rest the last two years. Not for anything longer than a few days at least.

But her distrust of safety was too deeply engrained. Always one to look a gift horse in the mouth, she turned over her first impressions of the members of this insular clan, wondering which one was most likely to sell her out first.

No one jumped out at her, but then she hadn't met everyone yet. *You just have to keep your eyes open.*

In the meantime, she would enjoy this ridiculously luxurious tub and that stupidly large soft bed for as long as it lasted.

"Hello, dearie."

Screaming, Valeria put her hands out, channeling her raw power to push all the water out of the tub. It streamed out in an arc, dousing the intruder and knocking them down with a loud smack.

She scrambled up, snatching a towel to cover her naked body. Valeria craned her neck to see a small figure wrapped in layers of wool struggling to get up.

"My apologies," a wet pile of rags said. This was followed by some grunting as the bent-over figure straightened, the gesture tentative because the tiled floor was covered in water and very slippery.

Valeria threw down another towel and stepped out of the tub, one hand up, ready to throw a defensive spell.

A rounded face peeked out of the layers of wool. "Hullo," the creature chirped.

Tense despite the friendly greeting, she pulled her head back, trying to blink bubble bath out of her eyes. When her vision cleared, she was staring at the oddest face she'd ever seen.

The intruder was round—round head, round nose, puffy round cheeks, and big round eyes. It was as if someone had animated a child's drawing of a face made of circles and brought it to life.

There was a crashing sound, and Rhys ran into the room.

He was big and moving fast so when his big boots hit the wet tiles, he had too much momentum. Sliding, he put his hands out to check his progress. He managed to shift his weight in time to stop himself from falling into the recently vacated tub, but only just.

Rhys straightened with a snap.

"*Agatha*," he began when he caught sight of Valeria, standing there dripping and naked save for the towel.

The towel she had grabbed was as large a sheet—indicating all the guests who stayed here were on the same scale as Rhys. But at least nothing was technically showing.

Not that it seemed to matter. Rhys kept staring at her as if he could see through the thick cotton.

"*Hey*," she snapped.

Giving himself a hard shake, Rhys cleared his throat. "My apologies."

He turned on his heel until he faced the wool-woman. "Aggie, I have asked you not to intrude on our guests. You gave me your word you would not do this again."

"I thought you just meant the men," Aggie said, her grin cheerful.

She shook out her many layers of wool like a dog shaking off water droplets.

Valeria's eyes watered, wondering if there was soap in her eyes. "Are your clothes completely dry now?" she asked.

Bending at the waist, Aggie bowed. "They are," she chirped.

Rhys turned to her. When Valeria glowered, he snapped his eyes up to a point above her head. "I believe I mentioned Aggie is a brownie. Once a brownie enters an agreement with a homeowner, they gain certain abilities—strictly powers over the domestic sphere. It makes them excellent caretakers, but it comes with drawbacks. They can appear in any room in their domain at will, which makes them lax when it comes to boundaries."

This last was said with a glare in Aggie's direction. She simply beamed as she began to flap her wool-covered arms at the floor.

"That explains why I didn't hear you knock," Valeria muttered, trying not to let her mouth fall open as the water receded. It was as if the brownie was pulling it back, tucking it away like a magician folded their many silk scarves back into their sleeve.

The brownie began to hum. Finishing up with the water on the floor, she began to fuss with the shelf of toiletries next to the sink.

Rhys pointed to the door. "We need to leave Valeria to her ablutions."

"Very well," Aggie shuffled to the door with a pout, her wool layers drooping. There was a little poof as she crossed the threshold of the bathroom and then she was gone.

Her host sighed heavily. "You can ask her not to come in without knocking. Brownies are mid-level caste Fae. They cannot lie, and Aggie's abilities end at the thresholds of this home. Within, her powers are significant, but she has no sway on the rest of the grounds or in another clan member's house. Her gifts are restricted to this one. Aggie is harmless. That being said, she will try to work around whatever promises you get her to make regarding privacy."

Valeria adjusted the towel. "So, asking her not to come in when I'm in the tub won't work?"

"Yes, it will. But then she'll pop in while you're changing in the bedroom or when you're using the other facilities," he said with the weariness of someone who had fought this particular war for centuries.

He gave the toilet a significant look. "It may take a series of promises to get to a place where you are comfortable with her."

"I'll remember that," Valeria said.

There was a long pause.

"Uh, I think it will take even longer for me to be comfortable enough to have a conversation with you while you're dressed and I'm only wearing a towel."

"Oh, yes. Of course." Red-faced, Rhys hemmed and hawed. "I will go."

He put his head down—an odd-looking gesture on someone so tall —and marched out of the room.

Valeria followed him to the door, closing it behind him with a heavy sigh. She turned around. The tub didn't have the same siren-like appeal of ten minutes ago, but there was a power shower built into the corner just behind it.

Pursing her lips, she looked in every possible hiding spot before dropping her towel, delighted to find the shower stall had a steam sauna built-in.

There is a bright side to having a peeping tom brownie, she told herself. *It's highly unlikely there are cameras on top of that.*

That would be overkill.

CHAPTER ELEVEN

Rhys was burning up—and not in the normal fire-breathing way.

He had been downstairs when he heard the shout. Part of him had been waiting for it. Aggie had a habit of intruding on his guests. Usually, she popped into existence next to them, eliciting a scream. That sort of thing tickled her.

But Agatha knew better than to interrupt them in the bathroom. That was why he'd run headlong into the room without thinking twice, only for the sight of Valeria in a towel to hit him like a brick to the head.

Her damp skin had glowed like a pearl under the gold-tinted lights Thomas had installed over the tub.

Was Rhys being tested? Because he was doing his best to be a considerate host. A potent temptation like this was the last thing he needed.

Before Rhys realized what he was doing, he was out the doors, striding down the mountain. Blinking in the bright sun, he took his bearings, gathered himself, and shifted, flying down to the lake. He hit the water a mere minute later, the splash rising at least ten feet in the air.

The ice-cold water ran over his scales in immediate soothing relief.

This was something very few in his clan did. Though they tolerated heat better than any other species, his kind was sensitive to the cold, more so in their winged form. They much preferred to bask in the sun after a flight, and only came to swim in the lake on the warmest of summer days.

But Rhys and his top lieutenants made a point of coming every few days in the winter when the lake wasn't iced over. It was punishing, but swimming in the cold built endurance and honed discipline.

Once his head was clear, he was able to reflect on just how badly he had made an ass of himself.

Yes, Valeria was a beautiful girl, a dead ringer for the woman he remembered. But the fact remained he was being pushed off the rails by a stranger.

His painful memories of Gabrielle were not something he cared to revisit often. But that didn't mean he didn't recall every moment they'd spent together.

Rhys had met Gabrielle over two centuries ago. He had just woken from a long sleep, taking his turn as one of the clan members to rise and remain awake while the others slept. It was a system they had abandoned—with good reason—long ago, but, at the time, it had seemed like a perfectly reasonable way to propel their small clan through the seas of time.

Intent on keeping up with the latest innovations in human society, Rhys had spent most of the early eighteen hundreds traveling through Europe. He'd made his way across the continent, visiting intellectual salons and seeking out the inventors and innovators who would lay the groundwork for the industrial revolution.

He had hated every minute of it.

At the time, he had a very low opinion of human society, particularly the ruling class, self-appointed arbiters of taste and culture. He saw them as preening fops and useless philosophers. In truth, the most elite humans of that time had little to recommend them beyond the lucky circumstances of their birth. That and the money that came with it.

His task of monitoring human progress had been an obligation, but it was one he did not shirk. The clan needed to stay on top of the sometimes-subtle transformations in human civilization—a dull but necessary task.

Then he had met Gabrielle.

He had been attending a lecture at the University of Vienna. The topic—recent innovations on steam engines—had piqued his interest in a way few subjects had at the time. Such devices had never been a part of his world, not unless they were a part of a larger military machinery and, even then, in a limited sense. What use were cannons to a dragon? It was the enemy who employed such tactics.

So, he had gone to the lecture, taking copious notes for the report he would eventually make to his superior.

It was there that he'd overheard a pair of dandies gushing about the latest opera. Though some of his people played instruments on their homeworld, none of his clan sang. It was not part of their tradition. However, their vocal cords were structured for cries across very long distances. It sounded almost as if the humans had discovered their version of the ability and turned it into a form of entertainment.

He'd attended as part of his research, buying admission to the pit in case he wanted to make a quick exit. It wouldn't have been the first time he'd been pulled into a human recreation only to beat a quick retreat after a few insufferable minutes.

However, Rhys hadn't heard a single note of music that night. Not after he looked up into the boxes and saw Gabrielle, who had been escorted to the performance by a member of her family.

One glance and he'd been lost.

Dark-haired with eyes like polished jade goldstone, Gabrielle had been radiant, a jewel universally admired. She had recently made her debut into society, and she was being courted by every eligible man in Vienna. Rhys spent the rest of the performance staring at her.

Memories swirled around his head, but he ruthlessly shut down the flood. This was simply a trick of time. The woman in his guest suite was not Gabrielle. His lost mate had been a hothouse flower, delicate and sensitive. Yes, this Valeria had the same lustrous beauty as his former fiancé. But this woman was...hard...suspicious. And more guarded than Fort Knox.

That and Valeria appeared to have very strong magic.

His clan dealt with witches about as often as they dealt with other outsiders—as little as possible. Nevertheless, Rhys' position meant that he'd met witches of all stripes over his long life, both light and dark. Gabrielle had been part of the light, a pure soul. He had no idea what Valeria was, but he strongly suspected her power was...not light.

Except witch talents were neither one nor the other, he reminded himself. It all depended on how they were used. There was also the fact that Valeria was being pursued by her own kind. Dark witches were monsters, cannibals who consumed anyone weaker than themselves. But she wasn't weak, which either meant she was light or untrained.

Yes, untrained made sense. Valeria would have known how to defend herself had she devoted herself to the black arts. Rhys breathed a little easier about his decision to bring a stranger into their territory. Figuratively, anyway, because he was still underwater.

After a few more laps around the lake, Rhys was back in control. He left the water soon after. He would learn more about his mysterious guest tonight at dinner.

She had to eat, right? Once he knew her history, he'd make some plans regarding her security and possibly theirs... Because, unlike Gabrielle, Valeria appeared to be alone in the world.

He might be all she had.

CHAPTER TWELVE

Valeria walked into the formal dining room, struck dumb at the sight she beheld.

The chamber was like something out of a medieval castle, with rough walls made of wood instead of stone and a very long table capable of seating at least two dozen people. Only two places were set at one end—a fact at odds with the sheer volume of food on the massive wooden table.

It was a feast.

A large fowl—a turkey or a goose—sat in the middle, the crisp skin a perfect golden brown. Next to it was a slab of meat, garnished with apples, a roast of some kind. There was also a ham, several savory pies, a cheese-crusted dish that appeared to be a pasta casserole, as well as several platters of cooked greens. Interspersed between the larger plates were bowls of fruit, some cut into bite-sized pieces, some not.

It was an embarrassment of riches. The sight and smell of so much food was a physical slap in the face. Forcing herself to walk slowly, Valeria reached the chair next to the head of the table—the only other place setting.

She reached out and held the back of the high-backed chair, making a desperate attempt to regain her equilibrium.

Rhys was tracking her movement, his eyes so black that she almost stopped in her tracks. But they weren't cold or angry. Instead, they glowed like burning embers. Just like in the mirror...

It was probably a dragon thing. Rhys was a creature of ash and flame. That was reflected in his eyes. It wasn't threatening, just a reflection of his nature, she assured herself emphatically.

His eyebrow twitched as her hesitation stretched a few seconds too long. "Are you all right?"

Despite having eaten Tom's second sandwich earlier, she nodded jerkily, her mouth salivating. Valeria cleared her throat. "Are we expecting more of your clan?" she said, gesturing to the mountains of food.

"Not tonight."

Valeria tensed as he approached, the hair on the nape of her neck rising. But Rhys didn't touch her. He gripped the chair, pulling it back for her in an old-world courtly gesture. Masking her discomfort, she sat, letting him tuck the heavy chair closer to the table.

She touched the satiny surface of the table. It was remarkable—a vertical cross-section of a huge tree varnished to a glossy shine. The natural whirls and striations more beautiful than any decorative carving would have been, the roughly polished edge retaining enough of the bark for her to feel the pitted and uneven surface. Frowning, she squinted down the length of the table. There were no lines to suggest there were separate leaves. There wasn't even a seam to indicate two slabs had been glued together.

"Is this a single slice of wood?"

He nodded in confirmation. "I made it," he added. There was the tiniest hint of pride in his voice.

She traced the darker mark of a knot of wood in the grain. "Did you use a laser to cut it?"

Rhys stared at her blankly. Then he shook his head.

"A giant saw?"

His mouth twitched. "Such things did not exist at the time."

She stopped fondling the wood. Good Lord. He made it by hand by *himself*. Awed, she twisted in her seat to examine the highchair back and then all the others. The backs were smaller versions of the table, each unique. The cushions attached to them were fastened with flat copper nails that echoed the reddish tint of the wood.

"It's incredible," she said, her hunger momentarily forgotten ."It must have taken a very long time."

Not to mention the amount of skill required to keep such a massive piece intact.

His shoulders rose and fell. "It was something to pass the time, and it serves a useful purpose. Many of my warriors dine here almost every day."

Her brows puckered. "Then where are they?" She didn't understand why there was so much food and only two places set.

Rhys leaned forward, taking a plate of what looked like little phyllo dough sacs. He offered it to her. Mouth watering again, she took one, unable to stop herself from biting it.

An explosion of savory flavor burst in her mouth. Thomas' sandwich had been delicious, but this mix of meat, mushrooms, and crisp layers of pastry was an onslaught to her senses.

"I've asked my warriors to see to their own needs for the evening," he shared, pushing a plate of cut fruit in her direction. "I thought a crowd might overwhelm you."

Swallowing reluctantly—the flavor in her mouth too good—she reached for the glass of water at her side.

"I guess dragons require a lot of calories," she said, feeling self-conscious.

Those smoldering eyes seemed to be studying her, as if he could see the spells of self-protection around her, assessing them for chinks, any weaknesses he could exploit.

She forced herself to slacken her muscles, feigning relaxation as he picked up his glass.

"Even I can't finish all this. But Aggie likes to show off when a guest first arrives. Also, the younger members of the clan have the run of the kitchen at all hours. They raid the icebox after their security shifts. Rest assured, nothing will go to waste."

He began to carve the bird, handling the knives so deftly she could easily imagine him carving up a person.

"Oh," she said weakly, subtly edging to the other side of her chair. Though Rhys ignored the small movement, she had the sense he was aware of her retreat. He put the knives down, loaded her plate with the efficiency of a steakhouse server, and then helped himself.

With a single nod, he began to eat. Her faux relaxation slowly became genuine as he consumed a startling amount of food. He wasn't glutinous or messy—he simply ate steadily, his table manners flawless until he'd eaten almost a quarter of the offerings, urging her to eat her fill with the occasional murmur.

Whatever half-formed ideas she might have had of being aloof or reserved fell away. Valeria began to eat, trying not to fall on the offerings like a slavering dog. She almost failed, carried away by the assortment and skill with which each dish had been prepared.

Only when it felt as if she was going to burst did she stop, wiping her mouth with a cloth napkin in a belated demonstration of good manners. She opened her mouth to compliment the chef when she hesitated, realizing the plates had thinned between one blink and the next.

Rhys, who also seemed more relaxed now that they'd eaten, reached over to pour her a glass of fortified wine she was sure hadn't been there at the start of the meal.

"Am I crazy or is Aggie clearing and switching out these plates with her magic?"

"You are not mad," he said, that dark rolling voice managing to sound crisp and vaguely British in its formality. "It is an aspect of her abilities. They are considerable in their way, not unlike a house-elf."

Valeria set down her glass. "Is that a *Harry Potter* reference?"

"It was required viewing."

She bit her lip to hide her sudden amusement. "Someone made you watch *Harry Potter?*"

An expression of resigned chagrin crossed his face. Rhys leaned back in the chair, the subtle motion managing to highlight how large his body was. "We make it a point to keep current with human innovation. I would prefer other subject matters for our film nights—documentaries are far more informative. However, Sanaa has argued that it's equally important to stay abreast of the cultural zeitgeist...whatever that means."

He sipped more wine. "We generally watch movies here a few times a month or outside utilizing a large screen in the warmer weather of spring and summer."

She was having a hard time picturing a bunch of dragons lounging around watching movies.

"What did you last see?" She already knew he hadn't seen '*The Terminator*'.

His tone grew dismissive. "Something frivolous with a caped strongman."

Her mouth quirked. "Superman?"

"Yes, that was it." He rolled his eyes. "Flying without wings...ridiculous."

A snicker escaped before she could help it. "I'm surprised you haven't nixed all comic book movies."

A corner of his mouth lifted. "I do try to be fair. Besides, I could hardly refuse given that it was one of my decrees that led to a regular movie night."

Her eyes widened. "You make decrees?"

"We are not a democracy."

She stared at him with a fixed expression. He leaned forward, his tone softening.

"It would be prudent for me to mention that the rules clan members follow are distinct from the ones we apply to guests. The clan strictly observes a coda of hospitality not unlike some Middle Eastern cultures. As long as you do not abuse our generosity or intentionally compromise the homestead's safety, you will be quite safe."

"And if I unintentionally compromise it?" she asked, chest tight.

"We will make sure that doesn't happen." He leaned forward without bending at the waist. "Did you sell them your blood? Is that how they're tracking you?"

Valeria's face flamed. "I'm not that stupid."

He leaned back in his chair. "My apologies for offending you. It's just that you said—"

She held up a hand. "I know. Although the offers were tempting, I've never actually sold my blood or hair."

Valeria hesitated. "Well, to tell the truth, I *did* sell blood once and I did say it was mine, but I was lying."

She stared down at the table. Her mother wouldn't have felt shame about her deception, especially under those circumstances. But Valeria had never felt comfortable with the incident.

Yet, you did it. She had needed the money.

A large warm hand covered hers. Flinching, she snatched her hand back.

Rhys froze, his hand suspended over hers. "My apologies. I should know better than to touch without permission."

He straightened in his seat, his face wiped clean of all emotion. "What about the hair that was taken by force?"

A corner of her mouth turned up. "I got it back."

She'd had to burn down a derelict building to do it, but that she did *not* feel guilty about.

"Then how do you believe they are tracking you?"

She shrugged. "Persistence mainly. Some of our kind are good at tracking. Others who aren't have outsourced the effort. I've been hunted by Fae and shifters. More recently one of those witches got close enough to mark me with a trace but I found it—eventually—and broke the hex. But I wasn't able to get far enough away after, and they ran me down in that alley. You know the rest."

"Your lack of resources must be a factor," he observed.

"Yes," she said stiffly. "I wanted to speak to you about that. Is there a way to earn money here?"

She fought the urge to cringe. Ravenna had never understood where Valeria got the stubborn streak of pride that made it difficult to borrow or scam people for cash.

"If you need to lie, cheat, or steal to survive, you do it," her mother had argued whenever Valeria's conscience had balked at a distasteful task. "No hunter will be merciful because you were honest in your dealings."

Thinking of her mother depressed her spirits, but Rhys' voice cut her reverie short. "Money will not be a concern here. You will not need it so long as you are our guest."

"Thank you," she murmured. "But what if I wanted to earn some while I was here?"

Without funds, she'd never be able to leave, and she wouldn't steal any of the glittering antiques she saw on almost every surface.

Despite Ravenna's best efforts, Valeria had her pride.

"I know this may be something of a disappointment for a witch of your rare talent, but we do not need spells or any enchantments—I know many of your kind sell their services in this way. I'm afraid we don't trade with the kinds of people who would buy such things. It would expose our location and that is something we just don't do."

"I wasn't thinking of selling spells." Doing that sort of thing had exposed them to danger too often. It might have even been the reason her mother was dead.

Wait. What had he said? "Fire wielders are not that rare," she said, wondering what he had meant.

Yes, it was an atypical talent for a witch, unless they had Fae blood.

Rhys hesitated. He fingered the rim of his glass. "But fire-wielding is not the natural form your magic takes, is it?"

Valeria feigned confusion, willing her heart to stop racing. "Of course it is. You saw me do it in the alley. Sanaa knows that. She said as much when I woke it. It seemed to please her."

The dragon's sculpted lips parted. "Sanaa assumed after she heard the details of what happened, and I didn't correct it. But I was there. I felt those flames...and I know that was not your fire. It was mine."

CHAPTER THIRTEEN

Rhys studied Valeria's face, wondering if he had miscalculated. Beneath her placid surface, she was panicking. He could smell her anxiety.

"I think we would be better served by being honest with each other," he said softly.

He didn't have that much experience with making people at ease. Being abrasive and blunt was second nature for a warrior at the top of the clan hierarchy. But this was too important for his normal hammer-to-anvil approach.

"I will not share the nature of your talent with the rest of the clan if it makes you uncomfortable. However, it would be disingenuous for me to pretend I did not recognize the fire as my own."

Pursing her lips, Valeria reached for the glass of sweet wine he had poured. She tossed it back as if it were a hard whiskey. "I faced a witch with fire talent once, and I used it against them. They were burned badly enough to stop attacking me. I got away that day."

Ah.

"It's my understanding that most fire wielders can't generate their own flames. They need a source. A lighter is enough. They take those flames and amplify them. But because it's not born of them, it can be used against them. My fire is a part of me. I cannot be damaged by it—

its source is the same wellspring of magic that allows me to change my form so dramatically—but magic alone is not its source. There is a biological component, enough that I would be able to distinguish the taste of it from the fire produced by the other members of my clan."

A subtle thrumming emanated from the delicate lines of Valeria's body. It was well-hidden, but Rhys was focused on her with a hunter's vigilance, and something more. He was honest enough with himself to admit that he desired her. There was no way he could miss her anxiety.

"I see," she said slowly, appearing to choose her words with care. "Well, uh, I would appreciate it if you did not share the nature of my talent with anyone else."

He frowned. "Is your kind of mimicry very rare among witches?"

"Apparently." She sighed, tired despite the much-needed energy boost the large meal had given her. "My mother was constantly warning me to keep it secret. I was never supposed to tell anyone exactly what I could do."

Rhys saw the wisdom of that. "It certainly works better as an offensive weapon if you aren't prepared for it."

"It has come in handy a few times."

"Only a few? Is it difficult to use?"

The lush lower lip thinned slightly as if she were pulling it into her mouth, worrying it with her teeth.

"I meant what I said earlier," he said, reading in her silence the need to preserve the secrets that had kept her alive. "This territory is a safe place for you. I would never share your confidence with my men, and none of my people would dare betray you to your enemies."

The look she gave him was frankly skeptical. "I don't mean to be insolent, but how can you say that? No one can know what's in the mind of another person."

Those last words held traces of pain. They were faint. She was trying to hide them, to shield herself from the world with impenetrable mental walls. This was a woman who had been betrayed over and over.

It was startling in a way, how easily he could understand what motivated her. No one had ever accused Rhys of being sensitive or even particularly understanding.

Only slightly more surprising was this pressing need to unravel her secrets. It was a desire borne of the most primitive part of him. He would *not* allow her to hide anything from him.

And if she ran, he would find her.

"I am the leader here," he said modulating his tone. The last thing he wanted to do was frighten her. "And I know my people. When I say that they won't sell you out, it's because they do not need to. They are fulfilled. They don't require money because we have wealth, quite a lot of it. Finding lost treasure is still a pastime, although we have learned to channel our innate acquisitiveness into updated and more conventional means of making money. Additionally, our kind is immune to most human-born magicks, so we wouldn't be affected by most of your spells in any case."

Rhys did not intend that last as a warning, but she seemed to take it as one.

"I wouldn't try to enchant anyone," she protested, her back stiffening.

"Good." He laughed, wondering at her choice of words. "You would find yourself rebuffed, and then very, *very* warm. But you do not need to worry about being fricasseed out of hand. No one will harm you while you are in my care. We are a disciplined lot out of necessity."

That earned him a tiny smile. "You must be a good leader if your people are that content."

If only she knew. But he fought the instinct to tell her everything. *Remember, she is not Gabrielle.*

That was enough to keep his mouth shut on the details of how his community's prosperity and hard-won emotional health had come about.

"Suffice it to say, we have learned from the lessons of our forebears. We don't allow the seeds of discord and discontent to take root," he said. "We are a martial people by nature, so we train in the tactics of battle a great deal, but we also recognize that our minds must be challenged regularly with difficult or intricate tasks. Conversely, everyone here has the right to leisure time when they want it. And although a small handful succumbs to the urge to wander the world in search of adventure, it's never for too long. My people always come back because they know they will always be welcomed home."

Her eyes met his before skittering away as if she found his gaze too intense. "Must be nice."

Damn. "My words were not intended to hurt you," he said softly, studying her averted face.

"They didn't," she said, bristling.

But he could feel the walls raising just a little higher. There was a whisper of desolation, like the wind in the desert. *She truly is alone, and has been for some time.*

Rhys let the lie pass. The silence stretched between them as he sensed her turmoil. It was there in her scent.

Her fingers rubbed around the stem of her wineglass. "My talent can be difficult to use," she said unexpectedly. "As an offensive weapon, it can be too slow. Just because you can copy someone's magic doesn't mean you can wield it. Some magic is too...foreign."

Eager, but trying not to show it, he kept his voice soft when she lapsed into silence as if she'd regretted sharing that.

"Can you shift in the presence of other shifters?" He was dying to know.

She shook her head. "No. That seems to be a step too far. But you had something else I could use."

He leaned back, understanding. "My fire."

Of course. It made sense. Her magic wouldn't have been compatible with shifting. That was too profound a transformation. It shuffled every system of one's body—skeletal, muscular, endocrine...The list went on and on. The ability to change was hardwired into a shifter's body. It began with DNA and ended with scales or fur.

But his fire-breathing ability was preternatural, something he could do in either form. The fuel was chemical, but the flames were kindled by magic. Else he couldn't have ignited them underwater.

"So, if a shark-shifter could freeze the water around him, that would be something your talent could copy?"

Her expression was priceless. Wide-eyed, she clutched the edge of the table. "There are shark shifters?"

Grimacing, he shrugged. "They're what Thomas calls really big jerks."

Valeria snatched up her glass, taking a big swig. "I'm never going swimming again."

This time, he allowed her to see his amusement. There was a corresponding hint of color in those strikingly carved cheekbones. His insides tightened pleasurably. "How close do you need to be to copy someone's magic?"

She sighed, something in her posture speaking to resignation. "Depends on how strong they are."

Ah, yes. The mirror would reflect brighter fires more clearly. "And once the person moves out of range, it fades in relation to that strength?"

Her brow wrinkled.

"Maybe?" She shrugged. "It's not like I've done tests. A lot of the time, I try to avoid picking up someone else's magic. It can be unwieldy. Especially if it's just some random passerby. In that case, I wouldn't want to use their brand of magic. That would just call attention to myself, and I have more than enough problems staying out of people's crosshairs."

Valeria rested against the back of her chair as if trying not to slump.

That was when he became certain. This girl wasn't a black witch. Whatever darkness she had, why his instincts kept going off—was a reflection of what she'd copied.

But though he and his people avoided witches as a rule, they knew one thing and it was universal—no black witch would ever think she had enough magic. The rites they practiced consumed it, eating it up, so they were constantly hunting for new sources.

Another question came to mind. What if the people pursuing her did have some inkling of Valeria's power? It could be she wasn't a target because she had so much magic. What if they thought they could exploit her ability to reflect theirs?

Did they think they could scoop off the extra magic the way cream was skimmed off milk?

"You'll need more clothing," he said, changing the subject to the practical and mundane after she stayed quiet for too long. "Do you have a cache of belongings hidden somewhere? Would you like me to send someone to get it?"

She shook her head. "No, thanks. I've had to learn to travel light, get clothes that wear well and can be easily washed in the sink. Everything I own is in my backpack."

He'd peeked into her small bag when she'd been unconscious. There had been two pairs of pants and three shirts, some underclothes, and a battered Ziplock bag full of toiletries. Other than that, there had been a small sheath of papers bundled together, written by at least two different hands.

No books, no jewels, and no gold. No jewelry of any type. Just some beautifully detailed sketches of flowers and birds, including a striking half-finished one of a hummingbird in flight.

The witch was a talented artist.

"I'm afraid your apparel isn't suitable for the area. But don't worry. The clan owns many companies, including a few clothing manufacturers. I've already taken the liberty of filling the closet in your room. I take it you didn't look inside?" he asked, gesturing to her clothes, which were her own.

"No, I didn't." Her face expressed discomfort. "But you didn't have to do that. I can make do with what I have."

He acknowledged that, but he couldn't let it go. "As I said I am the leader of this community. I am responsible for the well-being and care of everyone in my territory. That includes you for the duration of your stay. In any case, none of your clothing is thick enough. You need heavier gear up here. The terrain is rough, and the weather can be brutal, with sleeting rain even in spring."

She pursed her lips, but she didn't object.

"Sanaa chose most of your things," he lied.

Saana had given him the sizes, but it had been Rhys who had selected the colors and styles of the clothes in her room. He hadn't asked himself why he wouldn't let anyone else select what Valeria would wear.

"I can pay you back for the clothes," she said, fiddling with her napkin. "That's what I was trying to say earlier. I have waitressed, been a cleaning woman, worked as a hairdresser, and was even a nurse's assistant. I'm strong for someone my size, and I learn quickly. I can earn my keep."

Ah. "I understand some people can't stand being idle. In this, you are not unlike many of my people, but even we know when to rest and conserve our strength."

He tried to convey his reassurance with his hands, but the movement seemed to make her nervous, so he dropped them back to the table.

"Once you've recovered to full strength, we can discuss this topic again. In the meantime, take the time to recuperate fully. You have the run of the entire house and the grounds immediately around it. I'm sure Sanaa would welcome a visit soon. She's not as mobile at the moment, so going to her would be necessary. Beyond that, you should ask for permission or guidance. Some places are dangerous—like the training fields and certain unstable hillsides farther out."

She nodded gamely, but he could sense her exhaustion.

He rose. "You are fatiguing." He offered his hand. "Perhaps it is time to retire. You can get the full tour of the house and its amenities tomorrow."

"Thank you." She stood, but she didn't take his hand. Instead, she walked at his side to the stairs. "I...I am in your debt."

Satisfaction coursed through his veins at the acknowledgment. The dragon in him was greedy, but the man in him knew each concession this woman chose to make was a victory.

"Yes, but, in time, you may find, despite appearances, that isn't always a bad place to be."

CHAPTER FOURTEEN

Valeria knew never to take anyone's words at face value, which was why it bothered her that she wanted to believe everything Rhys had said at dinner. Enough that she had slept deeply all night—something that hadn't happened in recent memory.

She woke up angry with herself and irritated with him.

That won't do. Valeria might not have been comfortable enough to be a truly gracious guest but at least she could make the effort to fake it. Meanwhile, she didn't have to trust anyone.

I wonder if Rhys noticed I didn't eat or drink anything until after he had tasted it first.

She'd tried not to make it obvious, but that was the sort of thing that was difficult to disguise.

Valeria knew he wasn't telling her everything he knew. It was the way he watched at her like he was waiting for her to say or do something specific. Was he expecting that she'd incriminate herself somehow? What was he looking for?

It was tempting to stay in her room and hide from him all day, but that wasn't an option. She'd been fighting for her life in Los Angeles one night, lost consciousness, and woke up in an isolated rural community over a thousand miles away. She needed to get the lay of the land, to get her bearings.

Valeria went to get dressed, but her clothes were nowhere to be found. Her pack was there, closed. Her mother's notes and letters were exactly where she had left them, tucked into the inside pocket. But other than her toiletries, the bag was empty. The only clothes she had left were the worn t-shirt and leggings she had slept in.

Suppressing a growl, she threw open the closet door and jerked in surprise. Her walk-in was more like a large bedroom. It was bigger than her studio apartment had been.

Mouth dropping open, Valeria drifted inside, her suspicion and apprehension melting into bewilderment.

She tripped a motion sensor by coming inside. Soft golden lights in recessed niches turned on overhead, illuminating a space divided by rods and lined shelves. Every bit of space held new clothing and shoes.

At first, she thought this was an overflow of some kind. She didn't know how big this dragon clan was, but Rhys had said many people crashed here. It made sense that they would keep spare clothing for everyone.

Except all these things were new and in her size. Many of the tags had little holes where the tags had recently been removed.

Holy...

Slack-jawed, she went from rack to rack, examining the shirts, sweaters, pants, and dresses. It was organized by type and divided by color so precisely that Valeria briefly wondered if Aggie was OCD enough to do this on her own. It didn't seem likely.

Had Rhys arranged her clothes?

The closet had an island—something Valeria had only ever seen in pictures and movies. Silky intimates were separated from cotton ones in drawers on two sides. The third side held nightwear, both satin nightgowns and thick flannel pajama sets.

She almost cried out when she found the outerwear. Coats of all descriptions occupied a special section. Wool pea-coats shared a rack with puffy down-filled jackets. A full-length cashmere camel coat was next to a long trench with a lined hood.

Unable to resist, Valeria pulled down a three-quarter-length coat in a deep red shade that was trimmed with black fur. Touching it, she wondered if it was synthetic or something Rhys had hunted down and killed himself. Snickering at the thought, she picked out a pair of jeans, a long-sleeved t-shirt, and a light sweater. Dressing quickly, she slung the red coat over one arm, intending to wash up quickly before searching out the kitchen.

"Hullo!" Aggie popped into existence two feet away, holding a full breakfast tray.

Biting back a scream, Valeria fell against the door.

"Sorry, dearie," Aggie said, shooting her a gap-toothed grin. "Didn't mean to give you a fright."

Forcing herself to take a deep breath, Valeria didn't speak until she was sure her voice was even. "Agatha, in addition to never entering the bathroom, can you please always announce yourself before popping in here?"

"Of course, dearie."

Since that was the same answer she'd gotten for the bathroom issue, Valeria didn't have much hope of not having the stuffing scared out of her again.

Valeria had never met a brownie before. She was going to have to make a study on how to talk to the Fae. She knew enough about them to be aware that there were rules to it. Until then, she'd have to muddle through.

"I brought you some food," Aggie said. The tray disappeared from her hand, reappearing on top of the little table opposite the television.

"Did Rhys eat already?" Valeria assumed as much given how high the sun was.

"Oh yes. Hours ago," the Fae confirmed cheerfully.

Aggie blinked out of existence, reappearing next to the table with a carafe of orange juice. When she raised her arm, a diner-style coffee pot appeared. She poured a generous steaming amount into a thick earthenware mug. "You'll have to get up quite early to dine with him. He likes to wake with the sun, that one does."

Drawn to the siren song of the fresh-brew, Valeria sat at the table, murmuring her thanks.

Valeria added cream and sugar to the mug, sipping gingerly. She closed her eyes as the rich bold nectar hit her system. "This is excellent coffee."

"Thank you, dearie. I roast the beans myself—the master prefers mine to the store-bought stuff."

The Fae pushed the tray toward her. There was a pile of silver-dollar pancakes, eggs Benedict, and a bowl of creamy-looking oatmeal garnished with a crust of sugar that had been melted on, like a creme brûlée. There were also some interesting little things that looked like a cross between cherries and blueberries.

"This all looks incredible, and I'm very grateful for all the trouble you've gone to, but I should add I don't usually eat this much at break-fast—at any meal. So, there's no need to go to so much trouble. If you show me the kitchen, I can fix myself some toast and pour a coffee directly from the coffeemaker."

Aggie didn't seem to like that, but her voice was still upbeat when she spoke. "Oh, but it's no trouble. Besides, this is nothing to the meals I have to prepare for the master. Eat up, dearie. Once you're done, I can show you the house if you like. Or you can explore on your own. The master said you have the run of the place."

There was a question in her tone at that last part, but Valeria didn't know why Rhys wanted her to feel at home any more than Aggie did. So, she murmured her thanks and started to eat.

Shrugging, the brownie popped away. The minute Valeria finished and left the table, the plates disappeared as if her standing had been the signal to whisk them away.

In their place was a set of premium drawing pencils.

Startled, Valeria picked them up. There was a note written in a bold hand.

In case you need them.

How had Rhys known she liked to draw? Yet another mystery for her to solve.

Well, you're not going to accomplish anything sitting here. After washing up, she decided to explore the house first. She walked all along the second floor, skipping the upper level because it was Rhys' private domain.

In addition to the bedrooms, there were several meeting rooms. Some were minimally furnished, presumably so the clan could easily adapt them for whatever was needed. The doors were open, but she didn't know if they had been left that way so she could explore or if that was the normal state of things.

Then she found the library and was swept off her feet. The first thing that registered was the sheer number of volumes. Many were bound in leather, which fit Rhys' old-world sensibilities, but there were also plenty of modern hardbacks and paperbacks, as well as many magazines, equally divided between science, technology, art, and the financial world.

The stunning space spanned two levels of one corner of the house, extending from the second-floor, where a wide mezzanine wrapped around the room, down to the ground floor. Unnervingly, there was no railing at the edge, which told her exactly how often non-dragon visitors stayed in this mansion.

A beautiful spiral staircase connected one level to the other. There were also long and narrow cathedral-like windows extending up through both stories. It took her a while to realize that the light coming through them was muted as if the glass was polarized like certain office buildings.

It's to protect the books, her mind supplied.

For a second, she thought it was a missed opportunity to have beautiful stained glass, but then again what could compete with the richness of those wooden shelves?

Valeria had never fallen in love with a place before. Almost dazed, she walked along the gallery, her fingers trailing over the spines of the bookshelves bolted into the walls. Wide leather chairs were distributed intermittently around the mezzanine and in the corners of the first floor. Also below were two tables with four chairs apiece were set several yards apart—research spaces that had electrical outlets for computers just like a public library. On either side of the tables were long couches in a suede so soft, she wondered if it was synthetic.

Or is it from some exotic animal not of this world? Valeria decided she'd rather not know.

She could have spent all day—perhaps an entire week—in that library, but she pushed herself to move on to the rest of the ground floor. She walked through the big living room again, trying to picture it filled with men as large as Rhys. Even the thought of it was unsettling.

Skipping the dining room, she found the kitchen—also surprisingly modern with chrome appliances and granite countertops—but she wasn't allowed to linger long before Aggie ushered her out. Acknowledging that was the brownie's domain, Valeria retreated to the living room and ended up leaving the house via a pair of ground-floor patio doors.

She had known the house was situated at the top of the hill. But Valeria hadn't appreciated how high they were up from the driveway, because the grade of the road had built so gradually. However, it was clear enough from the back of the house where she stood. It was a steeper gradient here, but not so bad that she would have had trouble walking down. There was also a wide trail winding down to a sharply delineated valley half-hidden by the pine trees.

The air was so crisp and clear it almost burned the inside of her nose. Pulling on the coat she eschewed the path, choosing to walk around the house. There was little in the way of foliage so near the house, but the smell of pine was everywhere. More immediately plentiful were boulders—odd flat ones.

She half-suspected these were for basking lizards...very large lizards. But Rhys himself probably used the redwood deck on the top floor. Valeria could only see it by walking down the road a while because it was too big and high to be seen otherwise.

What she could make out was another wrap-around and rail-less balcony. It spanned enough of the upper level, making it accessible from both Rhys' office and the master bedroom.

She was tempted to go down one of the paths winding down the hill when she felt a strong gust of wind buffet her. Closing her eyes against the dust, she felt more than saw the shadow falling over her.

Stomach muscles clenching, Valeria couldn't stop the spike of fear that coursed through her as Rhys landed a few yards away.

"Hello."

Peeking cautiously from under her lashes, she saw him walking toward her on two legs, having missed the dramatic change from cottage-sized beast to intimidating man.

"Hi," she said. Forcing herself to stand straight, she gave him a sheepish smile. "I know I shouldn't worry about getting squished, but it's kind of hard not to when a mythical creature lands almost on top of you."

Rhys cocked his head. "I assure you that my control is excellent. The chances of accidental squish-age is so low as to be close to zero."

Tittering awkwardly, she nodded. "I'll remember that."

A wind that had nothing to do with his wings blew her hood against the back of her head. Unused to the cold, Valeria pulled the fur-trimmed hood up.

Rhys took a step back, blinking.

"Are you okay?" she asked, wondering at his stricken expression.

"I am well," he said, sounding more hoarse than normal. Reaching out, he touched the sleeve of the coat. "This color is becoming. I, uh, I believe it's one of Sanaa's favorites."

"How is she today?" Valeria asked. "Is she about ready to pop?"

He shook his head as if to clear it, then invited her to walk at his side. "The healer says her time is almost upon us. But it's been so long since we've had an actual pregnancy in the clan—and never one involving a bear shifter, which makes the healer's diagnosis less precise. He says it could be tonight, or it could be a week from now. Fortunately, Thomas has relented on the moratorium he put on visitors since Sanaa wants them. I believe she is getting frustrated with her lack of mobility."

"She seemed fairly active yesterday. I'm sorry she had to look after me so close to giving birth."

"Oh, believe me, she was quite happy for the distraction. She asked about you earlier, and she wanted to extend an invitation to visit whenever you feel up to it."

"I'd love to see her," Valeria said, surprised to find she meant it. The jury was still out on Rhys and the others, but she was sure Sanaa was good people.

"Perhaps tomorrow." Rhys' dark gaze roamed over her. She could feel his scrutiny like a physical weight passing over her skin. "You're still fatigued."

"I'm fine," she protested, hiding her displeasure at the observation.

She *was* tired, which didn't make sense. Valeria had spent years on the move. She was used to pushing past the point of endurance, running on empty until she could afford to crash somewhere safe. Well, she was safe now. She'd been in this community for a few days—some of them unconscious, true, but still enough that she should have recouped her strength now.

I'm not this weak, she berated herself.

It was also annoying how easily Rhys could read her. She had been trained to hide her flaws and frailty from an early age. It was second nature to her now. But it seemed this dragon could see through that facade.

Could someone *smell* exhaustion?

She blinked as Rhys offered her his arm. "Have you toured the house?"

You're rested enough to be in control. Touching him won't hurt him.

Feeling like she was in a period play, she put her hand on his arm. He began to walk, leading her back to the house. "I poked around the second and main floor. You have a nice library."

"Do you like to read?"

She shrugged. "I haven't had much in the way of leisure time for a while, but yes."

Public libraries had been some of her favorite places to hide. It had never mattered if she had a library card or how scruffy she had looked. As long as she'd been clean and quiet, librarians had, as a rule, never bothered her. Some had even gone a step farther and tried to help, passing her cards for women's shelters in the area.

Librarians were her favorite people.

"I have some rare books you might find of interest. There aren't too many on witchcraft, but I do have some diaries of notable practitioners."

"Why?" she asked as he led her back into the library. "I thought that sort of thing didn't interest you."

He led her to the couch. She sat as he went to a bookshelf near one of the windows. "It doesn't, but I mentioned treasure hunting is a hobby for my kind—some of the stereotypes humans have of dragons are true. I acquired some of these as part of such a search."

He handed her a small, worn volume. It was bound in cloth that had split at the top and bottom corners on both sides. "This belonged to the granddaughter of a German witch named Magaretha Ramhold, who was said to consort with a dragon. According to rumor, the demonic dragon was responsible for the family's newfound wealth. Her neighbors whispered that the dragon showered her with gold and jewels because she took it to her bed.”

Rhys sat in the adjoining armchair as she began to flip through the diary. Turning each fragile page with care, she squinted at the cramped script. “I don't read German. Does she mention the dragon?”

Had it been a relative of his?

His smile was a touch sardonic. “Only to scoff at the rumors. Magaretha was a matriarch whose business savvy and ruthlessness caused enmity and discord in her community. Scholars concluded envy was the reason she'd been branded a witch. But years after her execution, her descendent wrote that she *was* a witch, one who practiced healing magic. But there was no dragon and no horde of treasure.”

Her lips twitched. “I'm sorry.”

“It was a minor disappointment, I assure you. I mostly bought it because it clarified the dragon issue—I learned after the fact that what Germans of that time called dragons were more like a household spirit.”

“Were you looking for more dragons?”

“No. If we wanted to find others of our kind, it wouldn't be that hard. But I kept the book because the granddaughter wrote down some of her healing concoctions. We don't have any use for them, of course, but I thought they had enough historical significance to hang on to.”

He went to a sideboard. As in a historical novel, there was a bar hidden in a cabinet. He poured a few fingers of amber liquid into a pair of rounded glasses with flat bottoms.

“No, thank you,” she said, holding up a hand when he offered it to her.

Nonplussed, he peered down at the glasses. “It's sweet. More of a cordial, made of some kind of common nut—macadamia perhaps.”

She shook her head and he shrugged. “Sanaa liked it, back before Thomas stopped letting her imbibe spirits. Would you prefer something else?”

“Uh, well, I'm just not in the habit of drinking outside of a meal.” In truth, she didn't drink alcohol at all. Not only was it a bad idea to compromise her reaction times and dull her senses when people were hunting her, but alcohol was expensive. Food had always been the priority.

He set the glasses on the low coffee table, making a production of taking one and sipping it.

Valeria deflated slightly. "Oh...you noticed I didn't eat or drink anything you hadn't tasted."

Rhys didn't appear offended. "Being careful about what you consume is sensible. I can't expect you to feel comfortable here overnight. That will take time."

He wrinkled his nose suddenly. "Although, I should add that there are numerous things I can eat or drink that you would find unsettling, even incapacitating."

Collapsing on the couch cushions, she watched him with wry resignation. She hadn't considered that, but it made sense. Predatory shifters ate things they hunted down. There would be plenty of things she wouldn't be able to stomach. It made sense that a dragon's diet would be even more extreme.

"Thanks for being honest."

He paused, looking as if he wanted to say something, but he subsided. "I do understand," he said, picking up the glass again.

She could tell he didn't like the drink much. No, he'd chosen it because Sanaa liked it. The little dragon woman appeared to be his standard for all things female.

"Are there many women dragons here?"

"Just Sanaa and Eliana. Eliana is the mother of Naveen, my second in command."

Ah. That explained his small frame of reference. "And how many of you are there?"

A shadow crossed his face. He glanced away. "There are twenty-eight in total, including me."

The tiniest of warning bells sounded in the back of her head. There was a story there, but judging from his expression, it wasn't something he wanted to discuss. That was fine with her.

Ignoring the heavy atmosphere, she gave him a bracing smile. "Soon to be thirty."

His face softened. "Yes."

He sat there stiffly before taking a glass in each hand, and tossing back each glass in turn. Valeria laughed.

Rhys grinned back, a smile so unexpected and devilishly handsome it felt like a book had leaped off a shelf to hit the back of her head.

She was relieved when he left, called away by a younger man in leather who stared at her with wide curious eyes so long that she flushed, discomfited.

Why did they all watch her as if they were waiting for her to do something?

CHAPTER FIFTEEN

The master picked up the goblet his servant had brought him, flinging the entire jewel-encrusted piece into the flames burning in the massive fireplace. None of his followers had eyes on the witch. He flipped through mind after mind, but those who had been closest were no longer there. In their place was a yawing void, their small minds erased.

More pawns had been captured, or, to be accurate, they had been wiped off the board. And he'd been so close this time, his devout skilled enough to take her.

Yet, she'd managed to get away. Again. How she kept pulling tricks out her back pocket, like some sort of deranged magician, he didn't know. He'd have been impressed if all her efforts weren't to keep thwarting him.

How dare she?

He slammed his hands on the table, breaking it in half. Cursing, he flung the pieces aside. Losing the gold goblet was nothing. He had many like it in the vaults below. But trees for wood were a precious resource. Angry at himself for the loss of composure, he rose to feet and began to pace in order to spare the rest of the furniture.

He still had enough followers in this last group to make another attempt. And then another. If they failed, he'd find more pawns, more knights. The devout weren't as plentiful as they used to be, but there were enough kicking around the world. He'd burn through them all if he had to. Because he was never going to stop until he had her in his grasp.

CHAPTER SIXTEEN

Valeria woke up to shouting somewhere overhead. Rolling out of bed fully clothed, she pulled on a pair of hiking boots. Getting on her hands and knees, she was going for her backpack, which had been carefully repacked with heavier clothes, out from under the bed.

For the past few weeks, Rhys had spent a great deal of time with her, checking that she was resting up and updating her on the research his people were doing on the antique mirror. He offered her books to read and movies to watch, and when he discovered she liked to draw and paint, he showered her with art supplies, including the brand of oil paints she'd never been able to afford.

His attention felt strange at first. Except for her mother, no one had tried to take care of her before. Since he checked in with her ten times a day when everything was perfectly well, she knew the shouting followed by five minutes of silence meant trouble.

The loud knock made her jump. Figuring it was Rhys—Aggie never knocked—Valeria went to the door. But it wasn't Rhys.

Shrinking back, she tensed as the tall, muscled man snapped a quick bow. "Hello. My name is Naveen. I serve as second."

"Yeah, I know," she said, suppressing a grin. Naveen had been here multiple times. Rhys had even introduced her to him, as well as to several other warriors who'd been by to make reports or get orders.

Like any good boss, Rhys made it a point to have a lot of face-to-face time with his men.

But in Naveen's defense, he probably thought she couldn't tell them apart. They were all built on a scale similar to Rhys—huge, muscular, and hyper-masculine with the same bold but symmetrical features that would have turned female heads anywhere in the world.

The dragon's expression was inscrutable. "Rhys wanted me to tell you that he has been called away."

Oh. He must have been in a rush if he hadn't stopped by to tell her so in person. Over the past week, her host had been flawlessly polite and attentive to her, enough that she was starting to lose her wariness around him.

No one had ever won her trust so quickly, but Rhys was making serious strides.

"Is it Sanaa?" she asked, putting two and two together. "Is she in labor?"

"Yes." Naveen nodded. "Thomas and the healer are with her, but he's asked Rhys to come."

Valeria frowned, not sure if she understood him. "Thomas has? Or the healer?"

Naveen's lips compressed. "Both."

That was when she knew something had gone wrong. That bear shifter would not have wanted Rhys there otherwise. "Is there anything I can do?"

"I don't know," he admitted, his mouth moving as if the words were foreign to him.

Wincing, Valeria reached out, about to pat him on the shoulder before thinking better of it. It was never a good idea to touch, not with that other ability lurking inside her. Granted, she didn't have to be as cautious around Naveen as she had to be around Rhys, but it was better to play it safe.

She couldn't afford any complications right now.

"Most of the clan is at Sanaa's house." Naveen hesitated. "Rhys wanted you to know that so you wouldn't be concerned by the ruckus Jerik and I made coming to get him. But perhaps you should come, so he doesn't have to concern himself with your welfare. Unless you'd rather go back to sleep. It's late."

His tone held no judgment. She could have gone back to bed, but Valeria didn't consider it. This wasn't her community, but intentionally staying on the outside wasn't an option. "Would you mind if I tagged along?"

The line of his shoulders dropped as if this was an answer he'd been hoping for but not expecting. "I will drive you down."

"Are you sure?" she asked, running for the coat at the end of the bed. "I don't want to hold you up if you'd rather fly there."

He shook his head. "The roads are treacherous in the dark, and it's been raining. There are no street lamps, and the moonlight is weak. It's better that I drive. Aggie doesn't leave the house. Unless it's on fire, a brownie doesn't willingly leave their chosen home."

"I understand." Fastening her coat, Valeria closed the bedroom door, leaving her backpack next to the bed.

VALERIA WOULD NEVER FORGET the wild ride down the mountain. For someone who appeared so solid and dependable at first glance, Naveen drove like a demon.

He drove one of the clan jeeps with a speed that would have been barely acceptable in daylight, on a fine day. But in the dead of night, in sleeting rain, she was praying for them as the vehicle hurtled down the hill.

To make matters worse, Naveen did not turn on the headlights, insisting that the artificial illumination would actually worsen his night vision.

Gritting her teeth, Valeria just held on to the seat, trying not to show her fear, aware he could smell it on some level. That was the annoying thing about shifters. But at least Naveen was too preoccupied with driving to notice. That or he didn't care.

By the time they arrived at Sanaa's house, she was ready to get out and kiss the ground, but Naveen's urgency moved her to follow him inside the crowded house.

Regret was immediate.

A crowd of leather-clad men turned to them. It was different from seeing one or two dragon shifters in person with Rhys. But over two dozen? The visceral impact of it was almost like a physical blow. Not to mention the way they looked at her—their collective stares stopped her dead in her tracks.

I should not have come here, she thought, resisting the urge to flatten herself against the door.

None of these strangers were as large or as intimidating as Rhys. It made sense that, as their leader, he would be the biggest. Nevertheless, each of these men was bigger, more muscular, and more formidable than any of the mercenary shifters who had been paid to hunt her.

"Come," Naveen said, gesturing for her to follow him deeper into the house.

Forcing herself away from the door, she followed, unable to keep from swallowing aloud as she was forced to turn her back on those hulking specimens.

Naveen picked his way through the crowd, stopping to talk to another young dragon, this one with hair dyed a bright purple, one who didn't bother to disguise the fact he was giving her the hairy eyeball.

Aware she was the cynosure of every eye, Valeria made a beeline for a wooden chair against the wall, set a little apart from the couches and padded leather seats.

Making herself as small as possible, she waited for them to stop looking at her, but, apparently, she was the distraction the evening required.

"Hello." She glanced up to see Jerik. Rhys had introduced him as the youngest dragon in the clan, only a few years older than her. He was one of the 'informational team,' the group of dragons most comfortable with human technology. He and the others were in charge of their investments and spy apparatus.

Jerik pushed a can of soda into her hand.

"Thank you," she murmured.

Smiling broadly, he leaned over and smelled her before moving away. *He was just checking on your emotional state*, she told herself after piecing it together. Rhys was less obvious about checking her scent, but she knew he did it too. Still, it was weird. Nonplussed, she opened the can, sipping to have something to do.

Valeria almost collapsed in relief when Rhys exited the hallway.

He stopped short, his head jerking in her direction. "You're here."

Despite having dinner with him every night seeing him so suddenly messed with her equilibrium.

The man could unnerve her just by walking into the same room. She told herself that was fine. He was an apex predator. Any other reaction would have been foolish.

It's fight-or-flight kicking in, she'd told herself on more than one occasion. But that didn't explain why she would blush in addition to the racing of her heart. Tonight, however, she paled when she saw the expression on his face. That a hardened man could look this way— well, there was no question. Something had gone wrong in the delivery room.

Worried for the generous and sunny woman she had only met once, Valeria leaned forward to whisper. "I'm sorry, I shouldn't have come— this is private clan business."

Sanaa had cared for her when she was vulnerable but her impulse to come here had been wrong. This group was too thorny and insular for a stranger to insert herself and remain unobtrusive.

Apparently, Rhys disagreed with her unspoken desire to stay of out the way.

Drifting toward her he slipped his hand beneath the curtain of her hair, resting his palm on the back of her neck, fingers curling around her. The possessive gesture made her jump, but it had the opposite effect on him. His features relaxed as if he found touching her skin soothing.

The fact that it did the exact opposite for her appeared to go unnoticed.

"No, it's all right," Rhys said, looking down at her with that inexplicable warmth she saw in his eyes more often than not. "Sanaa will appreciate that you came. Thank you."

Well, damn. She really couldn't move now. *He's strong enough to snap your neck*, she reminded herself, the warning in her mother's voice. *Use the ability*, Ravenna urged. But Valeria didn't shift away despite her worries over the skin-to-skin contact.

It's okay, she reassured herself. She wasn't an ignorant teenager anymore. Valeria had spent years crafting safeguards and building in controls to that unwanted power. When she was rested and in full control of her faculties, it happened only when she wanted. Release had to be intentional.

Rhys raised his head to address the room. "The first child has arrived. It's male. He is a dragon, not a bear, and is healthy."

The men murmured. She could tell the news was welcome, but they didn't celebrate. Their leader's tone was too somber.

He didn't keep them in suspense. "There is a problem with the second babe. It seems the shell has broken within the womb. The dragon's crest has embedded itself in the muscle of the wall. The babe is stuck, and Sanaa is bleeding."

Santo cielo, they lay eggs. That bit of dragon lore was true. And, apparently, they busted out of the eggs as baby dragons. Was a humanoid baby too vulnerable? Or had they evolved to give birth to the dragon form because their home environment, the world they had come from, was too harsh?

The consternation to his news was immediate. The rumble of many male voices gathered in volume, sloshing like a rogue wave from one end of the room to the other.

Tensing under Rhys' holds, Valeria glanced up at him. He kept his eyes on his men, but his index finger began to stroke the side of her neck, soothing her absently. But he didn't let go.

"Does Veda require aid?" someone asked. Aside from Naveen and Rhys, she couldn't tell the men apart well enough to pick out who had asked.

Rhys shook his head. He looked down at Valeria "As clan leader, I can share some of our energy with Veda, our healer, the way native shifter packs do," he explained. "But Veda is in a bind—he can slow the bleeding by closing the wounds, but that means the tissue heals over the infant's crest, keeping it trapped."

He put his free hand on the back of his head to show her where the crest would be.

"And every time he dislodges it, the bleeding resumes," Naveen filled in the blanks.

"Yes," Rhys confirmed. "Veda succeeded in removing it once, but the little one is confused and scared. Thomas has attempted to calm him by singing to him, but the little one was too agitated to listen. My efforts had the same result. The babe just raised the crest again, re-embedding itself. Veda will try again after giving Sanaa a chance to rest."

"What about a C-section?" another man asked. He was blond and younger than the others, his tan face making him look like a body-building surfer. "The humans do it all the time."

"Thomas has already broached the possibility with Veda. It has to be our last option." Again, Rhys turned to Valeria. He put his hand on his abdomen. "In females, these muscles are critical to our flight because it's where the base of our wing muscles attach. Severing them once will compromise Sanaa's future ability to fly. But we will do it if we have to. The longer we delay, the higher the risk of losing both. Without the shell, our little ones will try to start breathing within a few hours, once the nutrient-rich sack disintegrates and the lungs unfurl."

Oh, God. Horrified, Valeria put her hands over her mouth. The eggshell meant the baby wouldn't be connected to Sanaa via an umbilical cord. It was going to start trying to breathe soon—and when it did, it would suffocate.

Rhys should have moved away to comfort the others, but he stayed at her side, letting his people come to him. But only Jerik and another woman—an older one she hadn't noticed—did so, speaking in hushed tones. The rest of the crowd proved too stoic. Some moved quietly, prowling to the kitchen and back. A few sipped from flasks, albeit discreetly.

Time began to go haywire, alternatively moving in fits and starts or crawling at a pace a sloth could have set their watch to. The men moved about the rooms, gathering in small clumps that dispersed and reformed according to some underlying pattern she couldn't understand.

At one point, she blinked, realizing the older woman was sitting next to her.

With only lightly lined dark skin, the woman was elegant with waist-length hair that was coal-black without a trace of grey. Valeria's skin prickled as the woman studied her.

After a moment, she seemed to relax. "I don't think you're her," the stranger whispered.

Valeria's eyes darted from the woman to the crowd, searching for

Rhys. The little hairs on the back of her neck were standing on end. She didn't know how, but Valeria was positive he wouldn't want her to have this conversation.

"Her who?" she asked, her voice dropping to the same low volume,

The woman's austere features warmed. She patted her hand. "Relax. It's a good thing."

Rising, she disappeared into the crowd.

Baffled and a little angry, Valeria stared at the floor, trying to make sense of the exchange.

At least now you know for sure. Rhys was hiding something.

The sharp pain in her chest took her by surprise.

Well, that is stupid. She had known something wasn't right. The mirror wasn't enough reason for her to be here.

And the way he looks at you—the way they all look at you...

A scream pierced the air. Thick silence descended, smothering the rumble of conversation.

Thomas appeared at the threshold of the room. His features were stark, his eyes glowing a preternatural shifter gold, the bear riding him hard. All of the animal's protective instincts were telling him to shift. But his mate didn't need the animal. Sanaa needed the man.

It must have been tearing him apart.

One glimpse of his face told her that Thomas didn't care about any of that. He looked at Rhys, and the clan leader disappeared into the hall as another scream punctuated the air.

Everyone stood, their eyes on the hall, a frozen tableau of an entire community at the brink. Valeria's pulse began to race. She stared down at her hands, wishing there was something she could do to help.

The skin over her forearms tingled as if someone were running an electromagnetic wand over their surface. This was followed by a popping sound, and then her arms were weighed down, filled with something slippery and warm.

Slime dripped from scales as the baby dragon blinked up at her, its little claws digging into her arms and thighs.

Valeria gaped, ready to scream, when a heavy hand clamped over her mouth.

CHAPTER SEVENTEEN

"Don't scream," Rhys ordered.

Valeria's eyes were wide and dilated, her shock at the unexpected bundle in her arms unfeigned.

He didn't need to look up to see that same shock reflected in the eyes of his men. His little witch had been keeping secrets. But exactly what those were would have to wait.

The babe's claws dug into Valeria's thighs. She whimpered, her head drawing back as the newborn snapped its head, trying to touch its muzzle to hers.

"If you scream, you will frighten the babe, possibly scarring it," he told her. "These first hours after birth are critical to development."

It was meant to be a moment of close bonding between mother and child. *And father*, he reminded himself.

He turned to the hall where Naveen had just exited.

"I explained the situation," his second murmured to Rhys in the old language. "And assured them the little one is well enough for the moment."

Sensing his man's discomfort, Rhys clapped him on the back. "Relax, old friend. You did not lie to them. How is Sanaa?"

"Better now that Veda can close the wounds without trapping the babe. He continues to work on her. Thomas will not leave her side until she's out of danger."

He broke off, letting some of his naked bewilderment show.

"How did she do that?" he asked in their native tongue.

"I'm not sure she knows," Rhys replied in the same language. "Let's concern ourselves with that later, once everyone is out of danger."

Sanaa's chances were much improved now that the babe was out of her body, those sharp spines no longer complicating matters, but the healer still needed time to do his work.

In the meantime, some things needed to be done for the babe itself.

"You need to turn the babe upside down," he told Valeria aloud.

"Please take it," she whispered, craning her head away from the snuffling, hooting babe.

Another dragon might have been insulted at the way she kept trying to get away from a newborn of his kind, but he could understand her reticence under the circumstances.

She had probably been expecting a human-looking babe. Shifters from this world were usually born in these softer forms—the better to blend in with the human majority.

But his people had evolved on a much harsher terrain. Their first form was the hardier one.

"I can't take her yet," he murmured, his tone deep and as soothing as he could make it. The female babe reacted to his tone, cocking its head and jerking a little less. "It's best that as few people as possible handle her until her mother can take her into her arms."

"Her?"

"I can tell by her coloring just here," he said, pointing just under the wing attachments. Those, he saw with some relief, were perfect. The first female born to the clan on this world had perfect conformation and a feisty spirit judging from her apparent curiosity.

Then the little one coughed. The sound was too wet. "Turn her upside down," he urged.

Valeria handled the babe like it was a bomb. It didn't want to cooperate, squirming in her grasp. Rhys tapped the little one's back, his palm making a small thudding sound that made Valeria flinch.

"You have to be firm, to get all the residual albumin out of the lungs," he explained as the child coughed up a viscous stream, making a pink-tinted puddle in Valeria's lap.

The nutrient-rich liquid would have been re-absorbed on its own, but slowly. But the child was out now and was starting to breathe. Oxygen was more important than those last dregs of albumin. Besides, Eliana had spent some time teaching Thomas how to prepare meals appropriate for the earliest days. They would get sufficient nutrition from those.

Valeria's breathing sped up as the baby wiggled and reoriented to bury its nose in her neck. "Are you sure you can't hold her?"

Deciding the healer had enough time to do his work, he took her by the elbow, biding her to rise. "We'll take her back to her parents now."

They left the room, making their way to the master bedroom.

Thomas gave them a black look, snatching his baby girl from Valeria's wet, sticky arms. Since he already held the male, it was a bit of a juggling act, but the father was determined.

"Be at ease," Rhys murmured when the bear snapped at his witch, showing his teeth. "It was an accident that in all likelihood saved your mate's life."

His aggressive expression softening, Thomas pulled the little girl against him more securely. "You're right. Thank you, Val."

Rhys frowned at the shortening of Valeria's name. Pet names were reserved for lovers among his kind, but Thomas did not share their ways, or so he told himself for the thousandth time.

The bear knelt by Sanaa's side, placing the babes on either side of her.

The female gave Rhys a wan smile, shifting to include Valeria in her greeting. "Commander, it's over. Aren't they perfect?" she asked, admiring her babies with maternal delight.

The boy was quiet, already sleeping, but the little girl continued to snuffle, raising her wings precociously.

"Yes," he agreed, resting his hand on her forehead in approval. "You're done remarkably well, Sanaa. You should be very proud of them and yourself."

He stroked her hair one final time, aware that Valeria was sniffling almost as loudly as the child—the cold weather taking its toll on her frailer constitution.

"Rest," he told Sanaa and Thomas. "I will be by tomorrow to give your children my official blessing, once you've had a chance to welcome them to your home and family."

Sanaa murmured her thanks, extending her hand to Valeria.

Stooping awkwardly, Valeria took the hand. "I hope you feel better soon."

Sanaa cuddled the young ones to her breast. "I am perfectly well now, just tired. Thank you for that little trick."

Noting how the little girl was straining toward Valeria, Thomas scowled again. Sensing her discomfort, Rhys said their goodbyes, guiding the witch out of the room before the bear took umbrage.

Things had just gotten more complicated.

He ushered her out the door and into one of the waiting vehicles. Driving slowly up the hill, he glanced over at the girl who consumed his thoughts, both awake and asleep.

"You seemed as surprised as the rest of us when you delivered the child."

Valeria put her hands on her pants. The albumin had mostly dried on the cloth, so she'd eschewed her coat, which had stayed clean since she hadn't been wearing it inside the warm house.

"I take it you mirrored a teleporter once?"

She glanced at him, studying him before nodding, sniffing. Reaching into her pocket, she withdrew a tissue, wiping at her nose.

"Was it one of the ones I burned?" he asked, keeping his eyes on the road because it seemed to make her nervous when he turned to watch her.

"No." The word was strained. She wiped at her nose again. A sudden suspicion crept over him, injecting little drips of acid into his blood.

"How long ago was your confrontation with the teleporter?"

"I'm not sure anymore."

Fear made his voice clipped. "*Guess.*"

Valeria scratched her head "I think it's been over a year."

"Did you always know you could do that? Reach into yourself to bring back earlier magicks you had copied?"

If so, good God. It was no wonder they were hunting her down like a dog. Every black witch on Earth would kill for power like that.

"It takes too much effort," she said as the SUV made a sharp turn.

"So, you *did* know?"

"It's happened that way before—on accident. It's rough, and draining. Well, not always, but mostly."

"So you never try to pull them back to the surface intentionally?"

"Mostly I can't," she said, the tiredness in her voice making him want to bundle her in his coat and carry her to bed in his arms. "They fade. I have to fight to keep anything longer than a few hours after contact. Keeping something for a day, or even a week, has been too difficult. The more time passes, the more I struggle to recapture it."

She paused, a hand on her head that told him she had a headache.

"The only time I tried to recall a talent intentionally was after visiting a healer of some renown. My mother took me to see her, on the pretense of consulting with her."

"She wanted you to have the ability to heal yourself should you be injured. And people don't know you can copy their talent, so it can be done with stealth," he finished.

When she had used his fire, he hadn't felt a pull—nothing to indicate his magic had been taken from him because it hadn't. She'd simply duplicated the flames, her ability elastic enough to encompass the ferocity of his fire.

And if she could copy his fire, then there were very few talents she couldn't copy. But that didn't mean she could use them all. Some magicks were never meant to exist, let alone be wielded without training.

Valeria dabbed her nose again. This time, the bright iron scent of blood filled the cabin. Rhys stopped the vehicle, slapping the overhead light on. "Turn around," he growled.

She attempted to shift away. "What?"

He reached for her. Valeria's delicate features hardened, and she pushed his hand back.

"I said look at me," he said, his innate dominance naked in his voice. But he made sure to keep his hands gentle as he tilted her face up. "How long has your nose been bleeding?"

Shying away from his touch, Valeria pressed the tissue to her face.

The red of her blood was stark against the white of the flimsy paper. "I'm not sure—I didn't notice it until I stood and we went to take the baby to Sanaa and Thomas."

Jaw tight, Rhys tore a clean corner of the tissue and balled it up. "Put this under your upper lip, underneath the side that is bleeding. The pressure will slow down the bleeding."

"It's both sides."

Swearing in his native tongue, Rhys reached into the backseat, where he'd tossed her coat. Ransacking the pockets turned up a little package of tissues, no doubt provided by Aggie.

He rolled another quick ball and handed it to her. She tucked them under her lip, deforming her perfect features...but not enough. She was still the most beautiful woman he'd ever seen.

And there is a spot of blood in her right eye. A pinprick hemorrhage. How much effort had she expended teleporting the babe?

"Did it hurt?" Of course it hurt. She was bleeding, the looming threat of cerebral hemorrhage still hanging over her head. "Are you still in pain?" he amended, forcing his tone to sound even, almost calm.

It must have worked because she slumped in the seat. "I have a little headache," she admitted in a small voice.

Marshaling the discipline honed from years upon years at the command of a militant clan, he cupped her chin with a firm but gentle hold. "You were already in a weakened condition from your earlier confrontation. Tomorrow, you must rest. I will call the healer to come and see you after he is done attending Sanaa."

"No," she protested as he resumed driving. "The man is exhausted."

"You will do as I say."

Anger, hot and sharp, filled the cabin. It made Rhys happy. He could work with anger.

CHAPTER EIGHTEEN

Spending all morning in bed was more than enough for Valeria's batteries to recharge. Aggie had bought her a tray and had shown her how to raise the television hidden in the console slash clothing chest set at the foot at the bed.

It was startling to see daytime talk shows on the screen, as if everything was normal, the earth spinning as it always had. *As if dragons didn't exist.* But here she was, sitting in a dragon's home, having delivered a dragon baby during a life-threatening emergency.

And pulling out a year-old talent from her arsenal—she hadn't known she could do that so effectively. Nor had she been aware of the true cost.

The healing talent was the only one she had actively cultivated, and it hadn't hit her the same way, perhaps because the healing ability had self-corrected any damage.

A few years ago, she had cut herself on a jagged piece of metal after climbing a fence to get into an abandoned warehouse where she wanted to sleep for the night. She'd used the healing ability then. Her nose hadn't bled, and there had been no headache. She didn't understand why it had been different with the teleportation. Yes, the latter could be classified as an offensive talent. The witch she'd copied it from had used it with vicious effectiveness, she remembered with a shudder. But last night, she'd used it to help someone. Apparently, the intent—to help or to hurt—didn't matter.

She lay in bed, trying to recall the other instances where she'd used a talent after the source was long gone. It had only happened a handful of times, but most of those had been painful enough to discourage her from trying again.

What if it was the source that mattered? The healer had been a gentle woman, her purity of soul so painfully obvious she'd almost glowed to Valeria's naked eye.

Valeria couldn't see auras, but, during that visit, it almost hadn't mattered. She didn't consort with good people all that often. Every other person she'd copied was almost universally bad—hunters and black witches who dealt in death and wanted her power.

So, what would happen if she recalled Rhys' fire without him close at hand?

Burying her face in her hands, she decided not to find out—not that she could. She'd knew without asking that Rhys wouldn't allow her to distance herself from him enough to test her theory.

I do like my theory. Valeria and her mother had lived on the fringe for so long, dancing on the edge of the black without quite going over. She'd felt her mirroring power inside her all her life. It was always ready to take, even without her conscious effort. That was one of many reasons she had feared it for so long.

But it wasn't the main one. No, Valeria had been inspired to fear her own abilities because of the way people watched her. Even as a child, she'd be in the street going somewhere with her mother and she'd feel someone's eyes on her. Nine times out of ten, it would be an old man or woman, watching her with fear or outright malevolence. Many had worn crosses, too. Come to think of it, those instances had always been higher around a church, or in very religious communities.

It was why, deep down, she had always believed she deserved to be hunted...because she was evil.

But if she could only recall the talent mirrored from good people without a harsh backlash, then maybe she didn't have to be as frightened of her ability as much as she believed?

What if, despite all evidence to the contrary, she might be...good? Or at least neutral?

That was something she had never considered.

Pursing her lips, she sighed. No, her power was too bright and brash, something that could blind her if she let it. The best she could do was to control it and not allow any more accidental lapses the way she had in her teens.

As for trying to recall past powers, she needed her brains in her head, thank you very much. Especially if she had to pit her will against a dragon.

She glanced down at her arms and legs. It was almost as if she could feel Rhys holding her arm, supporting her. He'd carried her all the way upstairs last night, setting her on her feet at the threshold of her bedroom.

Blush suffusing her cheeks, she was glad he was so old-fashioned. If he wasn't so proper, so governed by such a strict code of conduct, he would have come inside. And it wouldn't have been to tuck her in.

That's because he thinks you're someone else.

Spirits dampened, she dressed, sneaking out of the house to avoid Rhys.

It was a little immature, avoiding the man she was growing infatuated with, but she needed time to regroup.

Valeria had been alone so long, struggling to get by and just live. Now she was living in a mansion with an unreasonably handsome dragon who was not only protective, but also kind and considerate. Could she blame herself for these feelings?

It was tempting, so very tempting, to see home in her dragon's eyes. But that dark gaze didn't see *her*. When Rhys looked at her, he was seeing someone else entirely.

Annoyed and disgruntled, she started to walk outside, hiking down the hill. She was a quarter of the way down when she realized Sanaa and Thomas' home was too far to reach on foot. She turned around, taking a small footpath just off the main road. The narrow trail wound up through the pines, but it didn't look man, or, in this case, dragon-made.

It's too soon to visit Sanaa, she thought remembering the dirty look Thomas had given her when she'd handed him the baby.

Relax. For all his grumpiness, the bear had to know it had been accidental, and, under the circumstances, necessary. He'd get over it. Or at least she hoped he would.

She'd focus on the problem at hand, and it was a doozy—a mountain of a man called Rhys.

All those quiet nights reading by the library fire, the way he kept stuffing food in her face, and the clothes he'd provided... Who the hell was the woman Eliana had been talking about? If Valeria asked outright, would Rhys tell her or would he lie?

Frustrated, Valeria kicked the nearest pine tree, laughing when an unexpected shower of pine needles fell on her. Snoop first, ask questions later, she decided, resuming her walk.

She soon came to a small bluff with a view of the valley below. It was both gorgeous and brutal, the green hills dipping and rising in jagged peaks lightly dusted with snow, even now in April.

Why wasn't there more snow on this peak? Was it chance or had Rhys done something to get rid of it?

A mental picture of him in dragon form breathing fire on the ground to melt the snow flashed through her mind. The silly image made her smile before she scowled. *You are still mad at him,* she reminded herself.

But she wasn't going to find the answers she needed out here, beautiful as this mountain was. She turned back to the house, but quickly realized she'd lost the trail. That was all right, though. It wasn't possible to get lost. She just had to keep heading up to the summit. The house would be hard to miss.

Except, somehow, I did. That thought came an hour later. Valeria was surrounded by a thick copse of pines, with no idea if she was up or down.

It's because you were distracted, she scolded herself. She'd been too intent on the mystery of Rhys, too consumed by her desire to unravel his secrets. Well, look at where that had gotten her now. She was completely lost.

Blowing out a sharply annoyed breath, she picked her way through the trees carefully. Despite this part of the mountain being almost level, she couldn't be sure of her footing. This patch was more unforgiving, with more stones and boulders jutting out of the earth like jagged teeth.

To add insult to injury, the wind was picking up. It wound through the closely set trees and stones, the bite in it dropping the temperature by double-digit degrees.

She peered up, dismayed to find that the sun was much lower than she'd believed. It wouldn't set for another hour, but she was no longer certain she'd make it back to the house before dark.

Determined to try before Rhys sent out a search party, she kept going, stopping in another small clearing to catch her breath.

Her neck prickled. Valeria whirled, expecting to find Rhys or one of the other dragons at her back. But it wasn't one of the clan. She was at the mouth of the cave. A faint light came from it, but it was distant as if its source were far away.

She began to step away only to turn back around. Compelled by something she couldn't explain, Valeria walked into the cave.

The darkness inside was smothering. Her heart picked up, but she kept going, heading toward the source of the light. Unlike the area outside, the cave interior was clear of all obstructions.

This is dragon-made, she thought, feeling the walls. The same technology that let Rhys slice giant redwoods in two had made this passageway.

Leave or go on? Her chest was tight, the incipient panic making itself known, but her gut told her there was only one choice. She went on.

Well hell, how medieval. The light at the end of the tunnel was actually at the halfway point. There she found a large brazier—a disk as big as a child's sled, the round kind they used to fly down snowy hills. It was suspended from the ceiling from three chains high over her head. Three hundred yards down, there was a second brazier, then a final one before the passageway suddenly opened.

Valeria came to a stop at the top of a staircase carved into the rock face. She couldn't see what was down below, but there was a sense of space licking at her skin. There was a large chamber in front of her. She just couldn't see it.

Her stomach roiled, memories coated in blood, and the sharp metallic taste of fear rising to sap her will. But she'd come this far. Whatever Rhys was hiding, it had to be here.

Hyperaware there was no railing, Valeria put her hand against the wall, letting it guide her down. But she hadn't gone more than a few steps down when the world exploded in a wave of fire.

———

Sir, we have an intruder in the sanctuary, Kyrin informed him, his voice strong in Rhys' mind.

Freezing outside of Sanaa's home, he began to shout back across the mental link, telepathy being the sole means of communication of his people when they were in their winged form.

The punishment for violation of their sanctuary was death. Immediate death.

No! Do nothing. I am on my way.

He shifted in a blink and was slicing through the air, flying harder and faster than he'd thought possible, even for him—the fastest member of his wing.

Kyrin's voice returned. *Understood.*

Rhys could have fallen out of the sky right then—his relief was so great. But he kept pumping his wings, arriving at the entrance of the sanctuary in another minute before shifting back. Then he ran.

He found Valeria huddled a few feet from the mouth of the inner sanctum. The smell of brimstone and sulfur tinged the air.

His second youngest warrior stood over Valeria, his face like granite. His blond hair gleamed in the dim light as if the strands absorbed and reflected it. It tended to do that, even in the weakest moonlight, which was the reason Rhys made him blacken it whenever the young warrior ventured outside their territory.

Straightening to attention, Kyrin turned to face him.

"I found this intruder on the steps to the inner sanctum." His tone was cold, a flawless diamond in the snow. But while Rhys appreciated his man's control over his emotion and his aim—the scorch marks marking the cavern wall would have been well above Valeria's head when she was standing—he would have strongly preferred Naveen or Jerik on duty here during this particular intrusion.

The past had damaged his people in innumerable ways, but Kyrin's particular demons lived in this room.

Rhys put a hand on the younger man's shoulder. "You are dismissed."

"But—"

"I will take care of this."

A wash of heat flared from the young man, but he was too disciplined to argue further. He nodded.

"I give you leave to go see Sanaa," Rhys said, trying to mollify his most troubled warrior. "I've blessed the babes, but I'm sure you will want to welcome them yourself."

Kyrin knew what he was doing. "I thought Thomas forbade visits for the first week," he said, raising a blond eyebrow.

Rhys shrugged. "Yes, but Sanaa disagrees."

Their second-youngest clan mate wanted everyone to admire her brilliant children.

Kyrin continued to frown, aware he was being handled, but he had always been close to his cousin. He and Sanaa were related along the maternal line.

Aware that Valeria had lifted her head, Rhys gave Kyrin a small nudge to move along. Then he looked down at their intruder.

***

VALERIA'S MUSCLES were rigid after that panic-fueled flight. There had been darkness, and then, in the next blink, an explosion right out of an action movie.

Only this one hadn't been a fantasy because she'd been face to face with a dragon. It had been flapping its massive wings inside the chamber in front of her—the eyes glowing bright enough for her to see it after the brazier had been knocked down the stairs in the scuffle.

The dragon had stayed back as she scrambled into the tunnel even as the braziers' embers died on the stone steps. Expecting to be blasted into ash at any second, she hadn't run. In the movies that just brought the fire faster. Instead, she'd curled up into a ball, trying to protect as much of herself as she could, dragging up a shield made of pure magic.

Then the dragon had changed into a man. It had been too dark for her to see the transformation, but she'd known the blond warrior suddenly standing over her was the same shifter from the way he kept trying to eviscerate her with his gaze.

But she might have preferred that one to stay than face Rhys.

You promised not to endanger or betray his people. Well, it seemed by being in this cave, she had broken that promise. And she was about to pay the price.

CHAPTER NINETEEN

She waited, but Rhys didn't move or speak.

"Aren't you going to fry me?" she asked, holding her invisible shield of magic a little higher.

One thick black brow rose. "Do you think I could?"

He crossed his arms, leaning against the tunnel wall. "Or would you be protected by your reflective ability?"

He sounded more curious than angry.

"I honestly don't know."

Rhys pushed away from the wall. He gestured to the cavern behind him. "How did you find this place?"

"I was walking, and I stumbled on the entrance."

"Now that I have a harder time believing." Rhys reached down. Valeria dropped the shield, letting it dissipate just before he pulled her to her feet.

"There are several safeguards in place to prevent that sort of thing from happening."

He began to move down the stairs, his hand holding hers tightly. Afraid of letting go in this pitch blackness, she followed.

"What kind of safeguards?" she asked.

"Traps, misdirection. Good ones, too. But, somehow, I am not all that surprised you were able to circumvent them."

When they reached the bottom of the stairs, he let go of her hand. After a lifetime of avoiding touch, the loss left her suddenly bereft. She wrapped her arms around herself to keep from reaching out to him again. "I didn't do it on purpose."

Rhys moved away. She started to call out to him when he breathed fire at the cave floor. Valeria's eyes widened as a channel filled with an unknown fuel blazed to life.

Fire raced along the groove, going from one end of the room to the other, before looping around the back wall located about a hundred yards away. When it was lit, it illuminated a perfect rectangle twice as wide and long as a football field.

Rhys grabbed an unlit torch from the wall behind her. He dipped it into the liquid on fire in the channel and moved, lighting a series of braziers laid in an X-shape in the middle of the room.

Spinning on her heel, Valeria took in the space with open-mouthed dismay. Now that there was light, it was obvious what this place was.

"It's a tomb."

The central space was filled with sarcophagi. That was the only word for the coffin-like structures that radiated out in concentric circles.

"Yes and no." Rhys came to stand beside her. "This is the inner sanctum. Once it was the most important, most secret, and most sacred place of our clan. But now it holds only the dead, or close enough as to make no difference."

Startled, she looked at him. In this light, his carved features were harsher, more brutally handsome.

"Is *she* here?" Valeria whispered.

He turned to frown. "Is who here?"

She studied his face, looking for a hint of softness, of human caring. She didn't find it.

"The woman you think I am," she said. "Is she buried here?"

Rhys stared at her for a very long time. "No."

At least he didn't lie.

Valeria approached the ring of sarcophagi in the tightest circle. Each was carved with drawings and symbols clumped together. They were more elaborate than Egyptian hieroglyphics. She gravitated to one that looked just like all the others, aside from the way it made her skin prickle.

Tracing one with her finger, she glanced up at the too-silent dragon. "Who is buried here?"

He gave her an arrested glance as he shook his head. "I don't know how you do that—cut to the heart of the matter."

Rhys joined her at the sarcophagi. "Tell me, what were you doing when you found the tunnel mouth?"

"Nothing." She frowned. "I was just walking...and thinking about you."

He brightened. "Is that so?"

Her lips flattened. "I was wondering what secrets you were keeping from me."

"Oh." His expression darkened.

Valeria turned back to the sarcophagus next to them. "Who is bur—er...entombed here?"

Rhys smiled humorlessly. His hand swept up to encompass the room.

"This is where we once slept," he said. "That's our way, you see. My species is very long-lived. And time can be unforgiving. Sometimes, we just need to rest. The *somnara* is an exceedingly long slumber. You would call it hibernation, but it can span decades, even centuries.

"It was never widespread. On our homeworld, we'd live our lives and fall into *somnara* sparingly, and only once we reached a certain age."

His index finger stroked the carving at the top of the lid. "Then came the great wars. Not one, but a series. Our people were decimated, our lands laid waste, rendered unlivable."

"Then you came here."

He glanced at her, his dark eyes hungry for something he'd never ask for. "Not right away...but yes."

There was a long pause before he spoke again. "Compared to some places we found, this world is a paradise. There are abundant waters, cold and warm seasons, and life. So much life. We'd grown accustomed to endless barren vistas."

He rolled those big shoulders. "It was a shock."

"But a good one?"

After what he described, wouldn't it have been a relief to come to be in a peaceful place? The land they'd chosen to make their home was idyllic and wild if a bit cold for the current thinness of her blood.

He took a long time to answer. "You'd think so, but our people had just come through a century of war," Rhys confided, his eyes on some distant vista in his mind. "For some of us, it was difficult to appreciate or accept our new state."

He looked up. "After all that time, the endless fighting, we were too warlike to be at peace. But peaceful is what we needed to be according to the treaty we signed, the one that allowed us to stay here."

"You signed a treaty to stay on Earth?" Valeria asked in consternation. "With who?"

A corner of his mouth lifted. "That is a story for another time, I think, but suffice it to say we had a difficult time adjusting. There had been too much blood, too much loss."

He held up his hands as if he could still see it. "Despite the discipline instilled in me by my training, my impulses were too aggressive, as were those of the other men. Even our women were having issues. The only thing we were fit for was warfare."

"You could have conquered this entire planet." She knew it for a fact. But someone or something had stopped them. And... "Your people were tired. So, they slept."

"In unprecedented numbers," he confirmed. "We found a suitable unoccupied territory and built this sanctum deep in the highest peak, a safe place for the community to fall into *somnara*."

She tried to count the number of sarcophagi, but gave up after sixty. "Is it my imagination or are there more, um, beds than..."

Her voice trailed off at his bleak expression. "Yes. We lost more than two-thirds of our original colony."

CHAPTER TWENTY

Valeria would have been a terrible poker player.

The human card game was very popular among his men. They had learned it three decades ago, and like any endeavor requiring skill and money, they had mastered it.

Rhys wasn't the best in the clan, but his subordinates insisted his 'poker face' was superior to theirs. His guest didn't have one. Or, if she did, it did not occur to her to use it with him. He found that comforting.

"What happened?" she asked in a solemn tone.

He shouldn't say. The story revealed their vulnerability, something he'd drummed into his men's heads never to do. But keeping anything from Valeria was futile. If she wished to know something, he would tell her, even if the memories drew blood.

"We arrived when the civilizations on this world were young, primitive. It would have been safe enough to sleep. But we had learned the lessons taught by fire and bloodshed," he said. "Our clan leader, Markus, knew that things could change in a blink, our safety compromised."

She blinked rapidly. "You weren't the leader?"

"No, I served as second as Naveen serves now," Rhys said. "When Markus gathered our people here, he told us that the rest of us could sleep. He would stay awake to guard us during our sleep, to protect us in our most vulnerable state."

"But you didn't sleep." It was a statement, not a question.

"Not then. Not right away. We had seen too much for me to feel comfortable leaving without keeping tabs on the humans around us. I was the one who suggested that more should stay awake—one to stay on the mountain to guard the sleepers and two or three who would go out in the world and interact with the local inhabitants."

"That sounds reasonable," she murmured.

He lifted a shoulder. "We had seen civilizations become stagnant and wither away, but also grow in leaps and bounds. It could happen overnight, I argued. We had to keep abreast of human advances."

"To monitor them for threats?" she asked.

"Yes," he confirmed. "And to better emulate them if and when we chose to move among them."

There was a hint of amusement in her voice. "And perhaps to hunt for treasure?"

Valeria did understand his kind. He nodded. "That and we were not averse to exploration in and of itself. We like the variety—mountains, valleys, deserts, and vast oceans. Such diversity is uncommon in the cosmos."

She absorbed that for a moment. "What changed?"

"Not much, not for a long time. Most of our people slept, waking for a few years, but always going back to sleep in large numbers. Only a handful of us was awake at one time." He took his hand off the lid of the sarcophagus, his anger climbing suddenly but tightly controlled.

"I was one of the few who went out into the world. I enjoyed the exploration. There were many interesting sights to see, though I could not avoid the city centers when they developed."

"Much as you wanted to," she added.

He shrugged. "I have some issues with mankind, but mainly that's because I see them repeating our mistakes."

Rhys glanced down at the sarcophagus, his hand hovering over it as if he was contemplating smashing it with his bare hands.

"I made a mistake," he said, his voice flat. "We were so concerned with threats from the outside, we forgot to look for the rot within."

"You had a traitor?"

His facial muscles tightened. He felt as if they'd frozen into stone, the same kind they'd carved their sarcophagi. "Not exactly."

He studied her face. Such a familiar stranger. Although it was bizarre how much stronger she seemed than the fragile beauty he remembered.

She's been tempered in a crucible. Well, they had that in common.

"Markus. He'd been our leader a long time. He brought us through endless war, times of scarcity to eras of prosperity, and back again. Then here, when we were finally at peace, but broken...we left him alone too long, ignored the signs of his madness."

He wasn't looking at her, but he heard her sharp intake of breath.

She covered her face with her hands. "He killed them while they were sleeping, didn't he?"

"Yes."

RHYS FROZE when she wrapped her arms around him, but she held on.

This frustrating rigid man, she thought. Despite his secretiveness and the continued mystery of the unnamed woman, Valeria couldn't stifle the impulse to comfort him. So, she pressed herself against him, her forehead resting on his back, hugging him around the middle with all her strength.

He craned his neck in a futile attempt to look back. But he didn't shove her arms off. It was the first time she'd touched him willingly.

"Don't dragons hug when they want to comfort each other?" she asked, her mouth muffled against his muscular back.

There was a hesitation as if he were thinking about it. "The women."

"But not the men?"

"Maybe as children. It's been so long that I no longer remember."

Moving her hand up the carved surface of his chest, she covered his heart with her palm.

His voice was whisper soft. "It's lower and to the left on us."

Adjusting accordingly, she lifted her head away a fraction, surprised at the powerful drum under her fingers. "Does it always beat this fast?"

"No. But I don't think it will calm enough for you to learn its normal rhythm."

She rubbed her cheek against his vest. Today it was some sort of suede, not leather. "I don't understand."

"My heart won't settle into a normal rhythm unless you let go. But it will speed back up if you touch me again. A Catch-22."

Damn. Now she wanted to squeeze him harder, an impossibility given the unyielding density of his muscles. "Did you read Heller?"

His hand came to rest on top of hers tentatively, as if he was concerned their touch wasn't reciprocal and his would somehow be unwelcome. "I may not be entirely comfortable around humans, but I do like many of the books they write."

She turned her head, rubbing her face against his back to rest her other cheek against him. Aware she was rubbing against him like a cat, she stopped. "Tell me about Markus," she said quietly.

"He was the oldest of us. He was the model for everything I wanted to be. We trusted him implicitly, and why not? He had proven himself again and again in battle."

"But when you came here, things were different. You no longer had a war to fight."

"It's strange, isn't it?" he mused, his voice like sandpaper. "How the mind grows accustomed to strife and blood, but can't handle the quiet."

He shifted, but not enough to break her hold. "Only three of us were awake when he...back then. Naveen and I were traveling. He was exploring in Australia. I was in Vienna."

His hand closed over her waist, fingers convulsing. It was too tight, but before she could complain, he relaxed them slowly as if it took a great effort.

"For the first time since coming to Earth, I was happy. I had found something in Vienna—the greatest treasure of my life. But then Naveen and I received word that all was not well at home."

"From who?"

Rhys turned and took a deep breath, one so expansive his chest touched hers briefly. "It doesn't matter."

"All right," she said, hating the look in his eyes. Half of her contemplated shutting up, but she couldn't. And it wasn't curiosity but that damnable instinct of hers. It was telling her to keep pushing. Because he needed to talk about it.

"Then what happened?"

Rhys' gaze swept the chamber. "He was down here. The lids were off, the boxes overturned, and—"

He broke off. "We made the mistake of putting our most vulnerable together in the center. Our old wise ones were not infirm. Not as you would define it...but they were no match for him."

"Did they wake up and put a fight?"

"Some. When the threat finally registered. But it was too late. The *somnara* is hard to shake off. It takes days to fully wake, sometimes weeks. Our few younglings were already dead. Their bodies were too fragile."

"Oh, God." Her hands flew up to cover her mouth.

Valeria wasn't sure she wanted to hear anymore, but the words kept spilling out of him now as if he were purging them from his soul.

"There were only three women among our number, but he had already killed one. I supposed it was a blessing that he was working his way from the inside out. Else he would have killed Sanaa. That would have been devastating. She is the clan's little sister, and she occupies a special place in the hearts of many of our warriors. Her berth was next when I came in."

His voice was low, but it seemed to vibrate in this huge, lifeless chamber, an echo of the past.

"You killed him."

"I had no choice."

She reached out to touch the lid of the carved coffin in front of her. "Is he here?"

"Only his heart."

Valeria flinched, but Rhys knew it couldn't be helped. He would not hide that side of him, the part that did not forgive.

"He was our leader, and he led true for many years. But his mind became diseased. It lies with his bones, elsewhere, in an unmarked grave."

This time when she hugged him, she rested her head against his heart.

"I'm sorry."

He couldn't help stroking the silk strands of her hair. "So am I...you have no idea how much."

CHAPTER TWENTY-ONE

Rhys stood on the balcony outside his office, watching Valeria hike down the hill. She'd been down to see Sanaa and the babes, eschewing the offer of a ride. She preferred to walk now that her strength had returned, a full month after her accidental teleportation.

"Did you ever go back to Vienna? For your treasure?"

"Yes, but by the time I made my way back, the prize I sought was gone."

She hadn't understood, merely nodded, and resumed eating dinner the night after his revelations in the cave.

He was grateful she hadn't pushed at the time, but he felt guilty for not telling her about Gabrielle. But now he couldn't bring himself to confess, because she had finally started touching him.

It wasn't very much contact. A pat of her hand here, a brush of her fingers there.

She kept trying to comfort him for the decimation of their small band. Rhys didn't tell her his people weren't tactile, like some shifters native to this world. But with her, that fact never mattered. He soaked up each of Valeria's small caresses greedily, absorbing them like the parched earth drank the rain.

And she had begun to allow small touches back. He had to broadcast his intentions and never capture her unawares, but she no longer shied away. Not if he was careful. He was slowly building on that.

A sound behind him signaled his second.

"No harm seems to have come from confiding in her," Naveen said, coming to stand next to him on the deck.

His clan's sensitivity about the place aside, he had to ask… "What harm could she do down there?"

There were no longer any slumbering Draks to protect. Only the dead slept there now, making it a tomb in truth.

That had been Rhys' first decree as the newly elected clan leader. They would no longer bury their heads in the sand, sleeping the years away. From that moment on, what was left of their people would rise and remain awake, living their life as part of a community.

War, peace…whatever happened next, they would go through it together. None would be left to stew in their madness alone. Even when an individual broke off to travel, they were required to stay in touch.

The only ones who could slumber were the injured or soul-sick. But not here. Never here. If someone needed to enter *somnara,* then they would find a secret place, near but not too near—within a day's flight. But so far, no one had chosen to sleep, not since it happened.

"It's said some witches will pay any price to get their hands on dragon bones," Naveen murmured, his eyes tracking Valeria like she was prey.

Rhys weighed that for a moment, but only because that was his duty. "I don't think that's a concern."

There was a short silence. "Are you sure she can be trusted? I hate to be the one to remind you, but she did betray you once."

Rhys sighed, but it wasn't relief or exhaustion. It was acceptance of the things he couldn't change. *Finally*.

"I no longer blame Gabrielle for her weakness. She was a product of her times. In the end, she would have had no choice. "

There was a loaded pause, but Naveen eventually nodded. "My first, I did not mean to question your choices."

His tone was apologetic.

Rhys turned, clapping Naveen on the back. "That is your job as my second. Never stop questioning me."

Not allowing or accepting criticism was part of what had led to Markus going mad, to their loss.

"I do apologize, but my discomfort lies in the fact she circumvented all our safeguards so easily. She should be dead."

Rhys nodded. "Yes, I know." That had given him a shock as well.

Dragons did not do magic per se. But the closest they came to it had to do with their lairs. Protecting their hoard was something built into their DNA. Snares and traps were just the beginning. Dragons employed tricks of the mind, deceptions that had no name, but could drive a mortal mad....

Except for her. Valeria broke the rules without even trying. He'd stopped asking himself why she could do what she could do. The answer was simple.

"Valeria *is* magic. It's in her blood. It practically seeps from her pores." Rhys snorted. "The reason she found our sanctum is that she was wondering what I was hiding from her... She never guessed there would be more than one thing."

Naveen's answering rumble was somewhere between a laugh and growl. "Now I just feel sorry for her. Because if that's true, those witches will never stop hunting her."

No, they wouldn't. "I won't let them take her from me. Not again."

His second smirked. "I suppose I knew that already."

Rhys took his eye off his witch, scanning the horizon. "We need to keep a closer eye on the nearest human settlement."

"That little town? Why? It's so small that it doesn't have a name."

"You said it yourself. She is too great a prize. They will keep looking for her. When they find her, that's where the threat will come from."

Naveen grunted. "You're right, of course. Well, keeping an eye on the settlement shouldn't be too difficult a task. Enough of us have made ourselves known to the populace that people will talk to us. Not that a new group of humans could hide there. The place is so small that outsiders can't blend."

"Who would be best?"

"Well, actually, Kyrin has some friends in that community."

Now that was a surprise. "Is he still upset?"

Kyrin had never forgiven his grand-sire Markus for what he'd done. It was one of the reasons Rhys didn't like assigning him to guard the sanctum, but then, every member of his clan had difficulty being down here.

"Upset would be an understatement. But he won't disobey an order."

Of course he wouldn't. That wasn't the point. As the first of this clan, it was Rhys' job to make sure his people were of sound mind as well as body. And Kyrin had yet to deal with his anger and pain.

"Do me a favor and don't send him yet. Let a few others have a turn, show their faces in the township. Then Kyrin can go in."

That would give Rhys time to organize a few community-wide events. They hadn't had any recently, ever since Sanaa entered the last month of her confinement—the period when pregnant female dragons avoided flight in case the activity triggered premature labor.

But aside from Sanaa's delivery, the clan hadn't had a chance to interact with Valeria. He wanted her to become a familiar sight to his men.

I'll just set up a movie night.

Sanaa did it all the time. How difficult could it be? It was just popping in a disc.

A short laugh escaped his second.

Turning a questioning gaze to him, Rhys followed Naveen's hand down. A chortle got stuck in his throat as he spotted what had amused his man.

Valeria was being stalked.

CHAPTER TWENTY-TWO

There was a rustle in the bush to the left. Valeria tripped, checking her surroundings as her heart hitched high in her chest. *It's a rabbit,* she assured herself. There were no predators on this mountain. At least, she didn't think there were.

Were there cougars at this altitude?

Even if there were, there was no chance in hell they'd hunt in dragon territory. In the few months she'd been there, she'd seen multiple dragons flying overhead. The first few times, the sight had scared the poop out of her, triggering her fight-or-flight response. But after a few weeks, she'd grown accustomed to the awesome sight. Mostly. At least she'd stopped freezing in place despite being buzzed by one she was sure was Kyrin, the dragon she'd pissed off by visiting the crypt.

But her feigned blasé attitude lasted up until one of those big dragons swooped down not a hundred yards from her down in the valley near Sanaa's house and then took off, chomping a deer, eating it in mid-air.

In her dreams, the beast made '*nom-nom*' noises. *It would be much easier to eat me,* her brain supplied helpfully. Her hide was nowhere near as thick as a deer's.

Not that Rhys would allow such a thing. Which meant whatever was making that noise in the bush was a raccoon, possibly a fox. Something small.

At this point, I'll take a badger. Walking away, she put it out of her mind. But the susurration followed her.

Picking up the pace, she walked up the hill in double time. And then she was running. That was when the beast began to whine.

"Oh no!" Recognizing the sound, she pivoted, running back down the hill. She dug through the thick undergrowth, uncovering a small, mottled blue dragon.

"Lanaa, what are you doing here?" she cried, picking up the little female dragon. "Ow, ow, claws. Watch the claws."

She sighed with relief when the little girl responded, adjusting so her tiny, sharp claws weren't digging into the fleshy part of Valeria's arms. Resigned to adding another hour to her hike, she started down the hill.

"Your dad is going to kill me if this happens again," she told the precocious baby.

"He will not touch you."

Startled, she turned to find Rhys a few yards behind her. She looked up at the sky. "How did you sneak up on me?"

Dragons could be stealthy, as she'd discovered, but they were too big to land so close without whipping up the wind and kicking up a buttload of dust.

"I walked down here," he said, his mouth twitching. "You were so distracted with the babe that you didn't hear me."

"Oh." She felt a little stupid, but more than that, she felt...good. Being in Rhys' presence felt good.

Certain that acknowledging that fact was about to have an equal and opposite reaction in the universe, she glanced up, looking for a fireball that would signal an impending meteor about to strike her dead.

"Is something wrong?" Rhys asked after she twisted her neck far enough to receive a warning cramp in the muscles.

"No, although I guess I'm worried. Thomas is going to be pissed if this happens again."

Rhys raised a brow. "How many times has this occurred?"

Valeria showed her teeth. "This would be the fourth."

"Oh, I see." His mouth twitched.

"It's not funny," she admonished. "Thomas is going to be furious if this keeps on much longer."

Stifling a chuckle, he threw an arm around her shoulder. They stopped and stared at each other before she shrugged—but not hard enough to dislodge him. If he wanted to touch her, that was all right. She had a handle on their magic. Even the unwanted bits.

Lanaa snuffled, trying to reach Rhys. "Do you want to take her?" she asked, hefting the creature's slight weight a little higher.

He shook his head. "I'm afraid it would complicate matters."

"Is it still the imprinting issue? Surely that's not a concern anymore?" She glanced down at the babe before clarifying. "For you, at least. Haven't the twins had enough time to bond with their parents that being held by someone else—err, someone who didn't interfere at the moment of their birth—should be no problem?"

She had seen several other dragons holding both children during her brief visits.

"I'm afraid it's not that simple for me," he said. "I'm the first for this clan because of my strength and level of dominance. At this stage of development, my holding them might interfere with the parental bond. A few more weeks, and then it should be safe enough."

"So, this is normal?" She frowned, adjusting her hold on Lanaa as the girl turned her head in all directions, eager to see the world.

"Yes," he said. "Though we haven't had many young born here, we know such things from our writings, the most important that we managed to bring with us."

Valeria had been all over the library, but she hadn't seen those books yet. Those particular volumes that described in their history and biology must have been in his study or stored in their healer's home.

She didn't think he was hiding them from her, exactly, but it made sense that such precious tomes weren't left out for causal consumption to just anyone.

Rhys reached out to steady her when a rock in the road would have unbalanced her, her vision obscured by the wiggling child.

"It's a survival mechanism, isn't it?" she asked with her customary insight.

"Yes," he confirmed. There was no point in denying the fact now that she'd worked it out. He lifted one shoulder. "Given how seldom we breed, it likely evolved to protect the children should the worst happen to their parents."

"So, if the parents somehow died or were incapacitated, the babies would bond with the most dominant dragon around them—their clan leader."

He nodded. "It would ensure the babes obeyed him or her in exigent circumstances, increasing their chances of survival. But that particular biological imperative fades as they grow older. In a month or so, I will give them official welcome in the clan. They will recognize me as their authority without feeling the need to chase me around."

"Like Lanaa is doing with me? Why hasn't Sanaa banned me from the house?"

"Accidental imprinting sometimes happens. It will fade as the babes become more independent and the more time they spend with their parents. Your continued interaction with Lanaa may prolong the period a bit, but not by too much—a year or two at most."

Spinning to face him, she almost dropped Lanaa.

"A year or *two*?"

"It's not a long time to us."

There was something in his tone, a thread of sadness that ran deep. *It's the loss of their people, that terrible tragedy where their leader went mad.* But something poked at her, a sense of knowing that there was more.

She glanced down at Lanaa to find she'd fallen asleep. *Imagine this coming out of you.* Not that she was thinking about mating with a dragon, but given the fact this baby was part of an interspecies pairing brought up several questions.

"Thomas and Sanaa would still work if it went the other way—if Thomas was the dragon and Sanaa the shifter?"

Shifters were known for their resilience, so it stood to reason.

"It's easier if the female is human...or witch."

Her lips parted. "How do you figure that?"

He explained how humans and witches, which he called magically enhanced humans, were genetic blank slates, which allowed all sorts of creatures to make babies with them, even something as alien and extreme as a dragon.

"It's Thomas' shifter nature that may have led to complications, one less likely to occur in a human-dragon mating," he finished.

Her mouth thinned. "Because we're the breeding equivalent of tofu or plain potatoes? We take the flavor of whatever we're mixed with?" she asked, not bothering to hide her indignation.

Rhys' face contorted. It took her a second to realize he was holding back laughter.

"It's not a bad thing. In fact, in some circles, humans are valued and protected for this very reason."

She was tempted to say something scathing about brood mares and baby factories but discussing reproduction with Rhys was too much—just too much. So, she asked him something else.

"Is it my imagination or is Lanaa a bit more muted in color than her brother?"

She'd visited both babies earlier and noticed Galen's coloring was starting to brighten, getting hints of a brilliant cobalt blue around his wings and belly.

"Like many other dimorphic species, our males are the more colorful."

To attract a mate, her brain finished. It always came back to that. "This conversation is becoming circular."

His quick grin was like a thunderbolt—brilliant, devastating, and gone before she completely registered it.

It was a good thing he comes out of the shift fully dressed. She knew that wasn't true of other shifters. Wolves, bears, wildcats—all the more mundane beasts—ended up naked after the transformation.

She was suddenly glad Rhys had never actively flirted with her. She wasn't equipped to handle a lightning strike.

CHAPTER TWENTY-THREE

Thomas *had* growled at them when he'd seen them bringing the little one back. Snatching his child away with his characteristic impatience, he'd been just about to slam the door in their faces—something Sanaa had warned him not to do to Rhys particularly—when something remarkable happened.

Lanaa had looked up at her father and shifted in a shower of sparks, gaining her humanoid form several months ahead of schedule.

Taken by surprise, Thomas clutched the little girl to him, his stern face crumpling.

"Baby girl," he whispered, gazing at his daughter's human face for the first time. "You're so beautiful."

It was true. Plump and pink-cheeked with skin a deep gold that was only a few shades darker than his, but lighter than Sanaa's, the little one gave him a gummy grin.

Thomas' head whipped up. "Did you do this?" he asked Valeria.

His witch had her hands over her mouth, her eyes shining.

"*No.* At least, I don't think so," she said, inching closer to Rhys in case the bear's amazement turned to anger.

"I don't think it was her," Rhys said, returning the babe's smile when she turned it on him. "Lanaa is simply confident in the people around her. If she feels secure enough to leave the house on her own, then she'd be comfortable enough to be in her more vulnerable form."

"Well done, little one," he added, tapping the girl's small nose. The child responded by kicking her feet and drooling all over Thomas' shirtfront.

"Oh, yeah," Thomas said, cradling her. A look of resigned frustration settled on his face. "I didn't expect she'd be able to get out on her own."

"Did she fly out?" Valeria asked, glancing at the sky apprehensively. "Will you have to put a GPS tracker on her, so she doesn't get lost?"

"Her wings will be too weak to fly for a while yet, but she can glide. That's something she should start practicing now. Is Sanaa napping?"

"Yes, Galen kept her up most of the night. How did you know she fell asleep?" Thomas asked.

Despite the amount of time he'd lived in their community, he still treated Rhys with suspicion. It would have been insulting if Rhys hadn't come so close to being mated himself once upon a time.

He knew the drive to protect was a fierce one.

"Because, otherwise, she would have noticed the babe got loose." Rhys tapped his chest. "It's a tug here. As clan leader, I feel it, too. Don't worry that she'll get too far should she escape again. Her instinct will drive her back to someone familiar. In this case, it was Valeria, the first person she saw, but that should fade soon, as we discussed. For the time being, I'd advise closing the windows when Sanaa is sleeping."

Sighing with his whole body, Thomas agreed. Rhys jerked his head at Valeria, indicating they should leave.

They walked up the hill slowly, talking about books he'd noticed her reading in the library and about the places she'd lived and if she'd ever gotten the chance to develop any hobbies other than her drawings and painting.

It didn't feel like an interrogation, but Valeria ended up telling him things she had never told a living soul, about her mother and having to cultivate small pleasures for the sake of her sanity.

"What sort of pleasures?" he asked, his face carefully blank.

"Little treats I could afford, like finding immigrant bakeries—there was always something new to try," she said. "I liked finding Asian ones that made those little eggs tarts. Many big cities have a Chinatown or Little Koreatown."

Rhys made a mental note to introduce egg tarts to their menu.

"Have you made any progress on the mirror?" Her apprehension left a tang of metal in the air.

"My people have traced a few more names of the previous owners, but I'm afraid we don't know much more on the provenance than where we started. It doesn't seem to have a very notable history."

Except for the fact that the additional names belonged to men who had been known among their families as having exceptionally long marriages. But he didn't tell her that.

"Then maybe you've had some time to think about finding work for me?" she asked, the air around her continuing to be colored with her wariness and concern.

After what she'd done to save Sanaa, how could she continue to doubt her place here? If Thomas had any gold, he would have given it all to her already.

It was time. Rhys had been hoping to avoid this for a bit longer, but she was too smart to hide this secret from her anymore. Thanks to the little hints dropped by his people, she suspected it anyway.

No, it was better to tell her the whole truth now. She'd either be angry or... He shuddered, his need so sharp it physically hurt.

"Are you all right?" Rhys turned to find her watching him with wide eyes.

"I'd like you to come with me," he said, reaching out.

She studied him for a second but took his hand. When he led her upstairs, she began to turn to his office out of habit.

"This way," he corrected, guiding her to the other door on the third floor with a hand to the shoulder.

"Isn't this your room?" she asked, hesitating at the threshold.

"It's where I keep it."

She dug her heels into the thick carpet. "I've seen the mirror."

"I'm not talking about the mirror."

Valeria made a little *hmm* sound in her throat. He walked into the room, wondering if she would follow.

She joined him a minute later.

"That's a big bed."

He bit his lip to keep from grinning at her wide-eyed expression. It was earned. The bed was double the size of a California king. It had been custom made, with big wooden posts hung with draperies woven with intricate Draconian designs.

"That is also not what I wanted to show you."

Sucking a deep breath, he put his hands on her shoulders and nudged until she was facing the wall across from the bed, the one he would watch while falling asleep.

She stared at the painting of his lost love, completely motionless.

The frame was aged gold gilt, the canvas painted by a Venetian master who had been commissioned to paint Gabrielle's portrait by her family on the occasion of her marriage to Archduke Simion Ludwig Rudolf, a nobleman from Bavaria.

Gabrielle glowed like one of Rembrandt's subjects, her hair half-pinned up with the rest of her black tresses spilling over her shoulder against a wine-red dress. A magnificent ruby necklace was around her neck. With her pale skin and lips a deep mauve pink he'd found no match for in nature, she could have been Valeria in costume dress.

The blank spot in the corner of the canvas was when the artist stopped because Gabrielle had died, a mere three months after her wedding. The man had been uncertain the family still wanted it.

Rhys had stolen it before he got a chance to ask them.

Valeria walked up to the frame, touching it with tentative hands. "That's not me, is it?"

"No," he said softly, studying her instead of the painting. He knew every line of it by memory anyway.

"Who is she?"

"Her name was Gabrielle Rauch-Kastner. She lived and died nearly two hundred years ago."

There was a long silence. "What was she to you?"

"My mate."

Valeria turned away from the painting, sitting heavily on the velvet-covered bench at the foot of his bed.

"I met her in Vienna, but lost her far too soon."

Valeria's gaze jerked toward him. "What happened? How did you meet her? Who was she?"

The questions were tinged with panic, her voice unnaturally high.

"I saw her at the opera I attended by chance, then spent the next few days tracking her down," he said, putting his hands on his pockets to keep from reaching for her. "She was the only daughter of an old Viennese family."

He leaned against one of the bedposts. "Gabrielle's people were of noble blood but financially strained. They were counting on her beauty to attract a wealthy suitor to replenish the family coffers. Since my traveling persona of a student of the natural and engineering sciences would not impress them, I changed it, becoming a wealthy prince traveling incognito overnight."

She snickered. "You pulled out all the stops."

Rhys raised his brow. "I was not about to let their petty perception of my lack of wealth and breeding stop me from claiming her," he said with a nod at the portrait.

"Then what happened?"

"I began to court her," he said, sorting through his memories. "It was a slow process, too slow for a creature used to flying off with his mate right after meeting her."

Valeria's nose wrinkled, realizing that was what he'd done with her.

"Nevertheless, I stayed within the strictures of Gabrielle's society. It was the first time I had courted anyone, so I studied what needed to be done. I took her on carriage drives and walks in public gardens. I drank coffee from tiny porcelain cups in her family's parlor, all the while making sure to shower her with expensive gifts to prove my wealth and suitability as a mate."

Clasping her hands together in her lap, she shrugged. "If you wanted their approval, that was probably necessary."

"It wasn't enough."

Valeria's brow puckered. "I don't understand."

This next part was difficult to say. "My courtship was too new for them, only a month, but they allowed her to accept my suit. However, when I was unexpectedly called home, they balked at letting her come with me."

Valeria's lips parted. "The treasure from Vienna, the one you lost because of what happened here—what Markus did."

"Yes. I was speaking of Gabrielle."

Talking about these events had always hurt, but that was before he met Valeria. It was as if meeting her had turned down the volume on the pain, the one that never dulled because it was the agony of missed opportunities. Rhys had spent years living without his heart in his own chest...and then one day, it had just walked back in.

"After it was over, I broke the clan rules, flying back to Vienna non-stop, even during the day when there was a possibility of being seen. But over three months had passed. When I arrived, I found out she had married someone else."

Her mouth dropped open. "She didn't wait for you?"

"No," he sighed, before rolling his shoulders in a hapless gesture. "I was very angry with her for a long time for breaking her promise."

Valeria winced. "I'm sorry," she whispered.

"It's not your fault." And it wasn't. Blaming Valeria for what Gabrielle had done was the height of insanity. "As for Gabrielle, she was a product of her times. She wouldn't have been able to stand firm against the wishes of her family for long. It wasn't her fault, any more than it is yours."

She gestured helplessly to the painting. "Are you sure?" she asked.

He laughed. "You aren't her."

Valeria pursed her lips. "Obviously, some people here think I am."

"The resemblance is uncanny, I'll grant you. But Gabrielle wasn't a witch."

Her lashes fluttered. "She wasn't?"

"Not a drop of magic," he assured her. "I've grown fairly proficient at sniffing them out. Most witches have a distinct scent."

A spark of anger made it past the shock. "I *smell?*"

"Not bad. Bad witches are malodorous."

She appeared mollified. "I've heard shifters say that sort of thing before."

"It's the herbs they use, and the death they surround themselves with. It seeps into their pores so deep they can't wash it away."

"And yet, the shifter hunters always tried to capture me anyway."

"The bounty on your head must be very high."

She was silent for a time. "What happened after? You don't strike me as the kind of man who would just give up after you found your mate married to someone else. Why didn't you do the dragon thing? Why didn't you kidnap her back?"

It was strange. She knew him better than Gabrielle ever had. "I was going to, once I was able to think a little more clearly. Except, she did not want to be kidnapped..."

"How could she possibly have said no to you?"

The incredulity in her tone warmed his heart. "It was her brother who told me what happened, that she'd married a nobleman. But she did come to me one last time to tell me that she chose him, her new husband, willingly."

"Ouch."

He chuckled aloud. "I wish I could say I was magnanimous in defeat, and I let her go without a fight."

A corner of her mouth turned up. "So, you *were* going to kidnap her?"

He shrugged. "I was desperate. I needed to know if she'd say the same thing once she was alone with me, away from the influence of her family and new husband. But she died before I could go through with it."

Her eyes widened. She hadn't expected that. Valeria squinted at the painting. "How old was she?"

"In human years? Twenty-three."

Valeria's eyelid twitched. "That's how old I am."

"Oh."

The line of her shoulders crumpled. "I've often wondered if I would make it to twenty-four. I hope it's not an omen."

His face darkened. "No harm will come to you," he growled. "I will not allow it."

She gave him a sad smile. "Because you think I'm her."

"No," he said, shaking his head. "I don't. You smell nothing like her."

That made her laugh.

"Come..." He held out his hand. "I want to show you something."

Her reluctance was palpable. "Is it as dramatic as this?" she asked, gesturing to the portrait.

"I'll leave that to you to judge."

CHAPTER TWENTY-FOUR

This time, Rhys took her down instead of up. They left the house and took a winding path, one that ran along the side of the mountain, not away from it.

At the end, there was another tunnel mouth, this one concealed by a large boulder Rhys moved effortlessly despite the fact it was bigger than he was.

"Is this under your balcony?" she asked, looking up at the deck high above.

"Yes," he said, nudging her inside. The darkness engulfed them.

"No lights in here?" she asked, her voice higher than normal. "I take it you don't need them?"

His large hand grasped her by the elbow. "Like most terrestrial shifters, I have excellent night vision."

A few minutes later, he came to a stop. "Stand here for a moment."

He moved away. A stream of flame shot out of his mouth, lighting another one of those big dish-like braziers.

The sight that met her eyes should not have been a surprise, given what Rhys was, but the reality of it knocked the breath from her lungs.

She was in the middle of her dragon's hoard. Piles of gold coins, bars, and cups filled most of the space, with multi-faceted jewels and strings of pearls scattered over shelves.

Her host went around the cavern, lighting torches in wall sconces with nothing but the flames he breathed from his mouth.

"That's handy," she said when he was done, still not quite believing what she was seeing.

Chandeliers made of beaten silver hung overhead, but they weren't lit. There were also paintings and fine china, including vases that must have been Ming dynasty because what else would they be?

Overwhelmed at the sight of so many glittering objects, she closed her eyes, but the vision didn't disappear when she opened them. "I thought you preferred to be surrounded by your treasures."

"Many of my favorite pieces are upstairs, but I have lived long enough to acquire more than I can tastefully display. They wouldn't all fit in the house," he explained. "Not without making the decor unseemly."

That made her lips twitch.

"Also, when I made my pact with Aggie, I decided it would be prudent to have the main hoard nearby, but unconnected to the house."

He bent over, picking up a handful of necklaces that had been dropped over a statue of Venus. "Her purview ends at the basement. This cavern is deep enough that it's unconnected to the house. A separate entrance is required to keep her out of here."

"I thought she wasn't interested in gold."

"She isn't, but when I first met her, I took nothing at face value. I soon learned the error of my ways. She doesn't value these things. My treasure is quite safe from her, but that has a downside as well. She'll use a priceless ancient Greek bowl as a candy dish without blinking."

"So, you value our antiquities as well? Not just precious metals and jewels?" she asked.

His eyes moved down her body. "I admire anything beautiful."

Heat coursed through her cheeks, but then she saw something over his shoulder against the wall.

Valeria stiffened and rose to her feet. "That's the necklace in the portrait."

"Yes." He walked up to the piece housed in its own special niche. "I gave it to Gabriella as a pre-engagement gift. In our one meeting after she was wed, she tried to return it. But I wouldn't take it back."

"And you had her portrait done with it?"

"No. Her family commissioned the work. I assume they meant to keep the necklace, as was their right. It was a gift freely given and not part of my bride price. However, after her death, her younger brother returned it to me. He said she never wanted to take it off."

Her mouth tightened. "You didn't find that strange?"

Rhys shrugged. "I suppose, in retrospect, yes, but I wasn't thinking all that clearly at the time."

He pivoted, his gaze going from her to the necklace, a little frown on his face. "Do you want to try it on?

"No," she said quickly—too quickly.

"Of course," he said, leading her further into his cave, picking out other individual pieces from his treasure trove and telling her its story.

First, there was an ancient Sumerian tablet that he picked up in Iraq after a successful dive for gold coins in the Persian Gulf at the turn of the century. Then there was a tiara of dubious provenance. Created out of real yellow, white, and, pink diamonds, it was meant to be a forgery for the Eye of Light tiara, part of the crown jewels of Iran.

"The forgers intended to create synthetic diamonds," Rhys shared, enthusiastic about the tale. "But their technology failed to capture the precise shade of the Noor-ol-Ain, that central pink diamond. So, they cut one out of glass and hoped for the best."

"I take it their forgery was detected."

A corner of his mouth lifted. "Surprisingly, it came close to working. Unfortunately for the would-be thieves, the glass masquerading as the Noor-ol-Ain fell out and shattered on the floor. Everyone was arrested."

He held up the tiara. "I found it amusing to take the tiara after the ruckus had died down."

"So, you were there the night they were going to steal it?" Amusement lit her eyes. "Let me guess. You were going to steal it from the thieves, weren't you?"

"I may have had a plan in place, had they succeeded."

She arched a brow. "So, you wouldn't have taken it if it had been in the royal family's hands? Only from the thieves?"

"It's not treasure hunting if someone owns the thing." He nodded at the tiara. "I took that as a souvenir of a very interesting evening."

"Mm-hmm." She held up the diamond confection. The jewels glittered in the firelight with an unmistakable fire. "And yet, I'll bet the rest of the gold in this room that these are real jewels in here."

He beamed at her with pride, as if impressed she could tell genuine stones from fake. "Because they are—but these stones originated from my collection. It amused me to replace them with diamonds of higher quality than the ones in the original, which is why it's not a perfect replica. I believe in cutting stones to maximize their potential, not their intended setting. It took some time to find the right ones."

"Is there a master jeweler in your clan or...?"

"I did the work myself," he confirmed. "You'll be hard-pressed to find a dragon who would let another man or woman cut a stone for them. We all have our own tastes, and cutting gems is a skill we enjoy cultivating."

"So, it's a hobby?"

He leaned against a gold-tipped obelisk. "A rather competitive one. I upstaged Naveen with this tiara. His piece was a recreation of the Taylor-Burton diamond."

Her brow puckered. "Taylor as in Elizabeth Taylor?"

"Yes."

"So, it's not just crown jewels you copy?"

"Anyone that argues that Elizabeth Taylor is not a queen is mad," he said, making her laugh.

Leaning over, he plucked the tiara from her hand and set it on her head. It slipped over her eye.

"I didn't mean to make you sad with my revelation upstairs," he whispered in the sudden quiet.

Biting her lip, she looked behind him at the necklace on display. "Why did you show this to me?"

The painting she could understand. As long as she was staying here, she would have discovered it at some point. As it was, people were talking, dropping hints. This was a community that did not keep secrets. They had learned not to the hard way.

Rhys took a long time in answering. "I know you're wondering what your place here is. The truth is that I don't know what it is. But that doesn't mean you don't have one."

The corner of her mouth turned up. "Even though I don't smell like her?"

Rhys reached out and took her hand. He let her to a rectangular slab she thought was solid stone. Peeking underneath, she saw it was hollow, the interior lined with amethyst crystals.

She sat, a little surprised when he squeezed in next to her. "I don't think you're a reincarnation."

Of course she wasn't one. Rhys' one and only was a gentle pure soul who had never stolen or hurt a soul in her life.

Except for him, her mind whispered snarkily.

"Everything about you is different," he said finally. "It's not just your scent or the things you can do, but even your smile. Yours is... unrestrained," he continued. "But that doesn't change the fact that I have never felt what I feel for you before...save with her."

Moving slowly, the way one would reach out to a wild animal, Rhys took her hand. "I don't want you to leave. Even if you decide against me—against us—I would prefer you to stay."

She released a shaky breath. "For how long?"

"As long as you want."

CHAPTER TWENTY-FIVE

Your place is whatever you want to make of it. Rhys had told her that after walking her back inside the house.

She had stayed awake most of the night, tossing and turning.

Was she a copy or herself? Did she stay or go? Would staying even be ethical?

Rhys might say she was not Gabrielle, but it was clear he was letting her stay here because of the resemblance.

Her face had always helped her. She was pretty, and people mostly liked helping the attractive. That was what her mother had always said, only she had added, 'It's easier to take advantage that way'.

Well, now her face was a weapon, a stiletto knife sharp enough to push past a dragon's defenses, allowing her to play on what was might be his only weakness. How the hell was she supposed to deal with this?

At least you know why you're here now.

Valeria rubbed her temples. If she'd made a list of possible reasons why, never in a million years would she had put 'possible reincarnation' on it.

And where the hell did that damn mirror come into the picture? Rhys hadn't orchestrated her meeting up with it. That much she knew.

The next few days were tense. She avoided Rhys, wondering what the hell she should do, what it all meant... And she didn't sleep very much.

Eventually—when she almost stumbled down the stairs—Rhys put his foot down. He sent her to bed with one of Aggie's natural sleep remedies. When that failed, she went to the library, trying to find a book or diary boring enough put her to sleep.

That was where Rhys found her in the afternoon of the third day, standing in front of a bookshelf full of engineering texts and manuals. She must have looked like a zombie, staring slack-jawed at the books as if they were brains she was trying to decide between.

Wordlessly, he swept her off her feet, carrying her to the couch. That was when she finally slept, tucked next to him on the cushion. He was still there when she awoke, the moon high in the night sky.

A blanket had appeared in the interim. The soft throw was covering all of her and part of him, although she was one hundred percent certain Rhys hadn't moved.

The dim light flickered. Shifting her head, Valeria saw that the fireplace was lit. "I thought this fireplace was on the other side of the room."

"I had Aggie do a little rearranging while you were out."

"Oh..." Valeria yawned, no longer surprised that the brownie could move more than just furniture. "Why did you stay? I know you have a lot to do."

"Naveen came. Made a report. You were so exhausted that you slept through it." Rhys shifted her a little with a gentle touch. "I know why you're not sleeping. Fortunately for you, I've read enough of these books to know what is happening. I believe the philosophers call it an existential crisis."

She pursed her lips. "Is it philosophers or psychiatrists?"

"Is there a difference?"

"Hmm...good question. I have another one. Why are you so comfortable?" She patted his chest with her palm. "You're all muscle and hard bits. It should be like sleeping against a brick wall, but you're super comfy."

"I have no explanation, other than...you fit."

In a romance novel, of which the library had two dedicated shelves, that would have been the end of it. She and Rhys would have just accepted what the universe was trying to tell them. Then she would have been able to sleep because she spent every night in his arms. But Valeria wasn't a character in a romance novel.

I am living someone else's life.

That was the overwhelming feeling she couldn't shake. It accompanied her everywhere, on her visits to Sanaa and during her explorations of the wilderness around them.

She was constantly waiting for the other shoe to drop. Finally, she couldn't take it anymore. Valeria had to take matters into her own hands. But to find out the truth, she was going to have to betray Rhys and break into a dragon's lair.

CHAPTER TWENTY-SIX

Valeria waited until Rhys had gone down to the morning training session before leaving the house and taking the path to his private treasure cave.

Her host had explained about the bit of dragon magic he insisted wasn't magic—how his people created blinds and snares and small physic traps that would lead people away from any place they chose to protect.

Technically, it didn't matter that Rhys had brought her here once. Their little tricks were adaptive. They adjusted on their own, so the path down would have changed, making it impossible to navigate despite the short distance between the front door of the house and the mouth of the cave.

But she found it anyway. It had been easy. All she had to do was stop trying.

Valeria had come prepared this time, having raided the supply closet until she found a flashlight, one of those long, barreled-heavy ones that conveniently doubled as a weapon.

Also in her pockets were two sticks of chalk and a zip lock bag full of salt, as well as a bottle of water in case she was down there longer than she planned.

Once inside, she ignored the mountains of glittering gold and the displays of necklaces and crowns, except for one.

The ruby necklace was draped on one of those headless busts museums and jewelry stores used to display their special pieces. It was set in an alcove by itself, no other treasure within five feet of it.

Setting the flashlight down on the floor, Valeria fetched the nearest torch, lighting it with a match. It took a few tries, the material stubborn to light. Apparently, it was best suited to those who could breathe fire. It took six attempts, but the damn thing lit. She dropped the wooden handle into the sconce just above the necklace.

"Would it have killed him to install track lighting?" she asked, shaking her head.

If Rhys wanted to enjoy his treasure, that would have been the way to go.

The stones glittered in the fire, their muted twinkle—she needed more than one torch—mocking her.

"Just do it," she muttered, reaching out to take the necklace, but she hesitated.

Damn. Her hands were sweaty. Wiping them on her jeans, Valeria rubbed her fingertips together, hovering over the necklace.

One. Two. Three. Closing her eyes, she snatched the necklace...but nothing happened. No sirens, no flashing lights.

"That's all right then." What had she been expecting? It wasn't as if Rhys would have wired the bust with an alarm when so many other precious objects had been left lying around. Not even his version of the Iranian crown jewels had an alarm.

As for the rest of her plan, that was the reason she had brought the chalk. She put the necklace back for a second, then reached into her pocket.

"If you had taken any other piece—"

Screaming her head off, Valeria jumped a foot in the air. She turned around, gasping for breath, her hand over her heart.

Inclining his head, Naveen shot her a look of frustration with a soupçon of apology. "As I was saying, had you taken any other piece, I would have hauled you to the dungeon. But you'll be hard-pressed to find anyone here who would fault you for taking *that* necklace."

Valeria glanced down at the confection of rubies and antique silver. It was warm in her hand, as if it had just come off a living body, and not a display bust.

"Most everyone believes it's yours anyway," Naveen continued. "All you have to do is ask Rhys for it."

"Nope," she said firmly, widening her eyes for emphasis. "Don't want it."

Naveen raised a brow.

"*I don't*," she snapped. "But I need to use it."

Rhys's second stared down his nose at her. "So that's not a sack in your pocket?"

She huffed, realizing he expected her to steal the necklace because she felt entitled to it.

Nothing could be farther from the truth. This belonged to a dead woman, Rhys' true love. But Valeria would use it to figure out what happened to that girl because that was a question that needed to be answered before she did another damn thing.

Rolling her eyes, she reached into her front pocket, pulling out and raising a piece of chalk.

Kneeling, she began to draw a circle, embellishing it with runes and symbols.

"You're doing a spell?"

She glanced up to find Naveen frowning. Dragons tended to get irritated when someone failed to meet their expectations, good or bad.

"I met a psychometrist once, but it was a very long time ago."

She waited, but he didn't fill in the blanks. Rhys had not told him. *Of course he hadn't told him. He promised.*

Valeria said a little prayer of thanks. Because if Naveen knew what she was about to do, he would stop her. Fortunately for her, Rhys' flawless integrity was going to help her now.

Naveen tilted his head the tiniest fraction. "What is a psychometrist?"

Shuffling on her knees, she kept drawing symbols along the diameter. "It's someone who can see the past associated with an object. All they have to do is touch it."

Naveen straightened, his expression of disinterest disappearing. "That would be useful in determining the provenance of treasure."

One-track mind, these dragons.

"Yes, well, let me see if I can recall the power first."

"I don't know what that means." More annoyance.

So, she explained—part of it. Valeria left out the bit where recalling a past power hurt her. But Naveen was damnably perceptive. It was no doubt why Rhys had made him second.

He raised his brow, his mouth settling into stubborn lines. "Is this safe?" he asked when she sat in the clear spot in the center of her rune circle.

"Um, no," she said, deciding to be honest. "But I've been giving it a lot of thought since I accidentally teleported the baby. I think this protection circle should help me, which is why I've combined it with one for improving memory—well, extracting a memory would be a more accurate way of putting it. Regardless, this combination should do the trick, if I've calculated all the variables."

She added the last symbols to the inside of the circle. All that was missing was the final flourish on the rune just in front of her.

Naveen was starting to look uncomfortable. "You make it sound like a mathematical equation."

"It's more like a chemical one, a recipe with the runes and sigils as ingredients." She took a deep breath, reaching out for the last component.

Valeria stared at the ruby necklace in her hands for a long time.

Discomfited, Naveen took a step back. "I think I should get Rhys."

Valeria shook her head. "Not yet. Wait a minute."

"Why?"

She poised the chalk over the last rune. "Because this is either going to work right away or it's not, and if it's not, I'm going to need someone to carry me out of here."

"But—"

"You can't stop me," she interrupted. "Otherwise, I'll always feel like a thief, walking into this life that should have been hers."

They stared at each other for a long moment, Naveen's expression tight.

"I have to *know*," she whispered.

The dragon hesitated, his feet moving as if he was contemplating rushing forward.

Valeria drew the final slash to complete the sigil before he could stop her, tossing the piece of chalk aside and taking hold of the necklace with both hands.

Two seconds later, she started screaming.

CHAPTER TWENTY-SEVEN

Rhys resisted the urge to ram his second through the wall. It wouldn't kill him, but it would teach Naveen not to disobey him again.

Except he hadn't given explicit orders to stop Valeria from casting spells. The wily witch had used his second's ignorance against him. No doubt she had made the whole thing seem reasonable. Naveen had let her do what she wanted because the only one at risk was the witch.

And when it came down to it, his second hadn't believed she would do anything to hurt herself. He knew all this, but Rhys was no longer rational on this score.

"How could you let her do it?" he growled. "You are my second. It's your job to assess the danger to our people—that should have included her. She is our *guest*."

And in their culture, guests were sacrosanct.

Naveen hung his head, remorse and regret a thick cloud around him. "I accept full responsibility for my failure. I did not see the danger until it was too late."

He began to say something else but paused, closing his mouth rather than defending himself further. Silent, he awaited discipline.

Rhys sighed. "Just go assist Eliana with the search for a human healer."

It was the most important thing at the moment.

Naveen hesitated. "Yes, sir. But before I go, I should mention Valeria mentioned a witch gift called psychometry. She wanted to recall Gabrielle's memories because she wants to be yours without guilt that she's stealing from a dead woman."

He closed his eyes. Somehow, that only made it worse.

After his second exited, Rhys sat on the bed next to the too-still Valeria and put his hand on her cheek. It was cool to the touch, but her skin warmed with the heat of his hand.

"I am very angry at you," he told her, focusing on that emotion to block out all the others roiling in his breast.

Psychometry.

Rhys had researched many witch gifts in his time on Earth. This one, he recognized. It was a useful gift for those who cared about the provenance of treasure. But dragons didn't care whether a tiara was new or old as long as the precious metal and jewels it was made of were real. And really, what value should they assign to an antique who had belonged to a human king? Many of the Draconai were older than most Earth kingdoms.

Valeria's failure to bring back the psychometric magic had caused considerable damage to her brain. Veda had diagnosed her with a minor hemorrhage, and he'd done everything he could to heal it. But Valeria wasn't Rhys' mate, not yet. And Veda's power to heal a human outside their clan was limited, no matter how much he wanted it to be otherwise.

Even with Aggie's assistance, Valeria would not wake.

It went against every instinct to bring in an outsider, but that was what they were going to have to do if she didn't wake on her own soon.

Rhys stayed at Valeria's side for another few hours. Her condition was unchanged when Jerik came back with an update. "Sir, I found something that I believe you need to see."

Rhys reached out and took one of the ultra-thin tablets Jerik liked to work on. Frowning, he scanned the first line of the summary his man had written. "I thought I told you only human physicians. This is a male witch."

And any other witch was a threat to Valeria.

"I know, sir, but look at him," Jerick urged.

Resisting the urge to crush the delicate electronic device, he took a closer look at the healer's bio. "Is this a joke? I ask for a healer and you find me the scion of the most notorious witch clans on this side of hell?"

The Delavordo family was one of the Seven, the biggest and oldest witching families. Notorious for spawning black magic practitioners who periodically tried to destroy the world, the name alone was enough to inspire dread in weaker minds.

Still, letting any near Valeria was lunacy, even if this man's biography said he had been excised from the family by his own choice.

"Sir, look at his eyes," Jerik pressed.

Confused at his junior's insistence, Rhys obeyed. The color was distinctive, a hazel that was all green and gold with no brown in the mix. A combination that he could see now if Valeria would just open her damn eyes.

He sucked in a breath, understanding.

"It's the bone structure, too," Jerik said. "This Salvador Delavordo has the same ocular shape as her—the same cheekbones. His lips are thinner, but their overall shape is the same. And you can see his ears since his hair is pulled back. Those are the same, too."

The younger dragon broke off, rubbing his temple. "There are too many genetic markers in common for it to be a coincidence, not when you take in the magical aptitude."

Valeria, a Delavordo witch. It made a damnable sort of sense.

Rhys closed his eyes, praying for patience. No, he would not deny the evidence in front of him. But he did stop for a moment to wish the universe would stop jerking him around like a child's plaything.

"Whatever else is true, Valeria doesn't know or suspect a connection." She couldn't.

"Some of that clan have been known to cannibalize their own," Jerik murmured uncomfortably.

"I know, but that didn't happen to her." Valeria was too powerful, too precious.

Not everyone in the Delavordo coven was power-hungry or mad. A treasure like her would have been protected. The group hunting her was outside the Delavordo family.

They can't know. If they did, the hunters would be dead. He'd bet his horde on it.

Rhys rubbed his aching head. "Find me a human brain doctor," he said finally.

For now, he'd continue to shelve the idea of a witch healer. Valeria was hurt, but she was stable. If they failed, then he'd look into this outcast witch, Salvador Delavordo. But not before. It was just too risky.

CHAPTER TWENTY-EIGHT

Her head was pounding, but she moved it anyway. Anything to escape the light.

"Cut it out." Or that was what she tried to say. It came out in a garbled, "*Cut oot.*"

Suddenly, the light disappeared, and she was blinking up at Rhys' stern and impossibly handsome face.

"You promised never to do that again," he scolded.

Technically, that wasn't true, but Valeria wasn't about to argue with an angry dragon.

"I'm, uh, sorry." She licked her dry lips. "I guess the protection circle didn't work."

Lips compressing, Rhys' glare could have put out a fire, it was so icily controlled. "It would seem not."

Turning away, he spoke to someone over her shoulder. "Thank you for your service."

Valeria sat up to see a middle-aged Indian man with a paunch dressed in blue scrubs standing next to Naveen. He was wearing a stethoscope around his neck and held an otoscope—the source of the light shining in her eyes.

As she watched, the clan's second handed the doctor a full-sized gold bar.

"But I haven't done anything, only the most routine of examinations," the stranger sputtered, struggling to hold the gold bar. How heavy were those things?

"Our resident hea—doctor—is qualified to interpret the scans you ordered, thank you."

When Rhys signaled, the bewildered man was shown out by leather-suited men waiting at the door.

"Let me guess," she said, squinting to focus on the retreating forms. "He is a human doctor you paid to come up here, blindfolded the whole way."

"He was allowed to remove the eye covering on the airplane."

Valeria winced. "So, he's not a local doctor? He wasn't from around these parts? "

Rhys stared down his nose. "Dr. Sadi is a neurologist who specialized in brain injuries. We offered him his weight in gold to attend you. He offered several suggestions in transit and requested scans. But you woke up before his direct intervention could take place."

Her stomach tightened. "His *weight* in gold?"

Valeria had been hoping Rhys hadn't gone to too much trouble. So much for that...

"I would appreciate it if," the first of the Draconai Imperia began, "—given that you're being hunted by witches so they can kill you—you didn't help them along by trying to kill yourself."

He was yelling by the time he was done.

"I'm sorry," she said in a small voice.

Rhys passed a hand over his eyes, gathering himself. "Actually, I think it's best if the doctor continues monitoring you. I'm going to stop him, delay his departure."

He left the room. Once he was gone, she realized she still wasn't alone. Naveen had remained, standing guard on the other side of the bed.

"Hey," she muttered, her headache making it difficult to turn her head in his direction. Naveen obliged her by moving closer to the door.

"How angry is he?" she asked.

Naveen grunted. "Very. I'm not too chuffed, either."

Valeria wasn't sure what chuffed meant, but she got the gist. "My apologies to you as well. It can't have been too pleasant seeing me like that."

Her memory after the first bout of screaming was hazy, but she recalled the nosebleed that had poured blood down her front. There might have been a trickle from her ears as well.

"What was worse was telling my first what you'd done."

Damn, these dragons were excellent at the guilt trip.

"I'm sorry your spell didn't work," Naveen added, his face softening. "I know you were hoping to learn some details about Gabrielle's life."

Valeria's brow puckered. "Oh, that part of the spell did work. A little too well, actually."

Naveen blinked. "But what about the bit when you woke? You said—"

"I meant the circle failed its primary purpose—to protect. But the part where it helped me remember and use the psychometry, well, that went flawlessly," she finished dejectedly.

"Oh." Naveen glanced at the door as if debating calling Rhys.

"No," she said. "Don't."

"But..."

"I said no." Valeria shook her head, even though it hurt. "He can't ever know what happened to her, how she really died..."

She lapsed into silence, still trying to process all the memories that had flooded her brain.

All those screams locked inside her. That was why Valeria had cried out. Hundreds of years later, Gabrielle's screams for help had finally been heard.

Shutting down the replay of painful memories in her head, she opened her eyes to find Naveen sitting at the foot of the bed.

"I have been thinking about your dilemma," he said in a low voice. "You feel guilty for taking Gabrielle's place, for wearing her face, walking in her shoes. But she's been gone a long while. And you are here."

He paused. "Then there's the matter of the mirror."

Her shoulders slumped. *Not the mirror.*

Naveen must have seen the enthusiasm on her face because he said, "*Yes*, the mirror."

He picked up a pitcher of water, pouring her a glass and giving it to her. "Jerik and I are still researching the provenance, but we have discovered enough to be certain of one thing—the mirror shows your *vranai*—in human words, your mate."

Valeria parted her lips, but he forestalled her with a finger in the air. "Deny it all you wish, but the question of whether you are Gabrielle reborn doesn't matter."

She took a sip before putting the glass down. "How can you say that?"

"Because Rhys is not the one who looked in the mirror."

Frowning, she collapsed back on the pillow.

Naveen took the glass again, putting it to her lips until she drank. "I admit there would be room for doubt if he had been the one to gaze into its depths, because it could be either you *or* Gabrielle reflected back," he said, his air philosophical. "But that's not what happened. You, Valeria, were the one who looked in the mirror. And you saw *him*."

Footsteps sounded, signaling Rhys and the doctor's return.

Naveen got to his feet. "You saw my first as he is today," he continued. "So, stop tearing yourself into small bits wondering if you are his. The point is moot because no matter what else may have been true in the past, the reverse is most definitely true—he is *yours*."

With that, the clan's second snapped her a quick bow and left before Rhys walked in.

CHAPTER TWENTY-NINE

The dragons didn't have a direct translation for *carpe diem*, because they didn't need one. They seized life every day, whether they were training because they loved their mock battles or snoozing on a rock in the sun.

One would use a complex machine to make art out of a redwood log one day, another would carve a statue with a chisel, while yet another would hunt down a boar and then slow roast it for days just to make the perfect pork sandwich.

After her conversation with Naveen, Valeria decided to stop thinking so much and just enjoy her life. It wasn't hard. All she had to do was spend most of her waking hours with Rhys.

They walked along the trails near the house and drove to nearby lakes to swim. Well, he swam, and she basked on the shore, sunbathing like a cat. They also visited waterfalls that were only visible in spring because summer was too dry and they froze over in winter.

Every night, they returned to his house to dine with others in the clan, the men and women rotating in small groups. After dinner, she and Rhys would go to the library where she would pepper him with questions about his favorite books.

This list proved to be very short. It was basically *'The Art of War'* and '*The Count of Monte Cristo*', the first because human's understanding of war was quaint and the latter because the revenge was quote 'very satisfying'.

Almost all other classic novels were 'merely tolerable'. He would have tossed most of the newer novels into the fire after reading them if she hadn't stopped him. As it was, they would pick a book and sit in front of the fireplace, reading and drinking port or walnut wine. Then she'd fall asleep cuddled on the couch next to him and wake up in her bed the following morning.

It could be that this small oasis was an illusion or the eye in the hurricane that was her life. But Valeria had stopped asking if she deserved the respite. She savored every moment, hoarding each new precious memory like a miser afraid there would be no new ones.

The next one came early on movie night, one of the excuses the clan used to gather in its entirety.

Valeria hid a grin as she tossed the broken Blu-Ray discs into the trash bin. Rhys tried so hard to be gentle, but the fragile discs kept breaking when he handled them.

Jaws had cracked down the middle when he failed to remove it properly from the box. *The Godfather* had been fragmented into several pieces when he couldn't figure out how to slot it into the tray of the player correctly.

In the end, Valeria had volunteered to download *Jaws* online. Predictably, the crowd had rooted for the shark. They'd been rather disappointed when it died, but had cheered up quite a bit when she'd told them about the sequels.

"I can't wait until next movie night," Sanaa enthused, bobbing a wide-awake Galen in her arms.

The babes hadn't watched the movie. They'd played and slept upstairs, where one of the multi-purpose rooms had been converted to a nursery. Thomas, Sanaa, and Aggie had taken turns watching over them.

The brownie had been so pleased to welcome the babies, even after they'd taken a nip out of her hand.

"The series doesn't exactly improve as it goes on," Thomas groused.

The bear had finally stopped giving Valeria dirty looks despite Lanaa making a beeline for her when she came in. But the sight of so many new visitors, and the unfamiliar house, had distracted the little one enough that she didn't focus on Valeria too much. That and she was now fast asleep, her little hand curled around her papa's arm.

"I don't know," Valeria mused after a moment. "I rather like the second movie—teens in peril is a tried-and-true formula."

"Next thing you'll be saying is that the third one was better in three-D," Thomas groused.

"Never." Valeria took exception to that. "Although, I did enjoy the park storyline."

The bear reacted as if she'd stabbed him, his dramatics making his mate laugh.

They chatted for a few minutes more before Sanaa took the sleeping boy to their vehicle. Thomas shifted a slumbering Lanaa in his arms.

"I never thanked you for what you did," he said, looking down at his daughter with a warmth that made her heart ache.

Valeria had never known her father. Ravenna had always refused to discuss him, only telling her that he was dead.

She suppressed a wince. "I didn't mean to interfere with your bond—"

"I wasn't fishing for another apology." The bear scowled. "I meant what I said. Sanaa might not have made it if it wasn't for you. Complications aside, I will always be grateful."

He looked up, his face deadly serious. "If you ever need anything I can help with, ask."

"Thanks," she said, a little confused but relieved he wasn't holding a grudge.

Valeria walked him out to the car to say a proper goodbye to Sanaa. Many of the other men said goodbye to Valeria as well, their parting cordial, almost warm.

She walked back into the house, unsurprised to see that Naveen and Rhys were still talking. The clan's second was a fixture in the house. He came by every day, often multiple times, to make one of the seemingly endless reports Rhys demanded of him.

But they don't usually make him look like that. The expression on Rhys' face was troubled.

When they turned to her, she stopped at the threshold of the living room. Murmuring to Naveen, Rhys dismissed him. The second joined Kyrin at the door. The younger dragon gave her a look filled with distrust and suspicion.

Then they were alone. Even the tables were empty, Aggie having cleared them with her magic.

"Are you okay?" she asked.

Rhys nodded, holding out his hand. "Come sit with me."

He guided her to the couch, pausing to grab a decanter from a nearby sideboard and setting it down on a coffee table that suddenly appeared. Two crystal glasses were sitting on it.

"Do you have a mind-meld with Aggie?" she asked, raising a brow. "Is that how she knows what to do without you asking?"

A flicker of amusement crossed his face. "Thankfully, one is not necessary. Brownies anticipate your needs. Picking up the cognac was a signal, telling her to get the glasses ready. When she sensed me putting it down, she shifted a table from another room."

Valeria frowned. "That must be exhausting, being on duty twenty-four-seven."

"Not really. Her ability is autonomic, like breathing. Most of the time, she doesn't have to think about it. And if I didn't make it clear before—this makes her happy. Brownies don't reach their full potential without a home to care for."

He poured her a drink. "But that isn't what you wanted to ask me."

Her heart squeezed painfully. Something *was* wrong. "Do I have to leave?" she asked.

His eyes met hers. "I hope not."

Her lip trembled. She wanted to cry out, '*I like it here*'. But she'd been to hell and back before and knew pleading just made things worse.

"If you don't want me to leave, then what is it?"

He took a sip of his drink before leaning over to rest his forearms on his knees, the glass dwarfed by his big hands.

"You know we monitor the world outside for threats. We keep a particularly close eye on the areas just outside our borders...and for good reason. Someone came to the human settlement looking for you. They showed the locals your picture."

Her breath stuttered. "One of the hunters?"

Rhys shook his head. "It's a lone woman. She claims to be your mother."

CHAPTER THIRTY

Rhys watched the blood drain from Valeria's face. "That's not possible. My mother is dead. Or she's supposed to be."

Face carefully impassive, he nodded. She hadn't said so aloud, but whenever Valeria had spoken of her parent, it had been in the past tense. It hadn't been that great a leap to assume the woman had passed on to her reward.

"There is a high probability that it's a ruse," he replied. "But I don't want you to worry. I'm having the woman watched. The settlement is hundreds of miles away. Whoever she is, she can't get to you here. I promise."

His reassurance fell on deaf ears. Valeria remained pale.

"Did you bury her?" he asked.

"No, I didn't see her die," she admitted. "But I know she's dead because she failed to meet me. Not once, but three times. We had to separate—things kept going to hell so fast when we were together, but we always made plans in advance on where to go when things were quiet and safe."

"And?" he prodded softly.

Valeria shrugged almost casually, but her voice was desolate. "We had set up three rendezvous in advance. She didn't come. She never came."

"I see," he said. "How long has it been?"

A pucker appeared between her brows. "At least two years. That's too long. If my mother were alive, she would have contacted me before this."

Giving in to his instinct, he beckoned her closer. Something in him calmed as she came into his arms, resting her head against his chest.

"You are safe here," he repeated, savoring the silkiness of her hair against his chin. "But I need you to be strong. I have a photograph. Jerik took it with his camera phone. You need to look at it."

Straightening her shoulders, she nodded.

Rhys fished the lightweight device from his pocket. Handling it carefully—he tended to break them easily—he pulled up the photograph from the text message his man had sent.

It pictured a woman dressed in a patched-up down parka paying for dinner at Louise's dinner, the most popular eatery in the settlement.

Rhys had already studied the image, searching for a resemblance to Valeria, and found none.

The woman was middle-aged, with dry orange hair pulled into a messy bun with dark roots. Her features were sharply attractive, but there was nothing in the underlying structure that spoke of a specific region or nationality. And she did not resemble Salvador Delavordo or any of the other members of the clan that his people had managed to find photos of.

But even if he saw nothing of Valeria in the woman, he could see his precious guest's reaction.

There was recognition and a shock so brutal she needed support even sitting down. He gathered her to him, wrapping a protective arm around her.

"It might not be her."

He didn't have to tell Valeria that there were many ways to fake someone's appearance. The Fae's ability of glamour could be a damaging and pernicious trick. It didn't fool most shifters, the Draconai included because their keen sense of smell could see past the lie told to the eyes.

But for beings without a similarly sharp sense, glamour could be a damaging threat.

"Do you have anything of hers, something that would carry her scent after all this time?"

Her brow puckered. "No."

That had been his guess. Valeria traveled too lightly to have such a convenient possession in hand. Like the nomads of old, she carried only that which was the most useful. It was a spartan and severe way of life, especially to one who liked to hoard his possessions.

"I want to see her."

"This can be easily arranged," he said, trusting that Valeria would know if the woman were truly her mother after a short meeting. "We can take you to her. Once we establish who she is, we will re-evaluate, possibly extend an invitation for a stay here. Does that sound reasonable?"

Eyes glinting, she nodded. "It does. Thank you."

RHYS WATCHED her smooth her hands over the wool coat she'd chosen for the tenth time today.

Any minute, her mother was going to walk out of the back of the Rise and Shine Motel to grab breakfast from the convenience store.

Rhys' men had been watching her for a few days, and they had familiarized themselves with her routine. After eating, she would walk around town, talking to people. To a select few, she would flash Valeria's picture, explaining that her daughter might be nearby and asking if they had seen her.

"There is no need to be nervous," Rhys assured Valeria. "Even if this woman is an imposter, we would not allow her to harm you."

That was why he'd come, leaving clan territory for the first time in years.

He was in what he called his 'incognito form,' wearing 'human' clothing to blend in. For him, that meant jeans and a t-shirt. Somewhere high above the cloud layer, Jerik and Naveen were flying.

"One dragon is worth over a hundred highly trained soldiers," he'd told Valeria before they left. After seeing them train, Valeria believed him.

There was one surprising addition to their small recon group. Rhys had asked Thomas to join them. The shifter was in bear form, waiting beyond the tree line just a little behind them.

"I know. I'm more worried it *is* her," she confessed after a minute. The idea that her mother was here searching for her simultaneously made her heart ache and her stomach churn.

He turned to eye her sharply. "Why?"

She hung her head. "Ravenna has a way of sowing bits of chaos into everyday life."

It wasn't that Valeria didn't love her mother, but it was a prickly, difficult kind of love. *She's still your mother*, she reminded herself.

Maybe. But if this woman wasn't Ravenna, then they were going to have a fight on their hands.

"I can hear her stirring," Rhys murmured suddenly. "It shouldn't be long now."

"Right." She wiped her hands on her coat again.

It took a few more minutes before Ravenna appeared. She stepped out, glaring at the cloud cover as if it had personally offended her.

That was when Valeria knew. It was Ravenna. No one could imitate that expression.

Hailing her, she ran out to meet her mother, Rhys just a few steps behind.

EVEN VALERIA HAD TRIED to talk him out of inviting Ravenna back to the community.

"Things have a way of going wrong when my mother is around," Valeria had haltingly explained after the woman had accepted their invitation to stay at his home. "She doesn't have what I would call a well-defined moral compass. At best I would call it...flexible."

"Believe me, I know that." He'd gotten that message after Ravenna had explained what had kept her away.

"Some people were after me. I was in hiding for a long time," the older witch had said while they sat at a picnic table just behind the hotel.

"It was a misunderstanding, of course. I did the job they paid me for. It wasn't my fault they couldn't use the spells properly and someone died," she added defensively.

Ravenna had looked at Valeria then, her expression contrite. "That was why I had to miss our first two meetings. I chose to miss the third. I knew I was being watched and this group was vicious, more than any I'd ever met."

She'd stopped to cup Valeria's cheek. " I didn't want to bring down that kind of heat on you. I couldn't risk you that way. After that, I wandered, but I knew my baby was alive and well in the world. That kept me going."

As for how she'd found Valeria now, Ravenna had only laughed. "You are blood of my blood. Finding you was never the problem."

Rhys knew that answer had hurt Valeria, but she'd hidden it well.

That was around the time he'd called Thomas forward in bear form, the beast's posture and obvious intelligence marking him as a shifter.

He wanted Ravenna to think they were all bears. Valeria hadn't even asked why, but had nodded in agreement when he made the suggestion.

Now Ravenna was in his home. Her room was down the hall from Valeria, where he could keep an eye on her.

"I'm not sure it's a good idea to have brought her here," Valeria told him later after her mother had gone to sleep. His precious guest was second-guessing the wisdom of allowing her to stay with them.

"You have a lot of valuable things in this house," she said, red-faced with shame. "Items worth money have a way of disappearing when my mom is around."

"Come here," Rhys said, pulling her close. It took a long moment, but Valeria melted against him. "Whatever else she is, Ravenna is your mother. As long as you are here, she can't be kept away."

He would have to learn to deal with the mercenary female sooner or later. Better to get it over with now, so Valeria wouldn't be tempted to go off with the woman out of a misguided sense of duty or, worse, to try to protect them.

"But—"

"No buts. The fact is I would give every ounce of gold in my lair below if it meant keeping you," he blurted out.

It was no less than the truth.

Pressing her lips together, Valeria blushed. "Don't let my mother hear you say that," she muttered. "It's not a good idea to tempt fate when she is around."

He pressed her to him a little tighter. "Stop worrying. Now that she's decided to resurface, we have to learn to deal with her. I'd rather it be sooner than later. Besides, this house is Aggie's domain. Nothing can go missing without her knowledge. And brownies are not bribable in the traditional sense."

Even if this Ravenna were a quick enough study to figure out which of Aggie's buttons to push, he was confident she would fail. His brownie had lived without a home of her own for so long, he knew she wouldn't do anything to jeopardize it.

Nodding, Valeria's jaw clenched as if biting back a yawn. The emotional day had taken its toll.

"You should go to bed," he said, his voice soft as he rubbed a hand down her back. "After retiring so early, I'm sure your mother will be up at the crack of dawn. You can show her around."

He fished his cell phone out of his pocket, pulling up Jerik's number. Now that they had confirmation of her identity, he wanted Ravenna's whereabouts traced. They needed to know what she'd been doing these three missing years, and he didn't trust the witch to be honest.

Valeria murmured good night and was about to leave for her room when she changed her mind, coming to press a chaste kiss to his lips.

Heat rushed through every cell in his body, but Rhys was careful not to take more than she'd offered. This was a kiss of gratitude, not welcome. But if he were patient, there would be more.

"Thank you for inviting her," she said when she stepped away, her lips red as a rose.

"Anything for you. Your mother is always welcome here."

"Even if it means Aggie has to count the silverware?" she asked. "Also, don't let her into your office if you want her to keep thinking you're a bear. All those dragon statues are a dead giveaway."

"I'll keep that in mind," he said, his voice husky. He put his arms behind his back so he wouldn't grab hold to keep her from leaving.

Once she was gone, he unclenched the fist he'd made when she kissed him. The dust that used to be his cell phone slipped through his fingers to the carpet.

"Aggie," he called, gazing at the mess in dismay.

"I'm on it," the brownie called back.

CHAPTER THIRTY-ONE

It had been three days since her mother had come to stay at Rhys' mansion. But unlike Valeria, Ravenna took to the richness of their surroundings like a duck to premium bottled water.

"Well, you certainly landed on your feet," Ravenna murmured, her tone bordering on sly.

They were walking along a ridge just below Rhys' house after a sumptuous brunch in the formal dining room.

Her mother had no more experience of brownies than Valeria did, but that hadn't stopped Ravenna from taking full advantage, eating a three-course meal with delicacies that included quail eggs and puff pastries topped with caviar.

"Your young man is handsome," Ravenna continued. "And conveniently rich..."

"Who says he's mine?" Valeria said, averting her eyes.

The denial was automatic. It had never been a good idea to let Ravenna know when Valeria was interested in someone. It never ended well, which was how her mother liked it. "Never have an attachment you can't walk away from," she would say.

Her tune was somewhat different with Rhys. But then, none of Valeria's previous crushes—and they had never been more than that—had been remotely wealthy.

"Please, do you honestly want me to believe that all those long, lingering glances and close conversations are nothing?" Ravenna scoffed. "Not to mention the way he looks at you like you're honey and he's a minute away from sopping you up with a biscuit."

Realizing she still believed the whole group to be bears, Valeria snorted, trying to deflect. "He and I have done each other mutual favors. That's all."

Teleporting Lanaa had to count. It wasn't a complete lie.

"Too bad he's so young," Ravenna continued as if she hadn't heard her. "A rich old man about to kick off would be so much more useful."

"Don't even think about it," Valeria snapped, rounding on her mother.

"Tut, tut." Ravenna smiled smugly, and Valeria realized she had failed yet another test. "I'm hardly going to complain that you've found a rich and handsome man to take care of you. I would have done the same in other circumstances."

Her mother held up her hand, admiring the embroidered cuff of the designer sweater Rhys had provided her without her even asking. Diamond earrings winking in the afternoon sunlight, because her dragon never did anything halfway.

"Yes, I know, Mother." This was familiar territory. Had Ravenna not been cursed with such a magical child, she might have been able to stop and settle somewhere, have a normal life.

It was too old a complaint to cause guilt. Not anymore. Valeria had been grown long enough to realize most of the messes her mother got in were a direct result of her choices. Just not all, which was why Valeria had never thought of cutting her off.

Even if it would make life so much easier.

"If you need money—" she began.

"Why do you always assume I need money?"

"Because the sun is up?" Valeria shrugged.

"What would you say if it was night?" her mother sniffed.

"Then I'd say it's because the moon is out."

Ravenna rolled her eyes. "Were you about to tell me that your bear would loan me money?" she asked flatly.

"Yes, although it wouldn't be a loan. If I asked him, he'd give it to me. Just in case you were thinking of nicking something instead."

Her mother stopped walking, surprised. "Just like that? Because you asked?"

"The favor I did for him was a big one."

It would be a little embarrassing, asking Rhys for money, but given that he could smell gold and jewels, he could replace it easily enough. Keeping Ravenna out of trouble was worth that discomfort.

Her mother frowned. "But you're not sleeping with him? Or do you bone in closets when I'm not looking?"

"*Mom.*"

Ravenna sighed in exasperation sigh, rolling her eyes.

Her mother knew why Valeria disliked touch, but Ravenna didn't think it should stop her daughter from doing as she liked.

"As for the money, don't you find it odd that he's rich? I didn't think their kind appreciated the finer things in life," Ravenna said, pointedly ignoring Valeria's uncomfortable expression. "Granted, they are the shifter I know least about, but, by all accounts, most don't care about money. Supposedly, bears are perfectly happy to live in shacks in the woods."

"Well, this is a very old bear community," Valeria improvised. "And they learned a long time ago that money is an excellent way to safeguard their privacy."

Ravenna hummed, squinting at the rugged mountain landscape. "How many are there?"

Only Sanaa's house was visible at the foot of the mountain. But Valeria had since learned that at least a third of the clan had houses within sight of the house. They just couldn't be seen.

She was about to tell her mother the truth when the skin on the nape of her neck prickled.

"I haven't met them all so I can't say." That was a dodge. She hadn't met two of the clan because they were traveling on separate treasure hunts, but she knew their numbers.

And even though this was her mother, Valeria also didn't want her to know how many vulnerable people the clan had, young or old. Which was a problem because she was almost certain the rustling in a nearby bush wasn't a rabbit.

"I have to admit I didn't realize you'd have things so well in hand here." Ravenna said, avoiding her eyes.

Valeria stopped walking, her heart sinking. She knew that tone, and it meant trouble. "What does that mean?"

"That I think we can turn this to our advantage," Ravenna said in her stop-judging-me voice.

So well in hand...

"You already knew I was here," Valeria said, gorge rising up her tight throat. "Someone managed to track me. But they didn't know who or what rescued me. All they knew was that their people were gone, vanished without a trace."

The witches who'd cornered her in Los Angeles had been blasted to smithereens. Those three might have been ash, but it had been a windy night. There hadn't been enough evidence to pinpoint who or what had helped her.

"That's why they let you go," Valeria groaned, putting the pieces together. "They didn't know who I was with until you saw Thomas in his bear form."

Her mother pressed her lips firmly shut.

Valeria crossed her arms, staring until Ravenna caved, looking away to avoid meeting her eyes. "*Fine.* I was in more trouble than I let on. I...I may have made a deal."

There should have been a stabbing pain, somewhere near the vicinity of Valeria's heart. But all she felt was exhaustion, a bone-deep weariness of a life lived too hard.

It should have hurt more. After all, this was her mother. "And you gave them me."

"I never intended on following through," Ravenna cried, a little spittle flying out of her mouth. "I just needed time and some distance away from those sanctimonious cross-wearing assholes. But don't worry. I am going to figure something out. I always do."

Valeria had always had a sixth sense when it came to danger. The only reason she was still alive was because she listened to it. She scanned the horizon, searching for threats.

"Are they coming now?"

"*No,*" Ravenna snapped. "I made sure they would wait."

"How sure?" Valeria grabbed her mother's arm. "Did they mark you?

"Of course not." Her mother yanked out of her grasp. "You are not dealing with an amateur."

Then why was Valeria's skin still prickling?

"You've been feeding them information."

"It was nothing crucial," Ravenna protested. "Just a quick description of the men who were with you. I didn't even know their names at the time."

Valeria nodded, not in agreement but to get the information out of Ravenna sooner. The woman hated being called to account for her behavior. Nothing shut her up faster.

"Did you text them from the hotel?" she asked.

"Yes, while I was grabbing my things." Ravenna shrugged defensively. " I didn't send them pictures or anything. And I told them to wait until they heard from me before trying anything. I stressed that the men looked big and dangerous, so they better wait."

If only that warning were enough, but Valeria's heart wouldn't calm. Danger was coming. She could feel it breathing down her neck. "Mother, did they give you the phone?"

"Don't look at me that way. I am *not* an idiot." Ravenna passed a hand through her hair. "I turned it off at the hotel, and I haven't turned it on since."

"Good Lord, Mother." Valeria groaned. "You know that doesn't matter."

"How could it not matter? It's off! They can't track it."

"Of course it's possible," she shot back. "The police do it all the time."

She was already running when she remembered. Backtracking, she sprinted past Ravenna, peeking under bushes and crashing through others.

Valeria found Lanaa only a dozen or so yards behind them. It was probably part of her bear nature, something that drove the little one to stalk prey, rather than pouncing on it from the sky.

"Stranger danger," Valeria whispered, hiding the dragon from her mother's eyes. "Don't let them see your scales."

Ravenna was only steps away, calling for her.

My mother would not harm a baby, Valeria told herself. But people not knowing her power had saved her life. It would give the dragons the element of surprise, Valeria would protect the clan's secret, even from her own mother. Besides, her instinct was telling her that they were going to need all the help they could get.

She didn't know if Lanaa understood, but the little beast cocked its head.

"Be like me." Valeria banged her chest, willing Lanaa to understand. Something in her tone must have gotten through because the next thing Valeria knew, an adorable little girl blinked up at her.

Snatching a naked Lanaa up, Valeria whirled around.

Ravenna's eyes widened. "Is that a baby? What the hell is a baby doing in the woods?" She turned her head all around, scanning for people. "Where are the parents?"

Valeria ignored her, barreling up the hill as she shouted for Rhys.

She burst into the house, but there was no echo of big, pounding feet. "Aggie! Red alert!"

The brownie popped into existence next to her, wiping her hands on a dish towel. "Wot's that?"

"We may or may not be under attack soon," Valeria said in between gasping breaths. "I need you to get me the cell phone in the guest room."

Bending sideways to peek behind her at Ravenna, Aggie sniffed. "I knew that one was trouble as soon as I laid eyes on her."

The brownie flicked a hand, and a small smartphone appeared in her hand.

Ravenna crossed her arms. "*See.* I told you it was off."

Valeria ignored her. "Destroy it, Agatha, *now.*"

To her credit, the brownie didn't even blink. The phone disintegrated in her hand, the metallic dust steaming down to the wooden floor before being swallowed up by the bare boards like they were thirsty.

"Good," Valeria sighed, breathing a little easier. She pressed a kiss to Lanaa's soft baby cheek. "Is Rhys here?"

"He's out with the men." The brownie shook her head. "Are we really expecting an invasion?"

Valeria took a deep breath, willing her heart to stop racing. But the hairs on the back of her neck were still standing on end.

"I think so. It'll be witches. I have no idea how many."

She jumped as unseen lights popped out of the walls, glowing red. In the distance, a siren began to wail—the noise was muted inside the house because it would have hurt the baby's ears.

"Can you take her and hide her?" Valeria asked, knowing Rhys was on his way. If he were anywhere within a hundred miles, he would have heard that alarm. The second he did, he would fly back here.

"If you don't mind, miss, let's hold off on that." Aggie rubbed her hands together. On some people, it would have been a gesture of glee, but Valeria sensed she was nervous. "I've never had to hold off an army. I wouldn't want to put the little one in an inaccessible room only to get distracted and accidentally cut off the air supply."

Valeria clutched Lanaa closer. "Point taken."

"Do you think they are coming?"

Ravenna's voice was edgy, some of Valeria's panic starting to get through to her. When Valeria didn't answer, her mother turned and threw her arms up to encompass the room. "Look, that's no problem. We can start gathering some of these antiques and all the jewelry in the house. If we can find enough valuables—"

"You know it's not money they want," Valeria snapped.

If it had been, she would have robbed a bank, anything to get this target off her back.

"If I could," the brownie interrupted, moving her hands as if she were shuffling the house's room to her advantage. "If the master were here, he'd recommend taking the high ground."

A boom sounded, and the house rattled around them.

"What was that?" Ravenna cried.

Aggie gulped. "Not the master."

"Everyone will come, yeah?" Valeria asked, already backing toward the stairs. Getting to high ground was a good idea. Maybe she could spot them from the deck.

Sanaa would be nearby, with Thomas. They'd get here before the others.

Valeria was out of breath when she made it to Rhys' office. Ravenna was huffing behind her, but she stopped in wonder at the room full of bejeweled dragons.

"Come on," she said, pulling her out the doors. Both blinked in the windy sunshine.

"There's no railing on this deck!" Ravenna shied away from the edge. "Get back with that baby or you'll both go over."

"And wouldn't that be a shame?" a new voice broke in.

Valeria spun on her heel, her hand on the back of Lanaa's head so the monsters wouldn't see her face.

CHAPTER THIRTY-TWO

There were three witches on the other side of the deck. In a V-formation, a grey-haired man stood in the front and a younger blond on the left, but it was the red-haired woman on the right who had spoken.

Their presence up here meant one was a teleporter, who had probably seen them from the ground. Remembering how the alert lights had appeared out of the walls, Valeria knew that they hadn't come up through the interior of the house. Because a brownie's domain was everything in the house...even the deck under the open air.

Valeria clutched the baby to her.

"Aggie," she whispered, unsure if the brownie could hear. "We've been boarded."

The deck exploded.

Gasping, Valeria nearly lost her footing when the wooden boards rolled under their feet, lifting like asphalt in an earthquake.

Some boards splintered, becoming dangerous projectiles, a wall of flying wooden stakes flying like shrapnel.

Curling away instinctively, Valeria hunched over Lanaa as she braced herself to be pierced. But the shrapnel was only flying in one direction. Twisting her head, she saw Ravenna was already flat on the ground.

"Go," Valeria yelled, pointing to the door leading to Rhys' office.

Self-preservation had never been one of her mother's problems. Ravenna crawled toward the opening like a soldier in boot camp.

A chair flew in Valeria's direction, almost hitting Lanaa when she tried to follow.

The witches weren't dead. All three were on their feet, the one in front with his hands extended, his fingers pinched together as if holding a barrier in place. From the looks of the shrapnel falling around them, it was a shield of some kind.

The house responded by opening a hole in the deck in the area with nothing underneath. They should have fallen, but, after a quick jump, they popped into existence on another part of the deck.

Valeria didn't know if one of the witches were telekinetic—that gift was sometimes tied to teleportation. It was also possible that their protection was the result of a spell. Not that it made a difference. All that mattered was that they'd come prepared.

It made the house angry.

The deck kept disintegrating, throwing shards at the trio, but their spell held. The telekinetic responded by lobbing things at her, cutting off her avenues of escape.

Valeria's extra sense licked out, trying to identify and copy their magic. It should have done so automatically, the very instant they appeared. Instead, her talent bounced back...almost as if they had known and prepared for her gift.

Mother told them. That was why Ravenna wouldn't meet Valeria's eyes, and it was why the witches had come even after her mother had failed to report in.

They took the chance because they had already been prepared for Valeria's magic. But not right away, because whatever spell they were using to block her was complicated and likely took days, possibly weeks, to prepare.

She should have told me. Her mother's betrayal was a punch in the gut.

Then the rain of shrapnel around the witches stopped. Aggie had used up most of the space on the deck. If the brownie took any more wood from the frame the whole thing might collapse, taking her and Lanaa with it.

And then she heard a magical sound—the roar of a beast so angry and feral it vibrated the deck despite the fact it was still some distance away.

Every head on the deck turned to the horizon where two dots had appeared. They swiftly grew larger and larger.

Rhys and Naveen, the two fastest fliers in the clan, were the only ones visible, but Valeria knew they were just the vanguard. This was Rhys' home, the center of their territory. Every dragon would be coming.

"What the hell is that?" one of the witches cried.

"They're dragons," Valeria offered helpfully. "You've violated the territory of the Draconai Imperia. One of them thinks he's my mate, by the way, so even if you get me, they're going to kill you all."

"*Fuck*," the blond male witch spat. "I told you we couldn't trust that bitch Ravenna. She said they were bears."

And that had been dangerous enough for them to delay for a few days. But they must have been watching the bug they planted on the phone, noting that it didn't move after that message. So, they had chanced it, and now they had put targets on all their backs.

But that wouldn't save Valeria, because they weren't about to turn tail and run.

"It doesn't matter," the woman at the side said, her voice a whiplash of hurt and a blistering anger. "We finish this now—for Riaz. For Jude. Everyone but her dies."

Suspecting Riaz and Jude were some of the witches who'd died in the alley, Valeria stepped closer to the edge. Her ability couldn't reflect nothingness, but she had a lot of raw power. Without any other options, she battered at their shield with sheer brute force.

Lanaa whimpered in her arms, sensing her tension. Her lips parted, ready to ask Aggie to take the baby, when she remembered the brownie couldn't afford to split her focus.

"Lanaa, you have to shift back," Valeria whispered, bobbing the baby as she jerked her head back and forth between the witches and the incoming dragons.

Already she could distinguish the different colors on the wings that beat pell-mell in their direction. But they wouldn't get here in time. Meanwhile, the baby stayed resolutely in human form.

But Lanaa staying human wasn't an option anymore. Their secret was out, and the little girl was safer as a dragon.

"Please *shift*. You have to change," she cried, turning her back on the witches. All the while, Valeria continued to lob haphazard power strikes—they were raw and undisciplined, but she knew from experience that they hurt.

But none of that would have made any difference if Aggie hadn't been on the defensive. She kept the witches busy with a barrage of missiles thrown at them through one of the holes in the deck—her choice of weapon anything she could get her hands on.

Already, Valeria had caught glimpses of chairs, heavy-framed paintings, and an armoire.

One of her haphazard strikes hit, managing to crack the side of the shield. One of the witches fell from the deck with a scream.

A loud thud signaled from a stone jug she'd seen on a pedestal in the hall. This was followed by the pedestal. But despite their combined efforts, the remaining two witches were steadily moving closer. Was it the teleporter and the telekinetic? That would explain why they were so good at deflecting objects.

All this time, she kept bobbling Lanaa, urging her to shift by pointing out the wings on the horizon.

Valeria didn't know whether it was the sight of the other dragons barreling down on them or the sensation of air rushing past her soft human skin, but Lanaa finally got the message.

Valeria waited only long enough to see the glittering shimmer of the change before creeping to the very edge of the deck. With one eye on her adversaries, she stroked down the child's back, confirming it was scales under her fingertips.

Pressing a kiss to the top of Lanaa's scaly head, Valeria prayed Sanaa and Thomas had kept up with the gliding training Rhys had said they'd started. "You have to *fly*."

The words came out strangled. One of the witches had grabbed hold of Valeria telekinetically. They were trying to choke her. Already, her vision was starting to darken at the corners.

Valeria was out of options and time. But Lanaa wasn't.

Winding up, she threw the mottled baby dragon off the balcony. Someone screamed. In the distance, a bear roared in agony.

But little Lanaa's wings snapped out, the sight and sound remarkably like a kite catching wind. Soaring with a susurration that sounded like pure joy, Lanaa swooped down the hill—a winged creature taking flight for the first time and loving it.

One of the dragons altered course to intercept her.

Realizing they were so much closer now, a kilometer or two away, Valeria tried to reach out with her other sense. She couldn't reflect what was shielded by the spell, but there was another option—Rhys' fire.

Desperately, she reached out for his flames, but he was either too far away or she was too weak. Her vision was a narrow tunnel at this point.

Trying to pry away the invisible hands on her neck failed. So, she did the only thing she could. Valeria backed up few steps, getting a running start.

Then she jumped.

It must have taken the telekinetic by surprise because the invisible hold on Valeria's neck slid off abruptly as she cleared the wooden boards.

The wind rushed past her ears like a jet. Paradoxically, she saw everything in slow motion—Rhys and two other dragons were literally yards away.

Stretching out her hand, she strained her arm, trying to grab Rhys' clawed hand as he barreled closer...and missed.

Bouncing off his leg like a pebble glancing off a boulder, she fell backward.

Above her, Rhys tried to adjust, but it was too late. Tensing for the impact, she waited to hit the ground.

But the ground had other plans. It opened...and swallowed her whole.

CHAPTER THIRTY-THREE

Rhys stopped short of the deck with effort, angling his wings and beating them hard so he wouldn't crash into the redwood structure.

Below him, he saw Valeria fall. By human measurements, it was three stories.

Her fragile human bones would break on the stone and concrete path he'd laid by hand in a circle around the house.

But he didn't roar his rage until he saw the sigil circle spark to life directly beneath her.

A witch on the ground, his body broken, had somehow managed to toss a leather satchel he'd had fastened to his neck with a leather thong.

The curse had been prepared well in advance. Spreading open on impact, the spell unfurled, grains of dust scattered over an invisible shield over the ground making it look as if they were suspended in defiance of gravity.

It shouldn't have activated. Such an unnatural and pernicious thing needed a massive jolt of energy, a sacrifice on a major scale...but then the witch succumbed to his injuries. The man's death gave the curse the fuel it needed to rip a hole in reality, opening a door that should have stayed closed.

He could see nothing of the landscape on the other side of the portal before it snapped closed over his beloved. But that didn't matter because he would never forget *that* scent. Recognition was immediate, visceral.

His rage shook the mountains down to their bones.

Naveen landed directly on top of the dead witch. His bulk smashed the man's bones, his heavy legs stomping to snap and crush while he managed to hold Lanaa safely.

The female babe clutched at him with her tiny claws, nestling in the protected spot between his wings instinctively.

Sparing a second to thank the stars that Sanaa had not neglected her youngling's training, Rhys flew back up to maim the remaining witches on the deck.

Only one still stood. The second had fallen, a knife-sized splinter of porcelain from a priceless Ming vase embedded in his brain.

The remaining female took one look at him and jumped, letting herself fall through the hole in the deck. Tracking her by scent, he shifted, running through his office and down the stairs.

The witch was already at the front door when the wooden frame sprouted arms. They grabbed her and hurled her back into the room. She tried to get up, but the floor liquified around her.

Desperate to escape, the intruder tried to teleport out, blinking in and out of existence like a body visible under a strobe light. Except the light was steady. It was as if the woman herself was flickering, phasing in and out of existence.

Rhys grabbed her, his move lightning fast. It had to be to capture a witch trying to teleport away with every fiber of her being. That was why a teleporter should never invade the domain of a brownie.

A dead witch walking... Or at least trying to.

"In their home, a brownie's power is absolute," he told the invader. "No matter how hard a teleporter tries, they cannot bend the laws of physics while still inside, because those rules were already answering to someone else."

"Mercy!" the witch cried as his claws bit into the flesh of her shoulder.

He took a slow deep breath, smelling blood. Pinpricks of red bloomed in her eye, a million tiny hemorrhages coalescing into larger and larger ones as the witch continued to beat herself against the invisible walls surrounding her.

"Did you have any for Valeria?" he asked softly, ripping the cross off the woman's neck.

Face contorted, the witch continued to try to teleport out of his arms, but she was held fast by Aggie's power.

"I was doing the world a favor. Do you know where that thing was spawned?"

Rhys shook her roughly, making the woman's toes leave the floor. "I have a very good idea, and *I don't care*. I also don't care about the justifications you made to yourself for chasing her in the first place. I know them for the lies that they are. You were in this for the bounty. Well, I hope it was worth your life."

Her lips split to reveal bloody teeth. "My coven will reap the rewards."

Sneering, he shook his head. "No, they won't. Because I'm going to find every single one."

"You would kill the innocent?" A thick trickle of red slid from her ear down her neck.

"There are no innocents in your coven," a new voice said.

Rhys turned to find Ravenna had joined them.

"She's a lying bitch. Lies with every breath," the witch spat, twisting her neck to meet his eyes with a gleeful smirk. "You should have said they were dragons, Ravenna."

The woman knew she was dying. In her eyes was a spark that spoke more of fanaticism than desperation over her fate.

A true believer.

Rhys clenched his jaw at the proof these women knew each other. Every muscle in his frame was rigid with the effort not to backhand Valeria's mother against the wall. But he would deal with her later.

"The minute you breached our borders, you declared war on us," he told his captive. "And we give our enemies no quarter."

"Ravenna lies about our coven. I have a child—"

"You *attacked* a child," he pointed out, his lip curling.

The woman's stench made him want to toss her away. Instead, he forced his hand to open and let her drop at his feet.

She had done too much damage to herself to escape now.

"And I don't need to take Ravenna's word on who is guilty and who is not," he continued, his voice flat and obsidian hard. "I know evil when I smell it. The death you mete out in your rituals sticks to your very skin. It can't be washed off. When my clan hunts down yours, that evil will be purged from this world in fire. That is my promise to the mate you took from me."

The witch tried to regain her feet, but her brain was no longer capable of sending those commands to her legs. "So, you're...going to kill me?"

"In case you missed it, you killed yourself," he said, staring down at her in disgust and a cold that was so icy and unfamiliar he could barely speak. "But I choose not to save you. Because Valeria was good. And she was *mine*."

Turning her face against the floor, the witch coughed, spitting blood on the marble-tiled floor.

"You can't let...me die. Without me...you'll never...know where she ended up," she rasped, her breath weaker now.

The death rattle had begun.

Rhys turned his back on her. "I already know where you sent her."

Ravenna whipped around. "Where is she? Where is my daughter?"

He narrowed his eyes, his patience burned to dust. "Drop the pretense, Ravenna. We both know she's not your child."

Ravenna paled. "Of course she is."

"No." Rhys shook his head. "No mother would condemn her blood kin this way."

He was dead certain of that. The small cut on Ravenna's temple was the last nail in the coffin.

It was entirely conceivable that Valeria's mother might look nothing like her. His mate could have inherited her great-grandmother's eyes and her uncle's chin, or her father's ears. Genetic throwbacks were a biological reality.

But it wasn't possible that her mother wouldn't smell anything like her.

If Ravenna were Valeria's biological mother, half her DNA would have been the same. Her blood would have smelled like his mate, enough for him to tell. Familial scent patterns were strong enough when separated by a single generation. It was only after two or three that the pattern became muddled.

Rhys had held a bleeding Valeria in the alleyway—a lifetime ago. Ravenna was bleeding now. And there was no similarity in their body's intrinsic perfume. None.

The woman pretending to be Valeria's mother paled impossibly further. "That's not true. Stop saying that."

Glancing down, he noted that the cross witch was dead. Her eyes were glassing over even as he spoke.

"I'll stop when you do—no more lies."

Ravenna's lips pressed together, disappearing in her too-white face. "Rhys, where is my daughter?"

"Sheol," he whispered. "Better known as hell—the closest one anyway."

"A hell dimension." Ravenna closed her eyes, swaying slightly as if she were going to be sick or faint. "*No*. That's impossible."

Dismissing her, he began to walk away. Rhys needed to see Veda.

The man wasn't just their healer. He was also the clan historian. And Rhys needed to remember certain details, the knowledge he'd blotted out of his mind in self-preservation.

"You're wrong," Ravenna called after him, the words breaking against him like shards of glass. "You can't know for sure. Doors to other dimensions can't be opened with a snap of your fingers. There was no way you could have identified the location from that brief glimpse. "

Less wrong words had never been spoken. "I assure you that I can."

"How?" she cried, wiping the tears from her eyes that tracked him up the stairs. "How can you possibly know that was Sheol?"

He turned back at the landing. Whatever she saw in his face made her flinch and back away despite the space between them.

"Because my clan used to call it home."

CHAPTER THIRTY-FOUR

Valeria knew she was falling, but it had gone on too long. She should have hit the ground already.

And why did it feel as if she were being slowly compressed to death? Except it wasn't just her chest. The clamping sensation extended from the top of her head to the tips of her toes.

Mierda. I'm dead. It was the only explanation. Valeria had hit the ground and died on impact. That was why it was so dark.

Except it wasn't totally black. There was color at the edges of her vision, an oily sheen tinged with brilliant blue, magenta pink, and emerald green. She was just beginning to wonder about those unexpected tints when the world exploded into light and color—sort of.

Instead of a rainbow-tainted black, she was suddenly surrounded by dirty orange and brown sky. She could tell it was sky by the wind whipping past her so fast that her cheeks flapped like she was in a wind tunnel.

And I'm still falling. Shiiiiit. She could see the ground far in the distance. It was rushing toward her with a finality spelled with a capital F.

Rhys will catch me, she told herself.

Her eyes were watering so much she couldn't see him. Still, she should have been able to make something out—his house or the boulders surrounding his home.

But there was nothing. Not even a single pine tree. It was only the filthy sky and rust-colored dunes interspersed with cracked flat ground that she was about to get very up close and personal with.

Her cry was in her brain because the wind was rushing around her so fast that she couldn't even scream. Thoughts fragmenting, she tried to bring up images in her mind so her life could flash behind her eyes, but she was moving too fast. The speed was rubbing everything off like her brain like sand whittling away at a wooden sign.

The ground was close now. She could see individual markers—scars on the dunes and bits of stone or possibly concrete sticking out of the ground. Squeezing her eyes shut, she cringed with her entire body, tensing in preparation of going splat.

And then she stopped moving altogether. Valeria counted to ten, but the pain she'd expected at this point didn't materialize.

Holding her breath, she cracked one eye open. The ground was right where she left it—about nine feet below her head. She was hanging upside down, suspended in mid-air.

A voice spoke and she jerked, the bodily equivalent of jumping out of her skin had she been on her feet.

Twisting her head, she caught a glimpse of the bottom of a robe.

Flashing hot and cold, she waited, but no more words were forthcoming.

"Uh, excuse me?" Valeria cleared her throat, the blood rushing to her head making her throat tight and thick. "I realize you can't understand me. That's okay—I can't understand you. But I'm hoping you can help me down?"

The being didn't move. *I guess altruism was too much to hope for.* Story of her life...

She couldn't see the being's head, but she thought its weight shifted as if it were cocking its head.

At least she thought it had a head. Given the voluminous cloak, she could be looking at any kind of life form. She didn't even know how many legs it had. Or how many mouths...

"All right then. Given the landscape, fresh meat is probably at a premium. Are you going to be dragging some wood out here to start a little bonfire? Will I be served barbecue or rotisserie?"

This time, there was a sound, something suspiciously like a snicker. Then she was spinning as her body flipped the right way round.

The hooded being lifted an arm, and her entire body floated forward toward it. Except for the expansion of her lungs allowing her to breathe, Valeria couldn't move at all. She couldn't even kick her legs.

Clawed fingers appeared out of the sleeve, each tipped with a razor-sharp nail. They touched her chin, pricking her skin. She smelled her own blood and braced herself.

But the hand withdrew. Those claws took hold of the hood and brought it down, but she saw nothing except light. It was so bright she had to close her eyes.

Then the creature spoke again. Without the blood rushing to her head, she could hear it.

The voice was the purest and most beautiful thing she'd ever heard. It made her soul sing.

Valeria's brain flinched. "That's not right," she slurred before passing out.

CHAPTER THIRTY-FIVE

Rhys sat behind his desk, his jaw clenched so he wouldn't let the fire loose on the traitor sitting across from him.

Ravenna was pale, but she knew better than to try to defend herself at this moment. Not with his assistant holding proof of her lies in his hands.

Veda and Naveen stood on either side of his chair. Above the valley, the rest of his clan hovered.

Most were angry, their pride wounded over the fact that the enemy had struck in the very heart of their territory. Every last one had already pledged to come back to hell with him. They just had to find a way back to Sheol. He *had* to.

Only Sanaa and her family would stay behind. Thomas was still recovering from the shock of seeing Valeria hurl his infant daughter off a three-story deck. He didn't blame her. He'd seen what was happening, understood the circumstances. So, he wasn't angry, but he also wasn't okay.

There was a lot of that going around.

"The DNA results are back," Veda said from his left. "It's confirmed. There's less than a one percent chance that Ravenna is Valeria's mother—it's zero-point nine percent to be exact."

Ravenna finally reacted. She lifted her mutinous gaze. "I thought you could tell by how my blood smelled. Why would you need a DNA test?"

Rhys had told her about the damning scent print when she kept insisting, she was Valeria's mother.

"Thomas recommended it—he's the bear you saw, by the way. The one we used to make you assume we all were."

Rhys leaned back in his chair, studying her, trying to puzzle her out. She had lied to Valeria, used her, and, in the end, she had betrayed her to save her own skin.

But her grief at losing Valeria was real, too. And it was the only thing saving her from his fire.

Except in Ravenna's case, he might have to use his claws. He'd gone beyond anger to a cold place where ice flowed in his veins. It wasn't something expected or familiar. Even at the height of battle, Rhys had always burned hot.

When Ravenna didn't respond, he pushed without mercy. "We didn't need the DNA test to tell us that you weren't her mother."

"Then why did you test it?"

He took the test results from Veda, then tossed them in front of Ravenna. "Because people have a much harder time lying when confronted with irrefutable truth."

She stared at the paper without seeing the words on it, a flat expression in her eyes.

"Having the DNA results also opens another avenue of inquiry." Rhys templed his fingers together. "Say we wanted to compare Valeria's DNA with someone else's...Salvador Delavordo, for example."

Ravenna jumped up from her chair so fast it fell over. "You can't do that."

A lick of ice hit his mind. "He is her *blood*. Her family. You're just the woman who took her from him. From all of them."

Raising a hand to her head, she fisted her fingers in her hair. "Your ignorance is breathtaking. I saved her from those monsters. Do you know anything about them?"

"We know who all the major clans are. The Delavordos are one of the seven families who think they rule this planet. I have no love for them or any other witching clan. But I do not presume to pass judgment on their internal matters."

He leaned forward. "So, choose your words carefully. Explain why you think you had the right to take their child and raise her as yours."

"I carried Valeria in my womb." Ravenna fisted a hand and beat it against her chest, pounding it over her heart. "She was a part of my body and my soul."

So much was suddenly making sense…"You were a surrogate."

Ravenna sighed with her entire body, as if speaking the words aloud had taken something—perhaps the delusions that got her through the day.

Coming around the front of her chair, she let herself drop on the cushion, covering her face with her hands.

Given the Delavordo's reputation, there might have been a compelling reason Ravenna ran off with the child she was carrying.

"Start at the beginning," he said, making it clear from his tone that it was an order.

She dropped her hands. "Lucia Delavordo is a magical parasite, a tick that gorges itself until it has bloated itself with power."

Lucia. She was Salvador's mother. Wife to Fulgencio, the current patriarch of the Delavordo clan.

"That is not the beginning," he snapped. "I will judge Valeria's biological mother on *her* actions, not her reputation or your opinion, however colorful."

A spike of anger heated the air around Ravenna, but she wisely kept her mouth shut. It took her a few minutes, but she finally composed herself enough to speak.

"I am Romanian born," she said. "I grew up in a small rural village, but the strength of my talent was such that I was plucked from my home and sent to a minor noble house for study."

Rhys nodded, aware that while time and technology had advanced considerably, the underlying structure of the witching world was archaic by current standards.

Arranged marriages, a tightly regimented structure, and bloody internecine feuds and skirmishes instead of large-scale warfare. Elegant, deadly, and ruthless, the members of the major witch clans were arrogant, but, among their kind, they had reason to be.

An outsider witch with talent was their favored prey.

"How did you come to be a surrogate for the heads of the Delavordo clan?"

She lifted a shoulder. "I was approached by a third party shortly after my twentieth birthday. The man was a visitor who had stayed with the family for a few days, long enough for him to see how frustrated and dissatisfied I was."

Her eyes were distant, deep into the past. "I was grateful for their patronage when I was a child, but as I grew older, my talent outstripped theirs. They began to sabotage all my opportunities for advancement."

"But this man took you aside, whispering in your ear about an opportunity to get the power you sought?"

"Not power," she said. "Just buckets of money. But with the amount he quoted, I knew I could get as much power as I wanted."

She closed her eyes. "It was five million euros. That amount of money can change a person's world, open any door. The go-between also disclosed that despite having one child, the couple had suffered more than half-a-dozen miscarriages attempting to have a second."

Cocking her head, she lifted a shoulder. "I was young and idealistic back then. I thought I would be helping a wounded family complete itself. I had been an only child, and I hated it. I wanted to give their kid a sibling."

How altruistic. Sure, these reasons had probably crossed Ravenna's mind, but he would bet every piece of gold in his hoard that she wouldn't have made the deal without the cash.

"Did they renege on their deal?"

"No, I did." The words were so quiet that a normal human wouldn't have heard them.

"You discovered the identity of the biological parents and balked?"

She shot him a mulish look from under her lashes.

"I met the couple before implantation. And yes, I was scared when I realized who they were, but I told myself their reputation had been blown out of proportion. All the evil things I'd heard about the family were old stories. Legends. Nothing about the current generation."

If that were true, then it was less because Fulgencio and Lucia's hands were clean than Ravenna had been young, without access to the right whispers.

"But I eventually saw them for what they were. You just can't stand in their presence and not feel their evil. It's behind their every action, including the miscarriages and even resorting to using a surrogate."

"Explain."

"Lucia and Fulgencio had a son, a skilled and strong one by all accounts. But they weren't satisfied with him. I don't know why. They had done things to themselves, Lucia in particular, to enhance their magic—terrible things."

She closed her eyes. "They planned to concentrate all that potential in their offspring. They conducted rites, messed with things that should have never been touched...they were making a monster."

"Valeria is no monster."

"Yeah, I know," Ravenna snapped. "You're welcome."

The idea that this woman was taking credit for Valeria's morality, for her kindness and consideration, was too much.

"You traded her safety to save yourself, so save me the sanctimony, because whatever else was true, Lucia and Fulgencio would have guarded their child far better than you did."

It wasn't even a question. Perhaps the world might have had to deal with some Delavordo attempt at world domination, but according to rumor, even the son they claimed to have disinherited was closely monitored by his parents, any threats to him eliminated.

"I told you I was captured by those bastards. I crossed one too many people, and I ended up in a bad spot—a *very* bad spot," Ravenna said slowly, looking at her hands. "Things were...done to me."

"So you broke under torture? Offered up your daughter?" Rhys asked. He didn't even try to sound sympathetic. If it had been Sanaa, she would have never offered up her flesh and blood to save herself.

"Valeria would have understood. And I *didn't* give her up."

He raised one eyebrow, staring at her coldly. "Only because you didn't know where she was. You had to go looking for her."

Ravenna's lips compressed.

"Oh, I see..." Rhys sat back deeper into his chair. "I did wonder how you found her here. So, what is it? Do you keep a spare vial of her blood to do a tracking spell?"

"I'm not stupid," she snapped. "I used a tethering hex. It requires consent, but she was a child and I was her mother. She doesn't even remember doing the ritual. We did so many together. It was part of her training—and I did train her. We learned every spell I could get my hands on. I got her ready for the future."

Ravenna broke off and scoffed. "*Blood.* As if I were an ignoramus. Anyone could take a vial off me. A thimble full alone is worth a million dollars on the black market. "

"*Why?* I understand her ability is remarkable, but there are Elementals out in the world, four to be precise. And they are more powerful than any witch."

"You don't get it." Ravenna passed a hand over her face. "Lucia and Fulgencio weren't the only ones who were altered. Valeria was genetically modified at conception, her DNA spliced or mutated on every chromosome. She was meant to combine every magical talent the Delavordos could get their hands on. No Elemental could stand against her. Or at least that was their intention."

"Ah." And Valeria did possess all magical abilities, in a way. It just didn't manifest the way her parents intended. "She can copy any magic. But the ability fades with distance to the source."

Ravenna's voice was flat. "It doesn't have to."

Rhys' stare was flat. "Explain."

"Idiot man." Ravenna threw up her hands. "It should be obvious by now—whatever Valeria kills, she keeps."

She turned, staring out the window at the forested peaks around them. "I know this for a fact."

Suddenly, he grew very hot, his fire close to the surface. "I'm supposed to believe Valeria is a murderer?"

"No...it wasn't her."

He waited, and Ravenna rolled her eyes. "I *had* to."

"Sure you did."

Ravenna's chin jutted out. "There was an incident when she was young. A witch Valeria was copying realized what she was doing and figured out who she was. It was a miscalculation on my part. She was a known associate of the Delavordos, and she put two and two together."

"Did she plan on returning her for a reward?" he guessed.

Ravenna laughed. "No, idiot. She grabbed a blade—a cheap athame

—and she was coming up behind her, getting ready to slit her throat—Valeria was only nine"

He frowned. "You're certain? Maybe she was going to use it on you."

She lifted a shoulder. "I couldn't take that chance. I jumped up, pressed my gun into her gut, and pulled the trigger. Then I grabbed Valeria before she could realize what was happening. I didn't realize until months after that she'd kept that witch's power...permanently."

So it wasn't necessary that Valeria do the killing. Only the death mattered. "What is the nature of the stolen talent?"

"Something she would never use, not after she understood what it did to others—not even to save her own life." Ravenna put a hand over her eyes. "With extended touch and effort, she can pull someone to her, take them over and make them love her to the point of obsession. She becomes the most important thing in their lives—the only person who matters."

Well, damn. No wonder Valeria had kept so many barriers between them.

Like you were any different? In the beginning, he'd been so determined to prove she wasn't Gabrielle that he'd taken too long to realize it didn't matter.

Rhys knew his witch in a way he hadn't known his delicate Viennese flower.

Valeria was vibrant, brilliant, generous, and strong in a way Gabrielle had never been. And it was Valeria he loved—mind, body, and soul. He would for the rest of his life.

He cast his mind back to their early interactions, the way she would avoid touching him, every move in his presence careful and deliberate. "I can see why she would be reluctant to use that ability. I take it she has conscious control over it."

Otherwise, she would have never laid a hand on him. He would never know the sweetness of her kiss.

"Yes," Ravenna murmured. "Now."

Rhys wasn't good at subtext, but he knew there was a hell of a story behind that—an unpleasant one. But he didn't want to hear it from Ravenna. He and Valeria would have a heart-to-heart when he got her back. And he *would* get her back.

"My men are scouring every database on this planet, and every book in our libraries, for a way into Sheol. Can you help...or are you just going to write Valeria off?"

It was the only reason he was bothering with this interview now. That and he knew his mind was not clear enough for the painstaking research required. Rhys was better leaving it to his men. In the meantime, he would pry what he could out of this witch.

Ravenna gripped the arms of her chair, her knuckles white. "I thought that place was your home. Why can't you open the door you came through?"

"Because we did not open it."

No, that had been the Mother—the entity that truly ruled this planet. She had heard their pleas, and she'd opened a door. Her Elementals had been waiting on the other side, ready to destroy them in case they were a threat.

When they had asked to stay in peace, the Elementals had been ready with a contract detailing the terms and requirements of their asylum.

His people had been so war-weary they'd been ready to sign whatever the Elementals had put in front of them. But, to their credit, the pact had been fair. The clan had vowed not to make war, and not to disrupt the balance between good and evil. They would not try to rule. In exchange, they could live in peace.

Too bad that last had taken them so long to figure out.

Ravenna had lost color. "You didn't?"

"No."

Nodding as if this were expected, the witch pushed to her feet.

"Your clan can stop looking for the answer," she announced. "I can do it. I saw enough of the cross coven spell to recreate it, and I know how to tweak it so none of your people have to die to open the door."

Rhys raised a brow. An Elementals could do it without a death, but their spellcraft was the best in the universe. Could this witch pull it off?

It was possible. Ravenna had been wandering the world like a displaced Ronin, studying every spell and type of magic she could get her hands on. If there was a witch on this side of the barrier who could figure it out, it was Ravenna.

He crossed his arms, his fire flickering in irritation. She could have said so before. *Witches...infuriating creatures.*

"Are you sure?" he asked, resisting the urge to strangle her.

She nodded. ". But I will need supplies, some rare ingredients."

Rhys signaled to Naveen. "Get her whatever she needs."

CHAPTER THIRTY-SIX

Valeria woke up in drips and dregs, her head aching. Taking a deep breath to make sure her lungs still worked she rolled over and opened her eyes.

She took in her surroundings slowly, as if small bites would somehow make it more palatable.

The room had stone walls and a big bed underneath her that echoed the one she'd slept in at Rhys' house. Only this one appeared battered, the wood grimy. No one ever polished it.

A wardrobe and chest sat on her left. An elaborately carved fireplace was against the wall on the right. The windows were simple cutouts in the stone. No shutters, just some threadbare curtains that were pushed to the side to expose the light.

Beyond it was the strange, stained sky.

She hadn't imagined it. The only place she'd seen air like that had been in photographs of cities in China overwhelmed by pollution. Cheeks pulled tight, she went to the window, cautiously poking her head out.

More of that sky, only it was darker now. The ground below was barren. There was nothing green in the rust-colored dirt. The only sign of habitation aside from the dwelling she was in was a low stone wall that showed signs of having been repaired.

If the sky was real, then so was that man who'd kept her from turning into Valeria soup on impact when she arrived. At least she thought it was male. The voice, it had been male—so clear and strong it had been like someone rang a gong right in her ear.

Okay, so not a man.

The idea that she should go out and thank him crossed her mind before she smacked her own face for being a bloody idiot.

The stranger had to have known she was coming. He'd been waiting for her. Whoever the being was, he was the reason she had been chased, hounded to the ends of the Earth.

Anger coursed over her like a flashfire. Gripping her hands into fists, Valeria coughed, choking on her rage.

No, you can't kill him. First of all, she'd get creamed. Her ability was unique and powerful, but this was a creature who had survived this hellhole, had thrived even. If he were the reason she was here, then he had enough power to influence her world, sticking little tendrils inside it, dangling lures for witches like the ones who had attacked.

He—*it*—tempted them, making promises, waiting to snap up the unwary like that deep-sea fish they showed in ocean trench documentaries. A glowing lure, the shining promise of more power twisted into whatever form they wished.

Don't worry. You're not about to become dinner.

That much she knew. The stranger had gone to too much trouble to get her here.

If he'd wanted something as simple as sustenance, he'd have been satisfied with one of the cross witches.

But Valeria was here so he wanted her, or someone like her. She didn't want to know the reason why.

The temptation to hide here in this room was strong. Unfortunately, blissful ignorance was not something she could afford.

Valeria had to beard the beast in his den. The idea chilled the blood in her veins because she had a pretty good idea of what he was.

Given the evidence, there weren't too many options. Valeria had been taken by a demon.

VALERIA FOLLOWED the shuffling servant who'd come to fetch her down the steps, covering her mouth and nose with one hand. The servant smelled that bad.

The creature had appeared as soon as she worked up the courage to step outside the door of the bedroom she'd woken in. It had material-ized at the end of the hall, moving with a slow shuffling gait that would have driven her mad under normal circumstances.

However, Valeria didn't mind the snail's pace today. She wasn't in a hurry to get where they were going. Although stoic patience was hard to come by given the stench.

The servant's scent surrounded her like an eye-watering cloud of boiled urine. It assaulted her like a physical blow after she mis-stepped going down the steps and her hand slipped off her nose.

She would have used both hands to cover her nose, but she needed to keep one hand on the wall. The staircase was steep with stone steps so worn they were slick. The bottom of the stairs was so dark Valeria couldn't figure out how far down it went. If she fell, she'd break her neck.

Yeah, you're not that lucky.

"How long have you worked here?" she asked, picking her way down with care.

"Furrever, misss," the servant hissed in a voice that was more female than male. "Slank serves masster furrever. Honorrr."

"Slank? Is that your name?"

"Slank," Slank confirmed, continuing to shuffle forward.

Ten minutes later, Slank showed her into a large room that was one big open space. It was like the inside of a medieval castle's main hall, with stairs leading up to the second story.

The hooded being was sitting on a throne.

Well, someone thinks highly of himself. Taking comfort in snarkiness, she made sure no emotions showed on her face. Whatever the hell was going on, she had to keep those to herself. At least until she learned what she was dealing with.

The creature raised a gloved hand, beckoning her closer. Stomach twisting in knots, Valeria stepped forward.

Anger is fuel, she reminded herself. That was in Ravenna's top ten rules to live by.

The thought of her mother made her steps falter. *It wasn't a real betrayal.*

Ravenna would have told her the truth, and they would have come up with a plan together. It was just that when her mother was ashamed of herself—a rare occurrence—it took her a while to admit her wrong-doings. But she would have. Valeria had to believe that.

"WHY DO YOU TARRY, CHILD?"

She flinched, freezing to the spot. The voice had a preternatural resonance that rattled her bones. And it was so beautiful it hurt to listen to. Literally.

Startled, she lifted a hand to her ear. Her fingers came away tipped with blood.

"Could you lower the volume, please?" she asked. "You are going to blow out my eardrums."

Valeria was working under the assumption the being wanted her in some sort of functional order. At least she hoped so.

There was something that could have been a stunned silence from the throne. And then there was laughter.

"I am pleased with you. You speak your mind even in the presence of your gods. It's unwise but entertaining."

"I wasn't trying to be amusing," she said, deciding to ignore the 'gods' crack. Demons loved to brag. "Simply honest."

"Honesty?" The demon sounded surprised as if this were an alien concept. "How quaint."

Valeria bit the inside of her lip to keep from making a smart remark. "How is it that you speak English now?"

The words he'd spoken to her in the desert hadn't been intelligible. She hadn't recognized them despite her past travels and extensive study. It was either a dead language...or it had never been spoken on Earth.

"Aren't you going to ask me why I've gone to so much trouble to bring you here?" the hooded figure asked instead.

Despite modulating his tone, there was a creepy otherness to his voice that rubbed her the wrong way, as if she were a cat being stroked in the wrong direction.

Her shoulders slumped. "I'm not sure I want to know."

She hadn't meant to say that aloud, but when the being threw back its head and laughed, the hood slipped back a smidge—revealing shadowed features that were recognizable as humanoid.

That wasn't what she'd expected after meeting Slank.

And then the creature stopped laughing. It raised a hand and she shot forward, gripped by an invisible power stronger than any she'd ever experienced.

The toes of the expensive hiking boots Rhys had bought her scraped against the stone-flagged floor. Like the stairs, it was smooth, polished like a mirror. But there was no mortar in between. Each stone had been fitted so that they joined seamlessly, like a gigantic jigsaw puzzle.

Then the demon laid down the law.

"I realize the circumstances of your arrival were jarring. Therefore, I am willing to make allowances, but my indulgence only goes so far. Honesty, I will accept, but a word of warning—insolence will not be tolerated."

Realizing her throat wasn't compressed, she sucked in some much-needed air. "I understand and apologize for any offense my honesty might have caused."

There was a huff of agreement, and the creature stood. Despite the fact she was suspended in the air, the demon towered over her. "You are honored to be my guest."

Now she was going to choke out of pure spite, but she kept her voice level. "Sure, of course. Um...can you put me down?"

He didn't move or speak. "Please?" she added.

Her toes touched the floor, and she couldn't help a sigh of relief. "Thank you."

"Thank you, *master*."

Cabrón, he would have to be an egomaniac. Valeria looked down at her boots. "Thank you...master."

Another laugh. It was more muted than before, but still as affecting on a visceral level. Cold and beautiful like a glacier or a diamond.

"Why am I here?"

There was no escaping her fate now. She was going to have to deal with it. Better now than later.

The hooded figure tilted its head slowly, the move so smooth it didn't seem human. *That's because it's a demon.* And despite what she might have assumed from what she knew about the awkward way the possessed moved, a demon in the flesh was graceful.

"You're here to help me."

She took a step back, blinking rapidly. "What?"

"I said you've been brought here to help me."

He waited expectantly. *Great, the twenty questions part is required...* "Why do you need my help?" she asked.

"To return to your realm."

"Return?" She swallowed hard.

The cloak the being wore fluttered despite the lack of detectable wind. "I am in exile here. But Earth is my home, and I intend to return."

"Demons can't walk the Earth." That was demonology 101.

It threw back its head and laughed. "Who said I was a demon?"

Her skepticism must have shown on her face because her ribs were suddenly groaning. The head lowered until it was next to her ear. "I forgive you, child."

"Prove it," she gasped. "Let me go."

There was a chuckle, and the pressure around her chest eased. Another moment later, she was released.

"I understand your reticence and suspicion. It's only natural that you would make assumptions given the company I keep." The blade-tipped hands emerge from the end of the sleeves, pulling the hood back.

Valeria backed away so fast she fell on her ass.

Her captor's face was a reflection of his voice—in a word, stunning. Her flesh began to creep as he threw off the cloak.

Wings. *Feathered* wings. Blindingly white feathered wings. She was staring at an angel.

"Allow me to introduce myself. My name is Michael, and you, Valeria, are the most fortunate human alive."

He leaned closer, his radiance making her eyes ache. "You're going to help me save the Earth."

CHAPTER THIRTY-SEVEN

Three weeks later

Valeria blinked against the wind. She parted the sand, digging out the roots where Michael had directed. The coarse grains were like sandpaper against her fingers, but the roots Michael had instructed her to pick were too fragile to dig out with a spade.

Wiping her sweat on her brow, she flickered her lashes to shake off the grains. She had a cloth wrapped around her head, knotting it to keep it from flying off. The wind picked up a lot in the late afternoon, and her mouth would have been filled with metallic sand if she weren't covering her head.

Hell had a longer day than Earth and a very short night.

Valeria had been here for over twenty-seven days and twenty-six nights.

Despite her fervent prayers, Rhys had not come flying to her rescue. Valeria was in hell, not in a fairytale. And she was on her own. Again. Only this time, she was a slave to a ruthless entity who insisted he was divine and infallible.

Her captor wasn't some random everyday angel named Michael.

No, he was *the* Michael, the archangel above all others. And she was supposed to feel honored to serve him.

"You've been given a rare chance," he told her that first night. "Don't squander it."

He then proceeded to show her what had happened to the people who had done just that. Valeria had stared at the bones of her many predecessors, which were discarded in the basement, with undisguised horror.

"You're welcome to try to kill me *after* we reach Terra," he'd said as she pressed herself against the basement wall, trying to get as far away from the bones as possible. "That would be amusing."

He'd said that last with a grin so terrifying she hadn't been able to sleep that night after he dismissed her from his presence.

"*Mierda.*" Valeria pulled her hand out of the sand to examine her bloody fingers. Still no roots, but there were plenty of jagged little rocks buried out here.

If you're going to be this distracted, go slower. Valeria tried not to think about the past. But sometimes in between tasks, she'd become aware of a sharp pain in her chest. This was distinguished from all the other pains and aches she felt because it was over her heart. But she didn't cry. Instead, she put a fist over the spot and pressed hard until it went away.

Her dreams of rescue faded with each passing day. Valeria had been pulled too far, too fast. But she was sorry for all the things they wouldn't get to do, for what she had never gotten a chance to tell Rhys.

I never slept in his arms. She had desperately wanted to do that. *Damn.* There was the pain again.

When Valeria saw Michael unmasked, she had been sure it was a lie, some sort of illusion charm. Letting her sixth sense open, she'd squinted, intentionally making her eyelid twitch to see if she could break the glamour.

But nothing made the apparition disappear. It was still there—a face so perfectly formed it set her teeth on edge.

The archangel had golden hair so bright it glinted silver at the edges like the gold and silver alloy electrum. His head was a rising sun.

As if that weren't unnerving enough, his eyes were the same reflective silver of mercury. The irises were liquid, beautiful, and perfectly opaque. Despite Michael's usually benign expression, there was no emotion in them—not that she looked into his eyes. She could barely focus on them because they were just as toxic as the substance they reflected.

Valeria had never believed in any of the mainstream religions, but she was fairly certain that was one of the pacts humans had made shortly after crawling out of the ooze. Sure, the Greeks had gotten up to some tomfoolery but, by and large, the gods didn't walk around smiting their enemies anymore so human brains didn't explode.

None of the books back home had gotten the details right.

"How are you here?" she'd asked shortly after that first meeting, still having trouble believing what she was seeing. "Aren't you supposed to be up in Heaven bossing all the other angels around?"

Instead, Michael was ruling hell. Wasn't that Lucifer's job?

Michael's mercury-filled eyes flared with satisfaction. "So, you've heard of me," he said in a booming voice. "Good. It will make things much easier."

But he didn't explain why he was here, ruling this wasteland. She was starting to realize he never would. Instead, he began to strip off the top layer of skin on his hand.

Openmouthed with horror, she closed her mouth with a tiny snap when she realized Michael was wearing gloves. The claws she'd seen were pieces of metal that had been sharpened beyond razor-blade sharpness. The air whistled faintly with their every movement as if each were slicing the air itself.

She slapped a hand to her chin, feeling the sting of a small nick. "You cut me."

"I had to make certain you were the one promised. A drop of blood was enough to confirm. Those who sent you will receive their reward— once I return to Terra."

Cursing every black witch she'd ever met Valeria shook her head. "How am I supposed to help you?"

"I need a powerful assistant, a witch of true strength to fulfill my needs. Your bloodline has been monitored for generations. Whenever a witch of sufficient power was born in your realm, offers were made."

"To hunt us down," she filled in when he lapsed into silence.

"Yes. Precious few pursued the bounty," he said, sounding annoyed.

"Fortunately for me, your clan has many enemies. More than one group decided to take me up on my offer."

That last part made little sense. Aside from Ravenna, Valeria didn't have a single living relative. She sighed silently.

Perfect. Just perfect. Trust her mother to have made enough enemies in one lifetime that an archangel trapped in hell had been able to track her.

Sheol. She had never heard of it before landing here. Michael hadn't named this realm in her presence. It had been Slank who did that as she showed Valeria around the fortress.

Sheol was the closest hell dimension to earth and the place Michael had been exiled. By who, he did not say. But she'd gathered enough bits and pieces to realize he hadn't come here alone.

There had been other angels, and some were still alive. But not well...most definitely not well.

They didn't come here to this fortress, of course. Slank had made that clear while they scrubbed pots and cleaned mortars and pestles in the kitchen. "Fearr masssterr tey dooo. Is gudd. All other princesss are trashhh."

Valeria had hidden her surprise. "Err. Okay. But I'm curious, why aren't the other angels allies?"

Slank hadn't known, but Michael himself had answered the question a week later during a long and very loud rant.

The master disliked them because they had gone 'native'.

"You should see what Remiel looks like now—horns and spider legs," Michael spat as he stalked back and forth in front of his throne. His mercury eyes darkened to gold in his anger. "It's a disgrace."

He'd gone on about the current appearance of the remaining angels long enough for her to gather that they'd gone through some form of de-evolution.

Sheol bent them, slowly reshaping them into a form suitable to the environment. Something more like Slank but infinitely more dangerous. Of all the Host, as Michael called his former compatriots, only he had stood firm.

Every other angel had surrendered to their circumstances, becoming twisted and deformed...like the sparse population she never got to see.

Everyone succumbed. It was just a matter of time before she followed suit.

Unless you help Michael get back to Earth. Not that she had a choice. He was her only shot at getting back home. That and he'd snap her neck if she dared disobey. And so her life of drudgery continued—bouts of mindless work interspersed with bone-chilling moments of dread and dismay.

She got up at first light, gathering things in the 'garden' Slank had planted just outside the fortress gates. Things only grew near the walls because of Michael's grace. Ten yards out and the soil was barren. Slank had shared that in a hissing tone of warning as if Valeria were planning on making a break for it. As if she were stupid enough to run across a desert landscape on an alien planet.

After she finished the outside chores, Valeria would scuttle into the castle. Her tasks inside were varied. Sometimes, she would help Slank in the kitchen, a task that turned her stomach, but Michael never complained about the food they produced. Mostly she would work in the library, looking up things at the archangel's direction or occasionally dusting there or in the laboratory.

This last was where Michael spent most of his time. It was directly across from the library, the long rectangular rooms built as mirror images of each other with the throne room just above them.

Large double doors built on an archangel scale were set in the middle of each room, facing each other across the hall. They were left open so Michael could shout summons or yell instructions.

In the evenings, he dismissed her to eat in the kitchen while he sat down to a feast in the throne room, where Slank attended him.

One night, she made the mistake of asking him if Slank's smell bothered him.

"Her what?" he'd asked, looking at her blankly.

"Her scent. It's, um, rather strong, isn't it?" Valeria was grateful her mealtimes didn't coincide with Slank's because she was sure she'd never be able to choke down any sustenance.

The archangel had given her a look of such condescension and contempt in reply that Valeria had put two and two together. To him, *she* smelled just as bad. Humans, even un-mutated humans, were sacs of oil, sweat, occasional flatulence, and little more.

In Michael's eyes, she and Slank were both insects. They were useful in their way, but intimately they were just bugs.

As for her diet, Valeria only ate things from the garden. Her favorite thing, or at least her least disliked one, was the bulbous roots that reminded her of radishes but had the texture of water chestnuts, only sour. Almost everything that grew in the soil was either sour or sickly sweet. Michael would only eat the ones Slank managed to combine, balancing those two traits together. It took a lot of time and effort, however, so only Michael was entitled to eat those dishes.

He also ate meat.

Every few days, the archangel flew away to hunt, returning hours later with unidentifiable bundles.

She didn't want to know what it was that ended up on the banquet table, preferring blissful ignorance on this score. At least until Michael's dinner attacked her.

It happened early one morning. She had been gathering at the edge of the arable land, digging below the surface for the twisted vegetables that would be her and Slank's dinner—the farther from the castle, the worse their quality.

One second, she was adjusting the gloves that protected her from the coarse sand. Then she lifted her gaze and saw a face full of fangs inches from her head.

CHAPTER THIRTY-EIGHT

Yelping, Valeria scrambled back on her ass. She jumped up, sprinting to the fortress, expecting to feel fangs and claws rending her into tiny pieces at any second.

But the beasts didn't touch her. She made it to the garden where the nearest door was located—but no farther.

Michael exploded into her field of vision, landing in front of her with such force that the entire area was blasted with dirt and sand in a shockwave that knocked her against the wall.

Gasping and holding her bruised shoulder, she wiped her eyes with the cloth she had wrapped into a turban and faceguard.

Michael blocked her view of the newcomers. Edging to peek around him, all she saw were three small blurs and one very large one.

Blinking to clear her vision, she was eventually able to focus. The smaller blurs were sleek but subtly misshapen creatures—the Sheol equivalent of attack dogs.

Mierda! I'm looking at actual hellhounds.

Bulging with muscles and topped with horned heads, the beasts dripped saliva on the sand. Then one caught her eye and made a feint, its eyes red and reflective, like a warning reflector set in an animal's head.

But they weren't the ghastliest things. The entity behind them was almost the same height as Michael. It, too, had horns, but these were symmetrical, curling in for a single loop before pointing back out to act as weapons should they be needed to gore someone.

Their visitor's face was strangely featureless and flat, with bright yellow-gold eyes but only two tiny slits for a nose. As icing on the horror cake, the creature had a row of razor-sharp spikes running down his back. The black and burnt orange spikes jutted directly from the skin. They also dripped a green-tinged liquid. Poisonous.

And then the creature opened his mouth. She recognized the language. It was the same one Michael had spoken when she'd fallen to Sheol, delivered in the same ear-splitting volume.

Clapping her hands to her ears, Valeria slid down the wall. Only it wasn't enough auditory protection because Michael began to speak in kind.

Curling into a ball, she tried to protect herself from the sound, but there was no defense against *that*.

The words they spoke blurred in her brain. She half-suspected they were liquifying the organ—this was a language humans weren't meant to hear.

Which meant she knew who had come calling. Or rather—*what*.

Her suspicions were confirmed when Michael said something in a tone so cutting her ear started to bleed. His companion responded in kind, tearing off his face.

Startled, she watched the mask she hadn't realized was there fall to the ground. What lay behind it was an abomination—a hellish horror because the remnants of angelic beauty were still clearly visible in that wreck of a face.

This is what going native means. But who was he?

And then Michael began to yell impossibly louder, doubling the intensity and the pain in her head.

An argument between angels—it was something no human should ever witness. The sound and fury rattled her bones. Certain she was going to come apart at the seams, she tried to run, but she couldn't make her limbs work.

The visitor moved, and a blade flashed in the light. But Michael raised his hands and the demon-angel fell back, his body pierced by a blinding bolt of light.

Covering her eyes until her retinas recovered, she opened them to see the creature prone on the floor—conscious and furious.

The naked rage in the newcomer's eyes made her flinch. She would have run away but he was only moving his head as if the rest of his body were frozen. *Just like yours when you landed.* Michael was holding him telekinetically.

"Look at him," Michael hissed in a more normal tone of voice. "Look at what Camael has been reduced to."

She knew that name...but hadn't Camael been an archangel, too?

Twisting, Michael grabbed her arm, hauling her up. He flew her to the top of the castle wall too fast to let her regain her equilibrium. There, he released her, letting her fall on the stones of the battlement.

He spoke again, addressing Camael on the ground, but her ears were ringing too loud to make them out.

Then Michael raised his arms, and the entire castle shook. Scuttling to her feet, she whipped her head in all directions, trying to make sense of what was happening. Spaces appeared between the stones. Valeria jerked her left leg up, stepping to the side as the stones she was straddling grew farther and farther apart.

Then they began to turn—all but the stone she stood on. Every other block that made up the castle walls and floors began to revolve, rolling in one direction.

The reason Michael had immobilized Camael, then got the hell out of the way, became crystal clear.

Clapping a hand over her mouth, Valeria cringed as the entire fortress became a mobile monolith. Slow but relentless, the solid stone pieces rolled like a bulldozer, inching closer and closer to Camael's prone form while the fallen angel screamed, pleading for his life in that foreign tongue.

Blindly, unwisely, she touched Michael's arm as the first stones kissed Camael's feet. "Can't you spare him?"

Michael looked at her as if she were crazy. "Look at him. He has debased himself. There can be no mercy."

"Is the process irreversible? Can't he come back?"

Camael's screams were her only answer.

The shouts grew progressively weaker as the castle plowed over him. Closing her eyes, she turned away, her arms wrapped tight around her middle and throat so she wouldn't gag or throw up. That Michael could do this to another archangel—even a fallen one...

Then everything grew silent.

When she dared to open her eyes, she leaned over, craning her neck to see over the edge of the rampart. Valeria could see nothing but sand and dirt. There was no pool of blood. Every trace of Camael was buried underneath the stones.

Belatedly, Valeria realized Michael was glaring. He looked pointedly at the spot where she was touching him. Valeria snatched her hand away, murmuring an apology.

"Don't let this distract you," he warned. "Your job is to do what I say. Complete your tasks, and you may yet see your parents again before you grow bent and grey."

He assumed she knew the identity of her father. Valeria nodded, but couldn't help but ask. "My apologies, sire, but I thought we were close to completing the prep work for the spell?"

Why was he implying it was going to take decades?

"We are," he snapped before his irritated expression eased into a smirk. "I see. You don't know."

"Know what?" she asked, wondering what other elephant-sized shoe was about to drop.

Michael swept a hand imperiously at the horizon. "Sheol is not balanced. The barrier between this world and your own was twisted and thickened by that bitch you call the Mother. It's all her fault."

Her head drew back. Surreptitiously drawing away from his flailing hand, she tried to hide her fear and annoyance. "I don't understand."

He raised a golden eyebrow. "Time passes far more swiftly here than on Earth. It is of no consequence to me and my former brethren. We're immortal and do not age. But for you—unless you apply yourself to your task—you will be an old woman by the time we finish —while everyone you knew remains young in comparison."

He leaned forward, his voice growing colder. "So, I'd stop dragging your feet and get back to collecting those roots. I expect a new distillation made from them before daybreak tomorrow."

Nodding rapidly, she hurried to the rampart stairs to begin again.

CHAPTER THIRTY-NINE

Naveen watched Ravenna as she moved around the table they had set up in the desert. Behind her, his leader counseled the men. It would be difficult returning to Sheol like this. But he agreed with Rhys. Valeria belonged to him, and therefore to the clan as well. And no one took what was theirs.

The witch opened a jar. It was full of pufferfish poison, distilled and dried into powder form.

He'd had a hell of a time finding it, but it hadn't been the most challenging ingredient. No, that had been the fresh *tomar*—powder from a meteorite that had fallen to Earth.

He didn't trust the witch at all, but he knew enough about the dark rites to know Ravenna wasn't trying to lead them astray. She was genuinely trying to get her daughter back.

His cheek twitched, and he wondered for the millionth time whether Valeria would have been safer had she remained with her biological parents, the Delavordos.

Rhys had put him and Tanik in charge of keeping tabs on all their possible enemies, so he knew more about them than the rest of the clan. Enough to be uncertain.

It had taken some digging to confirm Ravenna's story about the surrogacy, but he had. Everyone thought Salvador Delavordo was the only child they had to survive to full-term. The fact that Lucia and Fulgencio also had a daughter was a well-kept secret. To everyone who knew about the surrogate, it appeared as if the couple had given up on finding their lost child. But Naveen had contacts all over the world.

Lucia and Fulgencio had never stopped searching for their lost child. Their search was quiet, and, to the unwary, deadly. It didn't make sense unless one knew what Valeria could do.

It must have been terrible, the urge to turn over every stone on earth in search of their baby, but not being able to for fear of painting a target on her back.

When he learned that, the sympathy he had for Ravenna dwindled to almost nothing. But he did not doubt that she'd do or say something to make her status go back up. It had happened several times already.

He forced his attention to the witch's hands. She was mixing a foul concoction, something pungent enough to make him take several steps back.

On second thought, perhaps it was best to give the witch room. He turned his attention to the desert.

The sky overhead was full of stars. Earth had only one moon, but despite the homogeneity of the night sky, he still enjoyed the view. Toward the end in Sheol, they could no longer see the stars. They had been permanently blotted out by the dust and grime that rose after the land had been scorched.

"How did you find this place?"

He turned at the sound of the witch's voice.

She flicked him a glance. "The layer between worlds is thinner here. I've already probed. To my knowledge, this is the best possible place to open a door out of this world. So how did you find it?"

Ravenna stopped mixing, rolling her eyes in exasperation. "I'm trying to punch a hole in the universe—the least you can do is tell me what you know."

Naveen was amused, but only for a second because he knew what was required to do what they had asked.

"This is where we came through from Sheol." He lifted a hand at the landscape. "There was no habitation, no town or villages nearby at the time. It's easier in inhospitable environments, like the desert or the northern and southern poles. The more life in the landscape, the thicker the shield."

Ravenna nodded. "That makes sense. I have been all over the world, you know, and made it a point to visit all the charged spots—Stonehenge, the Devil's tower, the Harz mountains in northern Germany. The air vibrated as if it were out of sync, responding to some kind of oscillation on the other side."

She held out a small flat stone charm fixed to a long leather thong. "This is spelled to Valeria's DNA. I took it from the hairbrush in her room. She grew a bit too comfortable in her time here. Otherwise, there wouldn't have been any hair to find. I thought I taught her better than that."

He took the necklace, studying it with a frown. The small carved heart was made of quartz that had been polished to a brilliant shine.

"Unless you already know where you're going?" the witch snapped.

He chose not to take offense at her tone. "We have a strong suspect, but this will help. Thank you."

Ravenna inclined her head and went back to her mixing, the brittle edge of hers a little more apparent. He knew why she was on edge, of course, although Rhys had not realized what would happen yet.

If his leader suspected, he'd hesitate. Not out of sympathy to the witch, but because the outcome would hurt Valeria and Rhys would never consciously do that.

Pity welled up despite himself. He stepped closer, letting his footsteps make noise so he wouldn't startle her, interrupting the potion-making.

"I know what has to happen to open this door—that you lied to Rhys. You can't do this spell without fueling it with death."

Ravenna was a skilled witch—she was recreating a spell she had seen only as leftover residue. But she wasn't an Elemental. She didn't know how to alter it to work another way.

The diamond glitter of tears appeared in Ravenna's dark eyes, but she didn't say anything.

He bent to speak in her ear. "We will get her back. When we do, she will know of your sacrifice."

She put the jar she was mixing aside. "I know he thinks I used her,"

Ravenna said quietly. "He doesn't understand what I had to become to keep her safe, to hide her from those people."

He wasn't sure if she meant the cross-bearing witches or Valeria's family. Regardless of which, he would bet self-preservation had been the bigger goal. But in light of what she was about to do, he held his tongue.

Ravenna bent to reach the Swiss army knife he'd provided. She turned to make sure Rhys wasn't watching. Once she confirmed the coast was clear, she pricked her thumb, squeezing her fingers to make the blood well into thick drops. Seven fell into the jar.

"Just get her back," Ravenna said quietly. "And when you tell her who I really was, make sure she knows that I never meant to hurt her."

She raised her head, the firelight making her appear younger than her years. "I was frightened, and I did what I thought was best."

CHAPTER FORTY

Valeria had taken a huge risk, but after Michael's demonstration of power, she'd known she could never allow him to reach Earth. Outright defiance was impossible. He was too powerful to disobey. The pile of bones in the basement had been enough of a deterrent. She had to work with him long enough to open the gate to Earth. But she couldn't allow him to go through it. So, she'd done the only thing she'd been able to do.

He did order you to use your power.

But all Michael knew about was her mirroring talent. He didn't appear to be aware of the other ability, the one she'd acquired as a child after that poor witch had a stroke.

Valeria closed her eyes halfway down the stairs, on her way to the library for the required reading Michael had assigned.

She was so sick to her stomach that she nearly pitched down the stairs. The memories of using her secret ability were that strong. Sitting on the stairs heavily, she let them come instead of pushing them away.

The first one she remembered had been the woman who'd broken down at the playground, tearing Valeria off the jungle gym and trying to drag her into her minivan. The hysterical mother of two told the cops that she was Valeria's mother, despite the fact her children were present, contradicting her. She'd had to be sedated before she'd stopped.

Who had been next? Valeria wasn't entirely certain because there were a few others in quick succession. The faces of her victims blurred. She had actively tried to forget them. But there was another burned into her brain— the boy from that Canadian coven she and Ravenna had visited when she was fourteen.

Fifteen-year-old Ryan had stolen a kiss. It had been perfectly innocent, and an infatuated Valeria had reveled in his attention—up until he'd grown dangerously obsessive. Things had deteriorated so fast that Ravenna had decided they had to leave. It had been one of the few times a hasty departure hadn't been because of her mother.

Ryan had threatened to slit his own throat when they started packing the car. He'd begged them both to stay. His parents had been forced to restrain him while they made their escape. For years afterward, she would hear his pleas echoing in her head as vividly as if he were standing right next to her.

That was the incident where her mother had connected the dots with what had happened years earlier.

She had been thrilled, Valeria remembered, stomach churning. Ravenna had even made her practice—what she called controlled experiments. Or, at least, she had attempted to control them.

Rubbing her head to scour the memories from her brain, Valeria debated the wisdom of trying to use that ability on Michael.

It won't work on him. He was a damn archangel. But what choice did she have?

Oh, he is definitely going to snap your neck. Well, that was some consolation, she supposed. Who else got to say they were struck down by an archangel?

Valeria scrubbed her face with her hands. *Don't get fancy. Call it what it is. Murder.*

She would get murdered by an archangel. The least she could do was make sure he had a good reason.

Picking herself up off the step, she continued to the library.

CAMAEL WAS CALLED Cernunnos because Camael was the one who slew the beast.

Valeria had come across the notation in the margins of a book, one that bore the markings of another library—that of Mammon the alchemist.

Many books bore that symbol in Michael's library.

Had another unfortunate witch made the note or was she seeing another devolved angel's handwriting? Or was Mammon one of the original 'natives' Michael had so much contempt for?

Valeria had found a map of Sheol in the library that had several familiar names marked on fortifications, things she recognized from her readings of Christian angels and devils. It was from the map that she realized the names of the demons were frequently synonymous with their fortification.

For example, Cernunnos appeared to be a title *and* a place. Camael became Cernunnos by inhabiting and ruling the castle Cernunnos. But Michael was not the new Cernunnos despite killing Camael because he didn't take over the castle.

He'd razed it to the ground, obliterating it along with all its inhabitants, all the servants and soldiers Camael had commanded. That last detail Michael had told her himself, tossing the fact at her casually like the books he'd nearly dropped on her head just yesterday.

The new books had come from Camael's library, the handful Michael had deemed worthy of inclusion of his own. *Another example of keep what you kill.* According to Slank, that was the way of life here.

Valeria had cataloged the volumes, adding Michael's mark—a star intertwined with a stylized laurel crown. It was a symbol of civility and power—and just as false as Michael's masculine beauty.

But it was this awareness of his beauty that Valeria exploited. She began to shoot him awed and admiring glances whenever she was in his presence. He didn't react, just accepted them as his due, but when she began to get flustered around him, he displayed an increased tolerance—after a few unfortunate missteps.

The first time she 'accidentally' bumped into him, he backhanded her to the floor. But he didn't use his full strength. It had been more like he'd brushed off a gnat. She'd been fortunate he hadn't killed her, walking away with only a cracked cheekbone. Fortunately for her, borrowed talents worked on this side of the barrier. She'd been able to heal herself.

Despite this less than auspicious start, she chanced a second touch when he'd handed her a list of chores. And then another when she bent to pick up something at his feet, brushing against his ankle with her pinkie finger. And then another and another. She kept engineering small accidents that led to skin-to-skin contact, courting death each time.

Valeria had just fetched a bottle from the wine cellar, a holdover from when the land was more fruitful, when Michael finally reacted.

She had poured him a drink, setting the glass just inside the circle of his arm as they rested on one of the library tables. Her forearm touched his, and she sent the largest pulse of possession she had ever chanced.

Valeria was pulling away when Michael grabbed her wrist. His hold wasn't painful, but it was unbreakable.

"Yes?" she asked, keeping her tone meek.

Michael tilted his head to one side as if he were studying her.

Forcing herself to stay still, she waited. *It's okay to show your fear. Your heart should race when an archangel holds you in his grip.*

"What are you doing?"

"Serving you, my lord," she said, eyes downcast. Valeria was dredging up everything she could remember about how servants acted in period dramas, hoping self-effacement would please him.

His eyes narrowed on her face, and she braced herself to have her wrist crushed.

"Do you admire me, child? Is that why you stand so close to me?"

"I, uh, I wasn't aware that I was," she hedged. "Please forgive my inattention. I will do my best not to forget my place again."

He sighed, then patted her head the way one would a dog. She was leaving the room when he called out to her.

"Valeria?"

"Yes, my lord?"

"I *do* find your scent more pleasant than Slank's. If you wish to take her place as my server at mealtimes, I permit you to do so."

She bowed, the gesture unfamiliar and awkward. Then she went to fetch his dinner.

The first dozen times she served his meal, he dismissed her with a wave as soon as she set down his tray. On the thirteenth, he invited her to sit down. On the twenty-first, he allowed her to speak. By the time they had shared a few dozen meals, he was ordering her to tell him stories because "I want to understand who the people I will rule have become".

She soon realized he'd caught glimpses of Earth. His questions were too detailed, too knowledgeable, for it to be otherwise.

Demons communicated with humans through a summoning circle. They could even travel there if the human doing the ritual was stupid or crazy enough to let them out. But she didn't think Michael had ever communicated that way. It was beneath him.

So how did he know that movies were watched on big screens or that humans had televisions in their homes? Because he had a million questions on how they worked and what people saw on them.

Many of these questions centered on a soap opera called *Days of Our Lives*. Michael was intensely disappointed when she couldn't answer a single one.

"But how did they bring Patch back from the dead? And why hasn't anyone defeated Stephano DiMera yet?" he thundered, promising that once he was back on Earth, he would force the creators of the show to write in a hero to do exactly that.

The knowledge he had showed signs of being acquired in snatches and only from a narrow or limited point of a view. It made Valeria recall all the times she'd been made uncomfortable by a person's gaze. It had happened by churches, the person wearing a cross more often than not...

What had she read in the library yesterday? The knowledge niggled and fluttered just out of reach for hours until it hit her as she was scrubbing the floors.

A true believer is an eye for the divine. That had been written in a book of history that she hadn't finished reading because Michael had snatched it from her hands. He'd scolded her, telling her not to waste time on things he already knew.

Now she saw his reluctance to let her read that book in a new light.

If a true believer meant a truly devout person, was it possible that Michael could use those people as channels? Could he hear from their ears or speak from their mouths?

That would certainly explain how he'd made deals with witches on her side of the barrier. And the vessels would either be willing or have no idea they were being used. Remembering the rabidness of the cross coven, she was betting on the latter. That made more sense than Michael making use of a circle where the summoner had the power to dismiss him at will.

Imagine what he could do once he's on the same planet as them. It was enough to give her nightmares, but since she was already living one, she said screw it and passed out every night, refusing to have dreams.

Not even good ones about Rhys. They would be too painful.

Would she be an old woman when they opened the door to Earth? Just how much faster was time running here? Double? A factor of five? Was the scale logarithmic? Would Rhys be there to help her beat Michael back before she slammed it shut again? Would anyone?

If only she could talk to the other side, leave them a message. But she didn't have the strength of a demon or an angel. She could try to send a message as the door was opening, but it would only work if Michael were distracted or he'd kill her on the spot. Unless she timed it so that killing her meant slamming the door shut on them both.

Provided she could pull off that miracle, what kind of message could she send? An email blast would be great. Or it would if she had a phone instead of the dead little husk she'd found broken in her pocket after her first day here. *And if you knew Rhys' email...*

Then there were the seven families. Ravenna had repeatedly told her that there was nothing that would ever get the witch clans to stop feuding with one another.

I bet the impending invasion by the head of all archangels would get them to stop it and work as allies.

Michael was the biggest threat to their power and vice versa. If her mother had survived the assault, she might know how to get in touch with one or more of the families. Whether they would believe Ravenna was another story.

Her mother had earned her poor reputation. They'd think she was lying as part of some big scam, or, worse, was trying to lead them into a trap.

I'll have to get Ravenna involved anyway. It wasn't as if Valeria had any other options.

But she hadn't counted on her time running out quite so fast.

CHAPTER FORTY-ONE

"**W**ake up, witch," Michael boomed.

Valeria jerked up in bed. "Wha—"

The archangel was in her room, his wings stretched so the tips brushed both walls.

"It's time."

He tilted his head at her, examining her nightgown—a threadbare shift made out of his old robes.

She pulled the equally tattered coverlet over her chest. "Time for what?" she asked, tacking on a '*my lord*' after a few more sleepy blinks.

"Our preparations are at an end. We cast the spell today. By tonight, we will be on Earth, the people's suffering at an end."

"Oh," she said dumbly.

He smiled at her beneficently before dropping a bundle at the foot of the bed. "I have had Slank prepare a gown for you for the occasion. It's only fitting that you look your best when our people welcome us home, their true rulers."

Our people? She bit her tongue to keep from pointing out his slip.

"I'll get dressed at once."

She joined him in the library a few minutes later. He glanced up, giving her an appraising glance. The dress Slank had brought her was the color of dried blood. It had long sleeves and a full skirt that went down to her ankles, but it was made from a lightweight cloth that didn't weigh her down.

"Thank you for the gown. It's lovely."

"Well, I can't have you wearing the rags you've been traipsing about in when we get there."

Since he'd provided all the clothes, she blinked but didn't comment. Valeria spent the rest of the morning shlepping books and supplies out into the garden where Michael had decided to cast his door-opening spell.

The archangel wasn't using chalk or salt—nothing so plebeian. His medium was the dried residue of the many potions she'd helped him mix.

He drew the circle and sigils himself, robbing her of the chance to sabotage them by making a small mistake. Superfluous after she'd carried the gear and supplies, she made herself invisible, watching him draw.

His rune work was genius, combining the powerful symbols in ways that shouldn't have been possible. The intricate work should have been laborious, but the symbols spilled from his hand fluidly, expertly. Her unease grew the more work he did.

Circles appeared within circles, one for focus, and one for enhancement. Valeria squinted at a series of smaller ones set in the inner layer. Were those reflections? *My mirror.* Michael was going to use it to bounce his power off her, reflecting it and repeating the cycle. Each one boosted the energy until it could rip a hole in the world.

Mierda. There was a very good chance this was going to work. Michael was immortal. He'd had an eternity to learn, to plan.

"Here, girl," the archangel said, reaching to take her hand. He guided her inside, directing her to place her feet in one of two clear spaces.

"This may sting a little," he said, "but you can't break eye contact."

Reaching up, he tilted her chin until she met his quicksilver eyes, the touch lingering. It may have been her imagination, but she thought this contact was gentler than the first time she'd met him. That along with his slip earlier gave her some hope that her stolen ability was affecting him.

Maybe.

By now, a human would have been obsessed to the point of stuffing pillows with her hair. Just to be sure, she sent another pulse along the small bit of contact.

"I'll try not to burn out your brain in this effort," he said, raising his hands.

"*What?*" That was a possibility?

Michael didn't reply. The wind had picked up, roaring around them. The angel's robes lifted, fluttering around him as if they had a mind of their own. Her hair was in her eyes. Risking movement, she pulled it behind her ears, wondering if the runes would be wiped away by the fast-moving air.

They didn't budge. The runes had sunk into the ground, glowing blue-white as if they were hot.

If she touched one, would she burn? *Not a theory you want to test.* Not that she could move at this point. Whatever Michael was doing was starting to build, making itself felt in steady, ever-increasing surges.

Valeria looked down at her arms. The fine hair on them stood on end. When she asked him what she was supposed to do, the angel only had one instruction.

"Don't speak. No big movements. Just hold your position and leave the rest to me."

"That doesn't sound hard," she muttered.

He'd given her a pitying glance and walked away. She knew why now.

The pressure in her stomach came at her from Michael, smacking her first in the stomach only to rebound from her core back to him. Then the cycle repeated, the intensity building steadily until the force was punching her with bruising strength.

Her nerves began to ache, and strands of energy became visible between her hands as if she were being filled with lightning. Unable to stop herself, she began to scream. But no sound came out—only energy. Brilliant white light spilled out of her eyes, her ears.

Michael's lips were moving, but she couldn't hear anything. Then her vision started to whiten out. The archangel's frown was the last thing she saw.

CHAPTER FORTY-TWO

Valeria woke to a damp cloth being rubbed over her face. She opened her eyes, expecting to smell and see Slank, but it was Michael. He was touching her, concern stamped on those perfect features.

She froze, wanting more than anything to fold in on herself like origami. Anything to get away. But she didn't have any control of her larger motor functions.

Her tongue felt like sandpaper. She had never been so thirsty in her life. Valeria licked her lips, but it didn't help. "Are we back?"

"No," he said shortly. "It didn't work."

"Oh." She was disappointed, but that was her selfishness speaking. Valeria wanted to be back on Earth, breathing the crisp pine-scented air. She wanted to walk in the woods with Rhys, and she wanted to touch him without worrying that she was going to ensnare him as she had succeeded with Michael.

He was tied to her now. She could feel the connections, but they felt weird. Sticky and fragile, they stretched between them like insidious silly string. If Michael became aware, he could brush them off or break them effortlessly. But he didn't know they were there, which was why he was wiping the dried blood from her face instead of killing her.

To the naked eye, the archangel looked the same, but she could feel his tiredness. "I'm sorry I failed you," she said and meant it. "Once I recover, we can try again."

Michael was silent long enough that she expected him to leave. But he didn't.

"If it didn't work with you," he said. "then it was never going to work. And that was my mistake."

Her head drew back. "I don't understand."

The spell they'd cast had boosted Michael's already awesome power to unimaginable levels. It was the most intricate piece of magic she'd ever seen or heard of. "It should have. No spell could have been crafted better."

Valeria wasn't trying to flatter his vanity now. It was a simple truth.

"No." His mouth twitched in bitter amusement. "Apparently, strength is not the key. I believed that if I could apply more force, I could punch a hole into the next world, but the more I battered at the barrier, the more it thickened. It was too well designed."

Valeria had no idea what to say to that. "Then we try a different approach. Start over from scratch."

He turned away, considering that. "It will take time," he said, lifting a golden eyebrow. "Perhaps the rest of your life."

She lifted a shoulder, tears she didn't think she had enough moisture for stinging her eyes. "What else am I going to do with it?"

Michael's laugh was short, like beautiful sharp little blades against her skin.

He stopped, tilting his head in that slow and slightly alien way that reminded her of a praying mantis. "At least I won't be in this endeavor alone this time."

It was the kind of line that would have prompted the old Valeria to make promises, to stay here, to be his partner. Her old self had needed something to hold onto. An angel trapped in hell would have been a good place to start.

But she'd had a glimpse of another life, another person she wanted to be. By some miracle, that woman had a partner, and it was a badass dragon, not a megalomaniac archangel.

CHAPTER FORTY-THREE

Ravenna cut her finger, squeezing several drops of blood into an earthenware jar before she signaled Naveen.

"The gate will slam shut only when this vessel is cracked over the circle," she said, placing a lid on the jar before she handed it to him.

He took the jar from her hands "How much longer?"

Her cheek twitched. "Give me a minute," she rasped, blinking and turning away.

Naveen nodded, understanding that the spell was done. But the witch needed a few moments before triggering it.

Pity welling, he left her to join his men. Every able-bodied dragon would join this fight except for Eliana. The elder had been a general in her day, and her skills in close-quarter combat were still sharp. But her endurance was flagging in her old age, so she'd been the natural choice to stay behind with Sanaa and the children. Naveen was confident Sanaa would be safe should the worst happen.

As for Sanaa's mate, Rhys had given Thomas another task.

Naveen and Rhys also knew that they couldn't leave a portal to Sheol unguarded. The men under them had drawn straws. Jerik had been selected to guard the opening from the Sheol side.

The junior was angry at being left out of the fight, but he hadn't argued. No matter what happened, they could not allow any of the inhabitants to come through the door to Earth.

As for the other threat, Rhys had decided that Thomas would handle it.

Naveen took the jar and handed it to him.

"How the hell do you expect me to stop an Elemental from slamming the door shut if one shows up?" Thomas asked.

Rhys came up behind him, clapping him on the back. "Charm? I've heard it works wonders."

The bear's growl filled the air.

"The Elementals are tied in with the fabric of reality in this realm," Rhys said, breaking the bad news. "It is inevitable that one will appear."

"And if they want to close the door, what the hell am I supposed to do? Throw myself on that grenade? Death before dishonor?"

"Of course not," Rhys said. "Just tell the truth. And hope for mercy."

"And if they don't show and you fail? "

"Jerik will come back through with whoever survives. Once he's back through, that's it. You close the door."

"Even if you don't come back through it?" the bear rumbled.

"The men will. They have their orders," Rhys said, his eyes distant. "As for me, I come back with Valeria or not at all."

He'd already said as much during their strategy session with the rest of the wing, but hearing it again hit Naveen just as hard as the first time.

The bear's reaction surprised him a bit. Thomas growled, crossing his arms. "Don't let it come to that."

When Naveen turned to question him, the bear sniffed. "Sanaa would be upset."

The corner of Rhys' mouth lifted. At his signal, Jerik began to hand out pots of paint. The men passed them around, putting their fingers in and beginning to draw symbols on their skin.

"What are those markings? Runes?" Thomas asked, his nose wrinkling in distaste. "Are they supposed to protect you?"

"No. We write the names of our ancestors on our bodies before going into battle," Naveen replied, as he drew both his grandsires' names down his arms.

"So, it's more of a prayer?" Thomas scrunched up his face, squinting at the complicated design taking shape under Naveen's hand.

"I suppose, in a way."

The designs were fresh but almost dry when Ravenna motioned him over.

"I may need some help," she said in a low voice, handing him one of the ceremonial blades.

His face tightened. "Does it have to be a painful death?" he asked quietly.

Ravenna met his eyes before turning quickly away. "It does. The more violent, the better."

It made a terrible sort of sense. "I see."

He glanced down at the blade, his discomfort making itself felt in the sudden roiling in his stomach. Killing the innocent went against the code of the Draconai, and his personal code as well.

"Never mind." Ravenna snatched back the knife.

"What's going on?" Rhys asked, looking over from his position by the men.

The witch's gaze darted back and forth between him and the knife. She stepped into the center of the circle, then gripped the blade with both hands. Ravenna raised it high before plunging it into her gut.

"What the—"

Rhys ran forward, ready to intervene. Naveen jumped in front of him, blocking him with a hand to the chest. "My apologies, my first, but you can't stop this. There is no other way to open the door."

His leader looked at him, shock and incredulity deepening the lines in his face. "But we can't let her *die*."

"Then the door stays shut," Ravenna panted, going to her knees. She pulled the blade out, her hand shaking as she flung drops of blood across the intricate design around her.

The lines of the circle shifted, the blood triggering a conformational change in the sigils.

With sluggish movements, Ravenna sat in the middle of the circle. Naveen winced as she used both her hands to arrange her legs in a lotus position. Given the way her shirt and pants had been soaked with blood, it was an unsettling sight.

Red bubbled from the witch's mouth, the distinctive rattle that signaled death beginning faster than he would have guessed. Perhaps the witch had tainted the blade with poison to help herself along. He hoped so.

"Ravenna, *why?*" Rhys snapped, his fire close at hand. "We could have found another way."

"There isn't...one," she replied. "Trust me."

"We could have asked one of the Elementals."

Ravenna laughed, her eyes sparkling with amused condescension. "Break...of the covenant. But now it's...on me...take care of...my girl."

Rhys passed a hand over his eyes. Naveen put his hand on his leader's shoulder.

And they waited.

"She's not even her real daughter," Thomas muttered in a subvocal whisper Ravenna couldn't hear. He was staring at the spilled blood with a green cast to his skin. The bear hunted because his beast demanded it, but he didn't like the sight of blood.

"Ravenna is the only mother Valeria knows," Naveen pointed out, his loyalty with the witch now. "We must let her act as such and make the most of her sacrifice."

He didn't lower his voice. Ravenna was past hearing them. The veil passed over her eyes, the life leaving them like sand running out from between a child's fingers.

Behind them the door snapped open, a shimmering hole cut out of the universe. On the other side was the lifeless wasteland from their memories.

Rhys bent over the witch carefully, making sure not to disturb the runes. He closed her eyes.

"Remember, when the Elemental comes, speak the truth," he said, his back to them.

Thomas swallowed audibly, but he murmured his agreement.

Strapping weapons in the special holster that would lie across his back in his other form, Rhys walked to the front of the wing. Naveen took his first's wrist, wrapping the necklace Ravenna crafted to track Valeria around his wrist, leaving it loose so the shift wouldn't snap the tie. Then he took his position behind him to his right while Veda took the left.

Naveen suppressed a shudder as Rhys walked through the doorway. But their ancient enemy didn't fall out of the sky to rain down hell on him. *That's what we'll be doing to him.*

"Hey!" Thomas called after them. "How am I supposed to explain the dead witch to them?"

Naveen turned back at the threshold. "As quickly as you can."

Then he followed Rhys back into hell.

CHAPTER FORTY-FOUR

Rhys shifted as soon as he crossed the threshold. The others followed suit, Jerik included. The young dragon would use his bulk to block access to the stone arch, part of the ruin where the doorway had snapped to life on this side.

The rest of the wing fell into formation behind him.

He consulted the tracking charm Ravenna had made. After his shift, it had ended up wrapped around one claw, the little stone touching his scales. It had been cold in his hand on Earth, like a little block of ice. But here on Sheol, it flared to life, warming incrementally. It would burn when they got close to Valeria.

Not that they needed it. Once they were aloft, the little homing charm confirmed what he already knew.

It's the archangel, Naveen said in his head.

As we suspected. Cold rage fueled his wings. He could set a record reaching that bastard's castle.

Bunching the muscles in his legs, he launched himself up, cutting through the fetid air.

The cataclysmic destruction that had begun before they left Sheol was complete now.

There were no trees, no water. Michael and the other angels had wiped those off the surface, turning the once-verdant landscape into a lifeless desert. Even the buildings made by their fragile neighbors, the Dareia, had been razed to the ground.

"It is a punishment befitting your defiance," Michael had told him after their last battle.

Rhys had never wanted to kill a creature more than he'd had at that moment. But his people and the Dareia under their protection had been compromised. Rhys had been forced to forego his vengeance, a choice that had nearly cost him his mate now.

But he was going to rectify that. And this time, there would be no quarter for the Host.

Spotting the battlements of the archangel's fort, he shouted the battle cry of the Draconai Imperia in his mind.

Fire and blood!

His men took up the cry, repeating it until it reverberated in his soul.

Hang on, Valeria. I'm coming.

CHAPTER FORTY-FIVE

Slank appeared at the door. "Master says go to your room."

Valeria frowned from her position on the bed of her chamber. "I am in my room."

She was finally mobile again, but it was difficult to get up and down the stairs, so Michael had allowed her to continue her studies from the comfort of her room. Slank would usually deliver her the books she needed, but her hands were empty this time.

"Ssstay inn rooom," Slank hissed, shuffling to the window. She pulled the curtain closed and left without clarifying further.

Frowning, Valeria went to the closed curtains, tugging them open again. She poked her head out cautiously, wondering if another former angel or feudal lord had come calling.

For their sake, she hoped Michael was in a good mood.

But she couldn't see anything from this particular vantage point. If she wanted to see what was going on, she'd have to disobey Michael's orders.

That was no longer as dangerous a proposition as it had once been. Yes, he was still sulking after their failed attempt to open the door to Earth, but his burgeoning feelings for her hadn't let him do it in isolation.

Thanks to her repeated attempts to snare him, he came to visit her in her room, sometimes three or four times a day, on paper-thin pretexts.

Once, he had swept in, demanding she give back a book he had sent with Slank. Another time, he had wanted to make sure she knew his preferences for dinner, although he had already eaten and there was no chance she could walk down to the kitchen to help.

"You can come and talk to me for no reason," she'd pointed out after he'd woken her from a nap to check if she were resting adequately.

For the first time in their acquaintance, Michael hadn't sneered or swept off in an offended huff. He'd simply shrugged before sitting in the only chair in the room to ask about all the movies she'd ever seen.

So if he were telling her to stay up here because he wanted her out of sight, it was for her safety. But the monotony of her days was enough motivation for her to get off her bruised butt to try to find out what was going on.

Valeria made her way to the ramparts, a little surprised to find them empty. She couldn't hear the thunder of angelic voices either, so it appeared she was wrong about the reason for Slank's message.

Or the servant was just being weird. Slank did shuffle to the beat of her own drummer—on a drum made from an animal she had skinned herself.

Valeria was about to begin the trek down the ramparts stairs when she caught movement in the sky.

She couldn't make them out very well, but that movement was unmistakable. It was wings.

Oh God, the other angels had found out about Camael. Had they banded together to kick Michael's ass?

For a split second, Valeria was elated until she realized that Michael's enemies would kill her, too.

"GET DOWNSTAIRS."

Startled, Valeria clapped her hands over her ears.

"*Now,*" Michael ordered in a less destructive volume.

She pointed at the fast-approaching cloud. "Are we under attack? But I thought you were the last angel left?"

Camael had lost his wings, she remembered. But those weren't birds coming at them. They were too big for one. Also, there were no birds in Sheol.

"I am," he snapped. "It's not the Host. My old enemy has returned. I don't know how, but they must have learned that the rest of the Host are gone. They've come back to strike at me now that I'm the only one."

He spread his wings, then put his fists on his waist. "They are fools if they think they can best me. Even alone, I can best a legion of their kind."

But Valeria heard the doubt in his voice. "I'll go, but before I do, can you tell me where they come from? Has your enemy been hiding in Sheol all this time?"

He gave her an arrested glance. "It's not likely, but I don't know where they went."

"So there could be a door open to somewhere?"

Michael spread his hands, the lightning playing between his fingers. "You are right. They could not have been hiding here all this time. But if there is a door open somewhere on Sheol, chances are it leads to a place no better than this. Sheol is not the only hell dimension. We must learn all they know. I will make sure to leave a survivor. Rest assured, I will make him speak."

Nodding because it was expected, she started to go down the stairs. Valeria was just about to cross the point where she could no longer see the approaching wings when Michael yelled a challenge.

Covering her ears again, she crouched, holding on until her ears stopped ringing. But her hands weren't enough to muffle the answering roar that returned.

A familiar roar.

Valeria scrambled back up the stairs. "*Rhys.*"

It was Rhys and all his men. They had come for her.

CHAPTER FORTY-SIX

Michael looked as if he was ready to pull her head off.

"You know these vermin?" he thundered, slashing at the sky with an imperious hand.

How angry would he be if she said yes? Grimacing, she took a step back. That was all the answer he needed.

Michael grabbed her by the arm, his grip punishing. "You're an Earthling. How can you know them?" he yelled, jerking her toward him.

He used only a fraction of his strength, but it didn't matter. She whipped around like a rag doll.

The bone under his hand snapped.

Clamping her jaw so she wouldn't cry out, Valeria put her hand on his, sending out another pulse of sticky threads full of need and want.

Abruptly, he let her go. She fell to the stones, cradling her arm and trying not to cry. Something that might have been guilt flashed in his eyes, but it was gone before she could be sure.

"I forgive you for consorting with the enemy," he announced magnanimously. "How could you have known?"

The caring in his voice was all the more terrible given that he hadn't even acknowledged he'd broken her arm.

Michael turned his back to her, spreading his wings and arms. "To think that all this time, the Draconai demons were on Earth. No doubt they've duped the populace into worshipping them. But don't worry, my dear, I *will* save them from these false gods."

He turned to her, his mercury eyes bright as hell frost. "We will find that door—just as soon I clear the path."

Michael beat his wings, taking off to meet the dragons, the lightning sparking from his fingers in eager anticipation.

Oh, God. Getting to her feet, Valeria covered her mouth, cringing as the dark purple dragon of her dreams met the pure-white electric fury of the archangel.

They moved fast and furiously, almost too fast for her eyes to follow.

The other dragons split into pairs, covering each other so one could breathe fire at the angel while the other tried to get past the bolts shooting from his fingertips.

Unfortunately, Michael's range was longer than theirs.

Valeria had seen the dragons hunt, but this was something else. To the naked eye, it was chaos, a choreographed dance with no rhyme or reason, but she could see their determination.

Michael's counter-assault was perversely beautiful. He bobbed and dodged just as quickly as the dragons, the angel light shooting from his fingers in a fierce primordial howitzer meant to decimate worlds.

Before her horrified eyes, Michael finally struck one of the flying dervishes—a black dragon with a yellow belly.

Her heart stopped, but the archangel was forced to break off his attack, diving to avoid the streams of flame that came at him from three different sides.

To her relief, the dragon who'd been struck seemed to shake off the hit, as if his scales had partially absorbed or reflected that violent power.

That was when Michael started aiming for their wings.

The air was filled with bolts that came so fast that her retinas threatened to burn out. She paced along the battlement, trying to cover her eyes with one hand to block out the excess light enough so she could see.

Then one of Michael's bolts split, passing through both wings of a mostly blue dragon.

Valeria didn't even know who it was, but she screamed anyway. She poured every ounce of pain and power into her cry. Pulling on Michael's telekinetic power was instinct.

But reflecting Michael's magic without the aid of a spell was not the same as doing it to a witch. The sheer level of power was staggering. Her ability was stretched to the limit and quickly beyond, even as the wounded dragon spun to the ground more slowly, his descent no longer fast like a cannonball hurtling to the ground, but a damaged glider limping down in circles instead.

Her mouth filled with the taste of meta and acid, but Valeria held on until two other dragons flanked the falling one. Somehow, they buttressed him enough to land farther from the castle—out of Michael's bolt range.

Dizzy, she went down to her knees, letting go of Michael's power. But her hands continued to tingle. Raising them, she saw the crackles of energy, the same one she'd felt and seen during the spell. *Mierda.* She hadn't meant to take his angel light, only his telekinesis.

Rubbing her hands, she realized the power wasn't leaving. She couldn't push it out of herself.

Chingado! The spell! Such a force shouldn't have come to her, but the spell had inadvertently prepared her, twisting her just enough to be a working receptacle. And she'd made the mistake of reaching for it voluntarily.

Her body wasn't meant to hold that kind of power. But she stopped trying to push it out because another glance at the sky told her the angel was holding his own.

Michael's prowess in battle was terrifying. He streaked across the sky some two hundred meters from the main body of the dragons, shooting bolt after bolt with no signs of fatigue.

But even the wrath of an archangel wasn't enough to stand again an entire squadron of dragons. Not now that he was alone.

Michael landed on the ramparts, hurling bolt after bolt into the distance. More must have connected than she realized because it looked as if there were fewer dragons in the sky. It was difficult to tell with them swirling and swooping so fast.

The dragons were closer now, inching forward. Their determination to reach the castle bolstered and ripped her heart to shreds at the same time.

Then another dragon went down. Again, she tried to slow his descent, even though she knew blood had started trickling from her nose *and* ears.

She couldn't even see Rhys anymore—and his scales should have been visible, even as a blur of purple and gold. But he was nowhere in sight, and most of the dragons she could still make out were backing away in retreat or already on the ground.

Some of these last were too close, well within the archangel's firing range.

She had to do more. These warriors had come to save her. Rhys wouldn't like it, but she couldn't sit back and let them get fried.

Wiping the blood away with her good hand, she edged closer and closer to the archangel.

Michael paid her no attention at all as she crept behind him. Then she jumped on his back. With almost frantic desperation, she sent more and more sickly sweet love tendrils into his body, trying to get as many as she could in him before he could shake her off.

The energy it took ran out of her like water from a broken glass. She was pushing everything she had at him, using the mirror to channel some of his energy and transmuting it into obsession, something she hadn't known was possible until she'd done it.

"*Michael, stop,*" she said, an unfamiliar resonance in her voice.

He turned to look at her, bewildered.

Valeria glanced at those flat mercury eyes, feeling her blood ice over.

Flawless features darkening, he brushed her off him. She fell on the stones, her world blurred white as the archangel spread his wings, looming over her.

The expression of betrayal on his face was something she'd never forget. He knew what she had done. Michael stared down at his arms as if he could see her tendrils sticking there. They weren't strong enough.

"Did you think you could ensnare *me? Do you know who I am?*" he raged.

Light began to glow all around him, suffusing his skin as he raised his arm. The tendrils began to snap, entire clumps at a time.

Michael's hands began to glow brighter than the rest of him. *Chingado*. He was going to strike her down with his lightning.

Valeria scrambled away from him, pushing with her legs and one good arm.

"I just want to go home," she panted, trying to make him see reason. "But you can't go with me, or Earth will end up just like this place."

"WE WERE GOING TO *SAVE* THEM TOGETHER!"

Cringing, she shook her head. "It's not just the witches, the dragons, or the other shifters who will resist you. Even the humans will. They change politicians like they change their clothes—humans don't want to be ruled anymore."

The light flared and she put her hands up, closing her eyes in expectation of death.

Except it didn't come. Her mirroring talent became a mirror in truth, bouncing the bolt back to its source. It hit Michael's chest on the left, buffeting him, but not hard enough for him to fall.

He was coming back at her, hands outstretched but not glowing, as if he'd decided to strangle her with his bare hands instead.

But he'd forgotten the dragons.

Black boots appeared in her vision. She recognized Rhys' unmistakable backside as he fell into his two-legged form, holding a bizarre spear made of his own purple scales. Fitted like overlapping arrows heads that had been sharpened to a razor-sharp point, the weapon sliced through the steely muscles in Michael's arm, pinning him to the stone.

With a sound like a thunderclap, another man-shaped object fell. It was Naveen, also bearing a scale spear. His weapon pinned the angel's right wing. Then there was another, a soldier whose name she didn't remember. He got Michael's left arm.

She looked up to see a dragon directly overhead. It rolled and shifted in mid-flight before landing hard. The fourth and final man pinned Michael's now-broken left wing to the ground.

Rhys bent in front of her, gathering her close. Too overwhelmed to cry, she clutched at him. "You came, *you came*," she whispered.

His beautiful onyx eyes filled with tears. "I'm so sorry," he said hoarsely. "You should never have been taken. I'm sorry."

"You're supposed to be on my side," the angel roared at her as she buried her face in Rhys' neck.

Valeria was crying too hard to answer.

"You can't demand allegiance any more than you can demand subservience," Rhys snapped, stroking the back of her head as he pulled her closer.

"Don't *do* that," Michael hissed. His voice sounded wet. "She's *mine*."

Rhys' disgust at the angel enveloped her. "You've never had anyone in your life that you didn't force to your side, have you? All you know is conquest. Well, human hearts don't work that way. And Valeria would never choose to be yours."

Michael laughed. It was such an unexpected and eerie sound that she twisted to see him.

"Take a good look at your saviors," he sneered, his breath labored. "Recognize them for what they are."

Frowning, she turned around, intending to ignore the broken angel, when she noticed something she had to have been blind to miss.

The dragons were in their human forms, but they were still winged.

Tilting her head back to look at Rhys, she fixed her wide eyes on the black wings sprouting from his back.

These were wide as Michael's but black as night. They stretched over bone and sinew, the tops peaked with protruding bony thumbs just like a bat's or a gargoyle's.

Her eyes darted back to Michael. His white wings were dirty now, stained with gold—angel blood. Then she turned back to the black ones.

Oh, shit.

Angels and demons. This was the source, the truth that global religions had been founded on. And it was all a lie. Because Rhys wasn't a demon. He *wasn't*.

Please let it be a lie.

CHAPTER FORTY-SEVEN

Michael spit on the ground, the saliva tainted with his blood. "Do you see now? Do you see the demons for what they are?"

He tried to rise, but Naveen had pulled up his spear and pointed it at his neck. Michael settled for waving a hand at Rhys.

"My cadre and I came here because we were asked," he said, pointing an accusing finger at the black-winged apparition. "The demon dragons had invaded this place, trampling the populace. We *liberated* them."

Dazed. she peered up at Rhys. His expression was fixed, remote. She knew then that it was the truth. "The one holding you so tenderly is infamous. His name is Berith," Michael sneered.

Her lips parted. Berith. That was one of the infernal names. Berith was Rhys.

Rhys stood frozen, gazing at her as if he were waiting for her judgment.

For a long moment she stared at his stricken face, trying to take it all in. *'Angels and demons'* her mind repeated on a loop, blotting out rational thought in a rising panic that had her heart drumming in her ears. How the hell had she gotten caught in a war between an angel and a demon?

And then she remembered all that Rhys had done for her—not the big gestures like saving her life, but the little ones. The way he had tasted all the food and drink in the beginning, until she grew comfortable with him to take what was given. And not all the fancy clothes he had bought her, but the drawing pencils he'd given her after learning she loved to sketch.

There were dozens of other examples.

Valeria's shoulders slumped in relief. She had spent enough time with both of these men, these creatures, to know their hearts. She had to trust herself, to trust in Rhys. Reaching up, she took his hand.

The ice that encased her dragon cracked. He squeezed her fingers back.

"Yes, you liberated them," Rhys began, addressing the angel. "But it was a *millennium* too late. We were living in harmony with the Dareia by the time you came to free them. Our war with them had been bitter but brief. We made peace, and we willingly intertwined our lives. Then you came, offering them a rescue they no longer wanted in exchange for subjugation."

He turned to Valeria. "They told him no, rejecting the Host's offer. They ended up begging us to save them from the angels."

The men around the angel holding the spears stayed silent as Rhys stood straighter. "We fought off the Host, expelling them from our territory and winning the war, but losing everything else in the process. As for the Dareia, they were much frailer than us. They died in droves, especially after the Host poisoned the land. Only a handful survived."

"Justice is eternal," Michael said, his voice weakening even as he continued to struggle against the spears pinning him down.

"Close your eyes, little love," Rhys murmured, but Valeria kept them wide open. She had to see.

Bearing witness was the last thing she would do for Michael.

Rhys' nod was reluctant, but he understood. Naveen raised his spear, then slammed it down, plunging it into his enemy's chest.

The angel's scream was terrible.

She pressed back into Rhys, trying to escape the sound. He tightened his hold, cradling her to his chest. But something was wrong. The hand she had pressed against his sparked with energy.

And it was growing brighter.

Valeria gasped in pain as the light began to open cracks in the skin of her hand and forearm.

Michael's power was running rampant in her. Too strong, too potent, her body wouldn't be able to contain it. No witch could.

Rhys slapped a hand over the crack. "What you kill, you keep," he breathed, horror dawning in his eyes.

He knew. Ravenna must have told him. A trickle of shame managed to work through the pain, but it didn't last. This wasn't something she would have chosen in a million years. But it didn't matter.

Michael didn't have to die by her hand for her to get his power. He just had to die.

CHAPTER FORTY-EIGHT

"Stop," Rhys yelled, spinning around to face his men. "Don't kill him."

Valeria's head lolled, and the cracks of light on her skin widened at an alarming rate.

Kyrin looked up at him, a wild light in his eyes. "He's alone here. We can finally end this."

"If you do, she dies."

His witch had stopped moving now. Her bare arms sported a spiderweb of lights as if she had a supernova about to detonate inside her.

Valeria was coming apart at the seams.

He wrapped his third-form wings around her. The move was instinctive and fruitless, but he did it anyway. Rhys couldn't lose her again. If she died, he would go with her this time.

Naveen clapped a staying hand on Kyrin's wrist. "The angel's power will migrate to her upon his death," he explained for Rhys, whose throat was tight with panic. "She won't survive it."

Kyrin's lips compressed, but he didn't argue. Lifting his spear, he backed away from the wounded angel.

Rhys took a last look at his oldest enemy. "You had a chance to stop this madness and let the land recover. You chose to continue the destruction. Now you have to live with that choice. But know this—from now on, Earth is off-limits. And so is she."

Michael's nostrils flared, the spittle from his mouth dripping down his chin. "You think...this is some sort...of end. It's just more...of the beginning."

Shaking his head, Rhys turned his back, snapping his wings out. He would fly back in his hybrid form so he could hold Valeria.

His men readied themselves behind him.

"It may be too late. His wounds are serious," Naveen said when the angel didn't get to his feet as they backed away to the edge of the ramparts.

"Then we need to get back home before he dies."

Michael's power alone hadn't been enough to punch through to Earth. With luck, the barrier would protect Valeria from the surge of power if the angel crossed the veil.

"Let's go," he told the others. "No formation. Just get back to the door as fast as you can."

Then he launched into the air, his precious burden tucked tightly against him.

CHAPTER FORTY-NINE

Are they back? Sanaa texted.

Thomas sighed. *Not yet,* he typed back, his big fingers introducing several misspellings. It was the sixth or seventh time his mate had asked.

He'd been sitting in front of this hole in the world for hours, and each second had been agony. It was wrong, this opening. Being in front of it was flipping every switch he had.

A nightmare of images played out in the big screen of his mind. In it, he saw a horde of demons pouring out of the door, ready to attack and kill everything in sight.

He'd known Rhys said anonymity was more important than brute force when it came to the doorway, but one guard on each side wasn't enough.

I should have called my old army unit. He would have felt better with that elite team of black-ops shifters at his back.

He wanted nothing more than to smash that little jar and slam the door shut, but he knew he couldn't. Despite their pompous bluster, the Draconai were good men, Rhys in particular. He deserved his fucking happily ever after. And despite the fact that Valeria had thrown Lanaa off a three-story building, Thomas liked the clan leader's witch. She didn't deserve to be dragged to the hellish place his wife had described.

"We must bring her back," Sanaa had told him with tears in her eyes. "No one must ever be abandoned in that terrible place."

So, Thomas had promised to do his part and guard the door. But he almost changed his mind and broke the jar prematurely when the wind blasted out of the opening, knocking him on his ass.

It had come out of nowhere. One minute, he'd been sitting on his haunches next to the circle and that poor dead witch. The next, he'd been flat on the ground. Only his excellent reflexes had saved him from accidentally smashing the jar.

Thomas jumped to his feet, tucking the jar into the inside pocket of his jacket. He'd been ready to do battle.

"Who's there?" he challenged.

But no one answered. He was alone. *Damn it.* Had it been a demon? Naveen had said they could discard their bodies and jump into this plane without them.

"*Shit*," Thomas added. What else could it have been?

Then Jerik poked his head out of the doorway. "Did you see them?"

"*Them?* It was more than one demon?"

"I'm not sure it was a demon—it was a woman. And some guy."

Thomas drew his head back. "I didn't see or smell anyone. There was just wind."

Jerik frowned. "It's my fault they got through me, but I'm fairly sure it wasn't demons. I think it was an Elemental."

The dreaded big E. Thomas wanted more of an explanation, but Jerik's head disappeared back through the door and he wasn't about to follow him to demand it.

Scowling, he turned back to the circle and almost had a heart attack. The wind had knocked the witch's body from a sitting position to the side.

Wincing, he took the jar out of his pocket and set it down before picking his way through the circle.

Thomas took off his jacket, then laid it over the top half of Ravenna's body. She was so small that it covered her like a blanket. Yeah, she was a kidnapper and had been more on the side of the black than the white, but he still felt sorry for her.

Too many mistakes for one life, and one big one so early. Passing a hand over his eyes, he sat down to wait, vowing never to let his life get to that point.

Except you're not a kid anymore. And his path had been set in stone when he met Sanaa. As long as he had her, Thomas would have few regrets when he met his maker. Whoever the hell that was.

Angels, demons—all the things his grandparents had taught him— were out the window now.

Just roll with the punches, and do this so your mate is happy and your kids are safe. As far as he was concerned, that was the most anyone could ask of him.

An hour later, Rhys popped out of the door, barking orders.

Thomas took one look at the unconscious witch in the dragon's arms and leaped to his feet. He handed the jar to the next dragon through the door, then ran to get the car.

In the end, he didn't know which Drak closed the portal to hell, just that it was done by the time he got back.

CHAPTER FIFTY

Valeria knew these sheets by texture. They were machine-made silk. Their softness was a comforting embrace, a reminder that she was home, because nothing that pure or mechanically perfect existed in Sheol. But she didn't roll around in them the way she wanted to. The cracks of light in her skin were still there, and they hurt like hell.

A hand touched her forehead very gently. "How do you feel?"

Rhys' blurry form sharpened into focus. "I feel like I got struck by lightning," she croaked. "About a million times."

"We're going to fix it," he promised, his fingers feathering over her skin.

She knew without asking that the spots he touched didn't have the cracks. Leaning over, Rhys poured her a glass of water, waiting with endless patience until she had drunk the entire thing.

His beautiful face was so serious it was breaking her heart. "Is it that bad?" she asked. Was she going to die?

His eyes dropped to her hands. "Veda has seen you. He came to set your broken arm."

"And?"

Rhys hesitated. "It's going to take a little while, but you're going to be fine," he said in a bracing tone.

She gave him a weak smile that stretched the light in her, the cracked spiderwebs illuminating a constellation against the dark silk sheets. "Liar."

"I'm not lying." Rhys sat on the edge of the bed. "We didn't finish off the angel. I had hoped you would normalize once we closed the door, but it seems the angel's reach extends into this realm. Veda's best guess is that the creature is in a state between life and death. Whatever happened to you over there, it's not progressing."

"But it's not getting better either."

He opened his mouth to tell her another comforting lie, but she waved him into silence. "It doesn't matter. I'm so happy to be home and with you."

Even if it's only for a few more days.

Rhys seemed to hear her unspoken words. He got on his knees, his hands hovering over her as if he wanted to touch her but was afraid of hurting her. "You *will* recover."

It was an order.

Valeria smiled despite the pain. She hadn't noticed it in Sheol—she'd been too overwhelmed to feel it there. She needed a distraction, which was why it was a good thing she had a million questions.

"Tell me about your war."

Rhys closed his eyes for a long moment before refocusing on her face. "I wasn't hiding anything from you."

Her mouth quirked up. "So, I imagined the bat wings? Or that you were at war with angels for God knows how long?

"No, of course not, you didn't imagine those things," he said with a little shake of his head. "The wings are quite real. It's what we call our hybrid form. It evolved for battle. Over time, we learned that it presented an advantage to keep it secret, so we don't flaunt it."

He looked down, uncomfortable. "But I admit I wasn't eager for you to see me that way. Thanks to the Host's influence here, those wings evoke a visceral reaction in the people who see them."

"They do make an impression," she said, trying for levity.

Rhys nodded, acknowledging her attempt at humor but not willing to step an inch away from his concern for her.

"As far as I know, no angels remain on this side of the barrier, but memories seem to have burrowed like parasites. We're automatically pitted against them as demons."

"It's a bit on the nose in terms of branding, but Michael's kind of a blunt hammer, isn't he?"

Rhys' face curdled. "I can't say that I know him as well as you do now."

"Not your fault," she assured him.

"I will never stop reliving that moment when you fell," he whispered. "If I'd known where you would end up, I'd have done everything differently—I wouldn't have left you alone for one."

But she hadn't been alone when the cross coven came. Figuring Ravenna was making herself scarce, she opened her mouth to ask about her, but Rhys forestalled her.

"I know it may have appeared differently in front of the castle," he said, "but I'm not ashamed of our hybrid form or our history. I was just concerned what you were thinking at that moment because I wanted to get you as far from the angel as possible."

"I know." She nodded encouragingly, prodding gently until his hesitation and reserve completely broke down.

In halting words, he began to tell her about the war, how it had started on a distant planet—not Sheol. But it had ended there after the Draconai and other dragon clans had hunted their old enemy, the Dareia, until they submitted.

"It wasn't easy, but we eventually brokered a peace," he told her.

"How old were you?"

His grin was like sunshine, genuine amusement crinkling the skin around his eyes. "I know I'm much older than you, but I'm not *that* old. This happened before I was born. The only battles I've fought were against the Angelii."

Rhys poured her another water, urging her to drink some more before he continued. "In the early days on Sheol, when we were still at war with the Dareia, they sent out a distress alert to anyone who would answer. No one came to their aid because our reputation was too fierce. So much time passed, we forgot they'd sent it. So did they."

"I gather the Angelii didn't?"

"No. We'd been living in peace with the Dareia for so long, many never knew we had ever been at war—compared to us, they were a short-lived species."

His mouth compressed, the memories darkening his handsome visage. "But some malcontents did remember, and they'd nurtured that hatred across generations. So when the Angelii came, offering liberation, those idiots accepted on behalf of all their people—imagine a tiny fraction of the population deciding what the rest wanted, how they would live."

She winced. It sounded too much like Earth's present day governments, and the way the rich bought politicians so they could dictate policy to suit them. "Didn't they know what they were inviting?"

He lifted a shoulder. "I'll never know. But the rest of the Dareia made their displeasure clear. We weren't a perfect society, but food was plentiful and there was no fighting to speak of between our groups, just a healthy rivalry."

He passed a hand over his eyes. "When the Angelii came the majority of the Dareia spurned them—something the Angelii never forgave."

Rhys trailed off.

"What happened?"

"What you'd expect—the Host gave no quarter. Most of the Dareia population was slaughtered in a matter of weeks."

"Did any survive?"

He lifted a shoulder. "A small group. Our closest neighbors were under our protection."

"What happened to them?"

"They came here with us, but chose to make their own way in the world. They were rather like your Fae in some ways. I think most made their lives with them, settling in Europe. Mostly Greece."

She frowned. "But how did you cross over? I spent months helping Michael try to get through the barrier."

"*Months?*" Rhys' mouth dropped open, his face paling.

Of course. He didn't know. How could he? "I guess you've been too busy to check a calendar since we got back. Time runs faster on the other side of the barrier."

"I had no idea." He broke off, swearing and covering his face with his hands and swearing. "I can't stand knowing you were in that monster's power for so long."

"I survived," she whispered. His grief was raw and real, and it soothed that damaged spot that had started to unravel in Michael's tender care. "But I'm still confused. How did your people get through the barrier back then? How did you get through it now?"

Rhys sighed. "According to our oral history, that wall wasn't always there. The lore suggests that it was constructed by the Mother to protect this world. Before, it was easy to go from this realm to the next—or at least feasible if you were strong enough. Some of our kind did it to prove themselves or for the adventure. And even though the barrier existed by the time I was born, it wasn't as dense at first. It took years for it to get to that state—as if it were building itself up in response to the amount of turmoil on our side."

"That almost makes sense. Every time Michael tried to punch his way through, it just got stronger."

"It's an intricate and cunning piece of spell-work," he acknowledged. "When the Angelii arrived, it became as it is now—impermeable if you don't know the right spell and designed only to be opened from this side."

The tiniest of frowns puckered her brow. Anything more would be too painful. "Then how did you cross?"

"This is going to sound strange under the circumstances, but I think it was prayer—prayer and pity." He crossed his arms, the memories making him edgy. "Our backs were to the wall. We'd beat the enemy back, but our small coalition was perhaps weeks from death due to starvation."

He sighed shakily. "Then the door was opened from this side. We were invited here and allowed to settle on a conditional basis."

The act of mercy was stunning in its implications. How often had Michael cursed the Mother, an entity Valeria had never really believe in.

But she existed, or at least she did then. "So did the Mother open the door again?" she asked.

"No, it wasn't *the* Mother. It was *your* mother."

Rhys stood, scrubbing his face roughly with his hands.

"My love, I'm afraid I have some bad news to share..."

CHAPTER FIFTY-ONE

"How did she take it?" Naveen asked.

"Badly." Rhys sighed, crossing the length of his office with ground-eating strides.

How else could anyone take news like that?

"Does she know all of it?"

Rhys sat at his desk, shaking his head. "Not all. She knows Ravenna was a surrogate and that she ran off with her while she was still in the womb. But I didn't tell her about her real family. The other news was bad enough. It took everything she had to hear that. She's sleeping now."

Naveen leaned against the wall. "With your permission, I'd like to speak with her when she wakes. There are some things Ravenna wished for her to know."

Rhys murmured his assent. His impulse to protect Valeria was beside the point now. She'd been to hell. How much worse could it get?

"I think you have to take that meeting now," Naveen prodded.

I'm wrong. It can get so much worse.

But his second was adamant. "I don't think you can put off meeting the Elemental."

Rhys suppressed a growl. "I don't want to leave Valeria."

"I know." Naveen winced. "But Veda says she's stable. And I'm afraid it's you they want to see—no other will do."

There are consequences to opening a doorway to hell. The Elementals, the Mother's chosen, were charged with making sure things like that didn't happen. But according to Jerik, there were extenuating circumstances —including the possibility that one of their own had made their own unfortunate detour to Sheol at the same time they did. And she hadn't done it alone. Jerik had recognized her companion.

Sometimes, coincidence was too inadequate a word to describe the way the forces in the world aligned.

So maybe, just maybe, they'd get a pass for violating the treaty they'd signed, which promised they'd live here in peace and not do anything to compromise the safety of this world.

Of course, it wasn't a good sign that their offer of reparation, a chest of gold and jewels, had been spurned by the Elementals.

"All right, set the meet for tomorrow."

"Tonight," Naveen pressed. "It's more than our trip back home. Rumors are running rampant about the Mother. Some are saying that she's gone."

Rhys' scowl was immediate. "Has the barrier fallen?"

Naveen shook his head. "It's as solid as the day we first crossed. But the witches from the high houses are manic. Valeria probably senses the disturbance, too, but she can't process it given everything else she's feeling."

Right. "Set the meeting for tonight."

"Don't you think you should let her decide? From what I hear, Valeria possesses a strikingly decisive mind and manner. And I don't think she would like you making this decision for her."

The words of Gia, the Earth Elemental, rang through his head.

All things considered, Rhys thought he'd acquitted himself well during the meeting. He was certain the Elemental hadn't known he was sweating bullets, waiting for the moment when she condemned him and his entire clan by exiling them back to Sheol.

Years of facing down the enemy had allowed him to cloak his face and form in arrogance. The camouflage had worked, too.

Gia had been more forgiving than he would have believed. Which meant the rumors about the Mother's departure had been true.

The Elementals would need allies once word left this realm. And the news *would* get out. It was inevitable. The Angelli were bad, but they were by no means the only threat out there.

To her credit, Gia hadn't seemed worried. As far as she was concerned, nothing had changed. The power granted to her and her sisters by the Mother was as potent as it had ever been.

But what was interesting was who had been there at the meeting with her.

Salvador Delavordo looked just like his picture. He was young, handsome, and guileless, with an energy that was not unlike Veda's. Except Salvador's healer energy was so deep and potent it made him feel ageless. And yet, he'd been raised by the family that produced Valeria. That meant he could do more than heal. His magical potential was off the charts. *Just like his sister's...*

When Rhys shared this with Naveen, his second, perhaps predictably, sided with the Elemental.

"It's inevitable that Valeria will ask about her real family once she recovers. And, as the Elemental pointed out, her brother has been disinherited, so he's safer than the rest of the family."

"You and I both know he's as entangled with them as he ever was."

Or else he'd have been hunted down, prey for the predators that swam in those waters.

"There is also the fact he's a gifted healer," Naveen prodded. "Rumor has it that's how he met Gia. She needed his services."

Rhys never asked Naveen who his sources were, but his network of informants was a marvel that never ceased to amaze him.

"I will reach out to Gia myself," Rhys promised.

Valeria was healing too slowly, and Salvador was a witch of her blood. He would be able to do more for her than Veda had.

CHAPTER FIFTY-TWO

Valeria's lashes fluttered open at the unfamiliar voice asking her to wake.

"Hello," the man said. Focusing on him, she saw smiling eyes, a straight nose, and skin a shade or two darker than hers.

The stranger was checking her pulse, his manner friendly, open. And Rhys wasn't tearing him apart for touching her so he must be safe.

"Hello," she croaked. Belatedly, she saw Rhys holding up the wall on her left. Next to him was a beautiful woman with cocoa-colored skin and cheekbones that could cut glass.

The woman was not safe. Not even close. Valeria knew it like she knew the man was a healer. It fell under the same category of knowledge that told her the sky was blue.

The healer turned his head, meeting the woman's eyes to have some wordless conversation that seemed to say a lot for such a quick glance.

The man turned back to her, and she noticed the fine lines around his mouth. This was someone who laughed a lot.

Putting his hands out, he let them hover over her a few inches, moving them up and down her body like a Reiki master.

"I can feel that," she said in surprise. This man *could* manipulate some kind of energy. How wonderfully weird.

"You must be extremely sensitive then. Most people don't feel anything when I do that." The smiling man put on a headset with magnifying loop attached. He bent over her hands for a long minute, examining the cracks in her skin with a focus that seemed preternatural.

"It appears there's a foreign energy in your body," he said, leaning back with a bemused expression.

"It belonged to an angel," she said helpfully.

"Ah." His thick lashes fluttered. But the man must have seen some shit in his time because he shrugged, unfazed.

"I'm better with curses and poisons, but I think we can come up with a treatment."

"We?"

His grin was sudden and infectious, lighting his entire face up. He looked over his shoulder at the dangerous beauty and back again. "I might need some help from my better half over there. Her name is Gia. Mine is Salvador, by the way."

"It's nice to meet you," she said, but then frowned. "Have we met before? You look so familiar."

The healer cocked his head, the same curiosity in his eyes. "Maybe. You look familiar to me, too, but, for the life of me, I can't remember from where. I'm sorry, I'm usually incredibly good with faces."

"Hmm. That's okay," she said, slurring slightly. The brief exchange had drained her. Tired, she let her head fall back on the pillow. Rhys stepped forward. He sat on the mattress, taking her hand. It only hurt a little.

The play of energy in the cracks of her skin reminded her of his fire. It may have been her imagination, but she thought they were smaller now. But if this healer could speed up the process, she'd shave her hair off to give to him for use in whatever spell he wanted as payment.

"What I think you need is a good old-fashioned purge," Salvador said after a while. "And by old, I mean ancient. I'm going to step out for an hour or so while we gather the materials we need. In the meantime, I'm going to have your brownie boil some water. There's a specific tincture I want you to drink to get ready."

"Will do," she promised.

The healer and his mate walked to the door. He paused at the threshold, giving her that puzzled, searching glance as if he were still trying to place her.

His mate touched his shoulder, and he finally exited. The woman did as well, with a last pointed look at Rhys.

She turned her head as little as possible to see her dragon. "What was that for?"

"Gia and I have come to an understanding."

"About her partner helping me?"

Rhys gazed down at her, his eyes possessive but guarded. "Among other things."

"Who is she?"

"The Earth Elemental."

"*What?*" she screeched. Or, at least, she tried to screech. It came out as a strangled cough.

"She's here to help," Rhys assured her. "They both are."

Crap on a cracker. "I thought Elementals were a myth."

His mouth curled up sardonically. "I'm afraid not."

"Wow," she said, sinking more deeply into the pillow. "What did you have to promise her to get her mate's help?"

"To get Salvador here? Nothing. It was her idea. She...well, she was..."

He raised his head as if listening to something, then opened his arms. "Can I show you something or will it hurt too much to be moved?"

It had to be important, or he wouldn't ask. Rhys had been treating her as if she were made of spun glass ever since he'd gotten her out of Sheol.

Valeria pushed the sheet off. Ever so gently, Rhys picked her up and carried her to the window.

Salvador and Gia the Elemental were having a discussion in front of the house. It looked heated.

The healer threw his hands in the air, then started pacing back and forth. His mate said something, but Salvador just waved her away, not wanting to be comforted.

"Salvador just received some unexpected news," Rhys said in a low voice.

"He looks so upset." Valeria felt bad for him. He seemed so kind.

She narrowed her eyes at Rhys. "You know what she told him, don't you?"

"Yes," he confirmed, his voice grave. "Salvador Delavordo just found out the sister he thought was dead is still alive."

She froze in his arms, going hot and cold. "Delavordo?"

"Yes. Salvador is the eldest child of Fulgencio and Lucia Delavordo. And you are their daughter."

Valeria blinked at him, expecting him to break into grin and tell her he was joking. But he didn't do that. Her lip trembled. "That can't be right."

Except it made so much sense. Michael had told her himself. *Fortunately for me, your clan has many enemies.*

Mierda. He'd known who she was the entire time. It was why he'd targeted her. The Delavordos were notorious for spawning powerful witches, many of whom had gone black.

It's why I can do what I can. Why I've had to fight so hard to stay in the light. She had too much power for one witch. So had many of the Delavordos.

Rhys held up a hand. "I know what you're thinking, my love, but everything about you is good. And the Delavordos aren't all bad. If one has won an Elemental for a mate, they can't be. Although, as Gia keeps reminding me, her mate is not part of that family anymore. He was disinherited."

Valeria didn't find that convincing, but she had done all her soul searching in Sheol. This wouldn't change the fact she was going to fight to survive this so she could be with Rhys.

Except it cast Ravenna's act in a new light.

"Have you ever met my real parents?"

Rhys shook his head. "No. I only know them by reputation. They are...formidable. And you should know that according to Gia and Naveen, they never wrote you off. They've been searching for you for your entire life."

There was a sizzling sound. Rhys wiped her cheek with the lightest of touches, stopping the tear before it could reach another crack of energy and evaporate like a drop of water on a skillet.

"That's unsettling." Her mutter was watery.

Rhys opened his mouth, but a knock interrupted whatever he was going to say.

The door opened, and Salvador poked his head in. His eyes were red.

"Hey."

She stared at him, studying him in a new light. Yeah, the resemblance was there. His eyes were a different color, but not by much, and they had the same shape. Also, his nose and mouth were the masculine versions of hers. And he was pretty close in skin tone, the darker cast it had coming from spending more time in the sun, according to the tan line on his shoulder.

"Hi," she said. The new knowledge she had must have been written on her face because he sighed, almost relieved.

He had been prepared to tell her, but he hadn't known how.

"Is it okay if we talk?" he asked. Salvador looked up at Rhys. "Gia is taking charge of gathering the supplies. This won't delay the treatment."

She could feel Rhys' reluctance. He didn't want to leave her alone with anyone...but this was her brother. *Damn. I have a brother.*

With the same care he'd taken in picking her up, Rhys set her on the mattress. "I will send Aggie up with the tea."

Salvador nodded and sat on the bed. He blinked rapidly a few times.

"Are you older or younger than me?" she asked.

His smile through his tears was genuine. "I'm older. You—well, I'm not sure what age you are."

"Because your parents used a surrogate. Was it a secret?"

Salvador's cheek twitched. "It was, even from me. I don't know the whole story, but Gia just filled in some blanks." His handsome face hardened. "I know this Ravenna woman sacrificed herself to save you, but I'm never going to forgive her for taking you. Neither will our parents."

He broke off, wiping his cheeks. "I'm sorry for what's happened to you."

Her grin was painful but worth it. "I was going to say the same thing to you—being excommunicated can't have been fun."

His lip twitched. "We're not a religion. Just a messed-up family. But even disinherited, Mother and Father poke their noses in my business. And even though they continue to be arrogant and argue like it's an Olympic sport, I do think they've mellowed a little in their old age. They continue to love me, despite our numerous differences and disagreements."

"That's good," she whispered, wondering what they would think of her.

Salvador leaned forward. "To be honest, I think your kidnapping explains a lot about why they are the way they are. Not completely, of course, but some."

Kidnapping. The word reverberated in her mind, her body reacting by losing cohesion. She sank into the bed, darkness rolling over her.

Salvador tapped her on the nose. "Don't think about it. We can talk about it—about her—once you're better. For now, you need to marshal every bit of your resources. The purge is going to take a lot out of you."

She held up her cracked hands. "Damn, I hope so." She tried to smile. "I want to hear more about our parents," she said. "And about you."

So he started to tell her about his life and their parents, including the fact they were about to have a baby sister—without a surrogate this time.

Just how old was her birth mother? "Is that what they call a change-of-life baby?"

"Maybe," he said, laughing. "I honestly didn't want to hear all the details. But a new life is always a good thing. I call her the miracle baby."

His eyes grew dark as he watched her process that. "I think I would have been a pretty good big brother to you."

She laughed, her eyes stinging. "I believe you."

He was a man who had that perfect big-brother air. The tears sizzled on her cheeks.

"That would have been nice," she added hoarsely. He had no idea how much. "But you get another chance with the new baby."

"And I'll do her proud," he said, his voice equally rough. "God knows she's going to need me to run interference with our mom and dad. But I'd like to think it's not too late for me to be a real brother to you."

She held up her hands. The angel light in her veins was beautiful in its strange, damaging way. "Well, not going to lie. I could use a little help."

"We will get rid of it, I promise," Salvador assured her. "In the meantime, can you tell me how you ended up with a dragon for a boyfriend?"

"Sure, if you tell me how you ended up with an Elemental for a mate."

"Deal," he said. "Who goes first?"

She wagged her finger. "Age before beauty."

Salvador burst out laughing. "I know you've never been a younger sister before, but it must be a natural talent. You sound exactly like one already."

He rounded the bed, kicking off his shoes and leaning against the headboard, settling in for a long story.

"Well, it started when Gia was poisoned..."

CHAPTER FIFTY-THREE

In the end, Valeria's treatment was simple. Salvador used a curse.

"Taking power is their intended use," he pointed out. "We have to make a few adjustments, but it's the easiest way to do this."

The biggest tweak he deemed necessary was to make sure that the angel light didn't end up bouncing around the atmosphere. "Don't worry," he assured her. "We organized an appropriate receptacle for the power. Well, Gia did."

The Earth Elemental put a hand on Valeria's cheek. Unlike the touch of the others, this skin-to-skin contact soothed.

"Either my sister Diana or Logan would work as a vessel," she told her and Rhys. "Both can absorb the kind of energy that we're seeing here, can even tweak it if needed so that it's at home in their body."

Valeria was skeptical but after Logan, the Air Elemental, showed up, she understood the genius of the plan.

Michael's lightning *liked* the Air Elemental. With her brother's help and a very special circle she helped him draw, the lighting left Valeria's body, sluggishly at first, and then eagerly.

Instead of keeping it, the Air Elemental decided to put on a light show for the clan.

Afterward, Valeria's skin was almost completely normal. Residual cracks remained, leaving her skin a little raw, but that problem was solved by soaking in an herbal concoction Salvador had mixed to speed the healing.

The two Elementals left soon after. Salvador stayed a few weeks more—to monitor her progress and to get to know her better. But after a long visit, he left, too. He traveled with Gia, maintaining a mobile healing practice he needed to get back to. Also, he had to go because he missed his mate.

"Before I leave, I wanted to ask something," he said on his last day. "I need to know if you're ready for me to tell our parents about you."

Valeria had been expecting the question, but she hesitated. "I...I think so."

His brows rose. "Are you sure? I admit I don't like keeping this from them, but once they know where you are, they will descend like Valkyries. Nothing short of Mother being in active labor will stop them."

Valeria hugged him, the gesture thankfully pain-free. "I dealt with an evil archangel for months, and I'm shacking up with a dragon. I think I can handle our parents."

His head tilted. "You say that now, but wait until you meet them," he said, making her laugh.

Salvador squeezed her once more before shaking hands with Rhys and leaving with Naveen, who was going to drive him off the mountain.

Rhys hovered over her as she walked to the couch.

"I'm okay to walk on my own," she chided as she sat in front of the fireplace.

"I know. But I may have a hard time letting you for the next few months."

Leaning over, he breathed on the logs, lighting them with his fire.

I'm never going to get tired of that. "Can you come sit with me?"

He was on the couch like a shot. Stretching his long legs out, he dropped an arm around her, tugging her into his side with palpable contentment.

Too bad she had to ruin his good mood.

Valeria leaned against his chest, afraid to look him in the face. "Rhys?"

"Yes, little love?"

"I have to tell you something bad."

His chest and arms turned to corded steel against her. "Is it about Michael?"

I wish. "No...it's about Gabrielle."

Rhys pulled away slightly, staring down at her in confusion. "What about her?"

You can do this.

Valeria took a deep breath reached up to stroke his face. "Remember when I touched her necklace? My experiment with the circle to protect me from the backlash failed, but the actual ability I was trying to recall worked. The psychometry showed me what happened to her."

"Her or you?"

She closed her eyes before opening them to look into his beloved face. He would not face this alone. "I honestly don't know. But I didn't want to tell you because she...she suffered."

He pulled away to stand in front of her. "Tell me."

Valeria stared down at her hands. "You were wrong about her not being a witch. Gabrielle had magic. And I think Michael was watching her, too. But he's not the one who harmed her. It was one of his agents, or a rival. An incubus who had possessed someone on this side."

Rhys started violently.

"An incubus feeds—" she began.

"I know what they do." His neck was corded so tightly that she was worried he couldn't breathe.

"I think the incubus betrayed Michael," she told him gently. "He was supposed to mark Gabrielle for Sheol, but the demon chose to feed on her instead, to get enough strength to stay on this side."

Valeria put a hand on his arm, willing the stone-hard muscles to soften. "She was hanging on by a thread before you met her. The incubus was in her sphere long before you arrived in Vienna, disguised as one of her many suitors. I don't think he planned on going through with the sham marriage until you appeared on the scene."

Rhys' voice was hoarse. "Did my proposal hasten things along?"

"No, I don't think so. What happened was inevitable."

Rhys closed his eyes, taking a moment to compose himself. "Did she know what was happening to her?"

"Yes," Valeria whispered. "That was why she suffered."

His face crumpled. "Why didn't she tell me? I could have helped her."

She grabbed his arm. "Rhys, she wanted to be with you, but she couldn't break free of him. Not enough to ask for help aloud. The incubus' claws were in too deep, controlling her every move. But Gabrielle still had the wherewithal to thwart the demon."

He closed his eyes, filling in the blanks. "She wasn't ill, was she? She took her own life."

Blinking back tears, Valeria nodded. "Laudanum—an opium overdose. It wasn't painful."

Not compared to the life she'd been living.

Heavily, Rhys sat in front of her. Even sitting cross-legged, he was so tall that they were almost at the same head height.

"You keep saying her..." he began.

"I know she was me," Valeria admitted in a whisper. "But I've been trying not to connect with her. I didn't want to identify with her any more than I had to. Seeing through her eyes when I held the necklace was bad enough."

He grimaced. "Because you've had enough bad things in your life."

"Hey." Valeria leaned forward to put her hands on either side of his face. "That would never include you. *Never.*"

His beautiful onyx eyes swam with tears. "I should have saved you back then."

"It was already too late," she whispered.

It had been from the moment he'd laid eyes on her. There hadn't been enough of Gabrielle left. And even if he'd succeeded in marrying her—eloping or something—she would have always been a beautiful shell, but little more.

"And you saved me this time," she reminded him with a squeeze of her hands. "You went to hell to get me."

Rhys tsked, wiping his eyes. "I seem to recall some mutual rescuing —taking the angel's telekinesis to save my men is enough for Veda to write your name amongst our greatest warriors."

She leaned back, pulling him on the couch. "Brilliant. I love that."

Beckoning him closer, Valeria plastered herself against him. He did the same, bending his head until their foreheads were touching. "I was always meant to love you," he said. "You've been mine for centuries, and you'll continue to be mine for eternity. And Valeria—it won't be nearly long enough."

She burrowed into his chest, so full of love she could barely see straight. "Then let's just make the most of today, every day."

"I can do that, my love." Rhys released a shaky breath. "I can do that."

EPILOGUE

Valeria stretched her toes into the sun on the rebuilt deck at the top of Rhys' house. Well, her house now, too.

The dragon clan's territory was home, and, slowly but surely, they were becoming her family—well, part of it anyway.

Her brother Salvador dropped by regularly during his wanders with his mate. So did her parents.

Lucia and Fulgencio had been everything Salvador had warned her about—aggressive, brash, and perhaps a little too morally flexible on some matters. But he was right about the other part. They loved each other, they loved her brother, and they loved the new baby sister they had brought to meet her. And despite what they had once wanted her to be, they had been through enough to give up their pretensions of power and care for her as she was now. And Valeria decided to let them.

After the way she'd grown up, it was strange to be the recipient of so much love and affection. First, there had been Rhys. Then the members of his clan, starting with Sanaa and her kids. Now her brother, sister, and parents.

The weirdest part was that their affection wasn't a transaction. She hadn't done anything to earn it except be herself. Turned out that it had been enough.

Valeria still had many mixed feelings about Ravenna. The mother who raised her had been laid to rest according to clan tradition, cremation on a pyre.

Sometimes, in her head, Valeria would rail against her and what she had done. Other times, she was able to see from Ravenna's perspective and she found it easier to forgive.

It was likely she'd always be conflicted about Ravenna, but, after a while, Valeria decided that was okay, too, as long as it didn't hold her back from living the life she had now.

And that life was good.

She hadn't expected it, but, strangely enough, her biological mother and father approved of Rhys. They liked his wealth and his strength, seeing him as a fitting protector for the child they had once lost themselves.

Not that either had brought that up. Fulgencio and Lucia did not mention Ravenna's name during their entire weeklong visit. It was still too raw a subject for them.

Her parents had left a few days ago. They had kept pushing her to visit them on their estate in South America. Valeria was excited to see it, but she had plans for her first post-Sheol trip out of clan territory. She'd been researching like mad, determined to impress her dragon mate with her cunning plan.

A baby's laugh attracted Valeria's attention. Lanaa was enjoying a snack with her dad on the other side of the pool while her brother paddled with his mother.

Rhys had stubbornly added the pool to the new deck, despite her objections over the extravagance. There was no such thing to a dragon with a horde of treasure. And now that there was a temperature-controlled option to the freezing lake, the other dragons took full advantage, especially the little ones.

There was also a very sturdy rail on the deck now, one with a door Rhys could open to launch himself out over the valley without having to worry she'd fall off the third-story roof.

She was distracted by the sight of the man in question climbing out of the pool in his skin-tight swim trunks. A drop of baby-blue paint was stuck to his shoulder from when he'd helped lift her to the ceiling so she could finish the mural she was painting in the children's nursery.

It depicted a dragon wrapped around a sleepy bear in a gumdrop forest.

Rhys saw her watching and preened a little, shooting her a private smile. That last came a little easier than it had in months past. The love of all her lives was only now calming down with his overprotectiveness. He was also starting to lose some of the reserve that had characterized him when they first met.

For instance, the bat-wings made a brief appearance as he walked toward her. They beat hard for few seconds, pushing the water droplets to the waterproof deck before he sat next to her on the extrawide pool lounger.

"I don't know where you found this reclining chair thing, but it is officially my favorite place to sit in the entire house."

"I thought your favorite place was in front of the fire."

She had told him so yesterday when she had burrowed into his arms after a sushi meal because she hadn't had fish since before Sheol.

"That may be my second favorite now."

He raised a brow. "What about last night in bed?"

"That's not technically sitting," she pointed out with a grin.

A picture of her draped over Rhys after they had made love flashed through her mind. She wasn't afraid of touching him anymore—not after a particularly memorable conversation in the library.

They'd been messing around, reading whatever took their fancy, when he'd crossed her path unexpectedly. Despite everything that had happened, she still jerked away to avoid brushing up against him. Having used that gift intentionally so recently had made her wary of it all over again.

Rhys had apologized and had been ready to take her back to bed because he assumed her skin was still tender after the angel light. When she admitted it was because she feared ensnaring him, he'd laughed.

"How could it be dangerous?" he'd asked dismissively.

"Aside from making you my unwitting love monkey if I'm not careful?" she'd shot back.

He'd shaken his head, taking her face in both his big hands. "Unmindful simian's aside, believe me when I say that this power of yours is of no consequence. Not to me. Not to *us*."

"How can you say that?" she asked, bewildered. "Aren't you concerned that I might be pushing you, leading you to think or say something that you don't want to do?"

His amusement had been reassuring. "I love you as much I can within the bounds of reason and possibly beyond. That's been the case since before this life and will continue into the next—of that, I have no doubt."

He'd pressed a soft kiss to her lips. "No witch's gift of ensnarement could compare."

It was clear Rhys meant every word, so Valeria had slowly begun to pull down that last wall between them.

It wasn't easy. She had to alter the habits of a lifetime, but dragons could be surprisingly patient. And now she had a relationship that was emotionally loving and breathtakingly intimate, something she'd never dreamed she'd have.

But something was nagging at her, one last thing she had to do before she picked up and moved on with the rest of her life.

When he first heard what is was Rhys had scowled and went out back to break some boulders for fun. But after an hour or so of cathartic smashing, he came back inside ready to listen.

He hated the plan, but loved her enough to humor her, especially after she convinced her brother's mate to get on board. Only an Elemental could open the door to Sheol without a human sacrifice.

"You know this is a frivolous reason to break the Covenant," Gia scolded with a maternal-sounding tone as she prepared the opening.

Valeria shrugged. "It's more like bending it. And I don't believe it's frivolous. I think it's important for Michael to see how humans live now. His window into this world is too small. He inevitably takes things out of context. I think he needs a bigger picture. Michael needs to learn how we actually interact with one another."

"And you think soap operas are the way to do that?" Gia asked skeptically.

"I do," Valeria said, laughing.

"Hey, there are plenty of documentaries in there, too," she added, pointing to the piles of books, movie discs, and the specialized video player Michael would need to play them.

There was a duplicate of the latter and several solar-charging devices just in case the first one crapped out or the archangel broke one in a rage.

"Soap operas are something he knows," she continued. "I'm hoping they'll be his entree into figuring out how people tick—the way they love despite adversity and how sometimes they have to compromise to make their way in the world."

She broke off to add another book to the pile. "I'm sure there are a million other things I should have included and didn't. But it's a start."

"You could have preloaded a laptop and e-reader with all this material," Naveen pointed out, picking through the discs that had comprised the Sight and Sound list of the world's greatest movies.

"True, but he is most familiar with what the devout people he uses to look into the world know. Most of these individuals are older and less tech-savvy. But I'm hoping there is enough common knowledge in his memory for him to figure out how to work a disc player."

"He could be dead," her brother added hopefully.

"Evil never dies," Rhys said ominously, unaware he was quoting several movies.

Valeria brushed off her hands. "Michael is immortal or near enough. I think he survived. And, if he did, he's going to be angry. This won't stem that anger, not at first. But it might give him food for thought—if he doesn't smash it to bits after its arrival. I figure that's the best I can do."

If it meant he'd stop targeting witches to help him get to Earth, she had to try. It might even inspire him to take a closer look at where he was and try to make that place better.

That was a big ask for a pile of films and books, but Michael had to start somewhere.

Gia opened the door and pushed the pile through it, sealing the opening shut in less than two seconds. When it was done, Valeria felt a thousand pounds lighter.

"Happy now, love?" Rhys asked, leading her back up the hill after her brother and his mate departed.

"Yeah," she said, slinging an arm around his waist. "I am. It feels like a fresh start, a new beginning."

He put his arm around her shoulder, propelling her to the house. "So, what do you want to do with this new lease on life?"

"Well, it so happens I have a plan," she said, her excitement catching his attention enough to make him stop walking. "I want to go treasure hunting."

Rhys's amusement lit his eyes. "If that's what you want to do, I will take you wherever you wish to go. But we could do anything—sailing around the Azores...shopping in Paris. Or I can fly you to Rome for the perfect dish of pasta."

He raised his arms wide to encompass their surroundings. "There are no limits. I plan on giving you the world. There is no need to restrict yourself to treasure hunting for my sake. "

Valeria stopped, crestfallen. "But I want to go! And I thought you'd leap at the chance to get back out there. Isn't seeking treasure a dragon's favorite pastime?"

He rubbed her back. "Oh, don't get me wrong. I would take great pleasure in guiding you on your first hunt—to see you experience the thrill of finding a gold coin or precious gem for the very first time. But I no longer feel the need to search for such trinkets myself."

"You don't?" she asked skeptically.

He squeezed her to him. "I already found the greatest treasure there is."

Valeria snickered, hugging him around the waist. "So cheesy," she said, laughing.

Rhys grinned, nudging her with his hip. "You love it."

"I do." Valeria leaned her head against him, sighing contentedly as they reached the house. "I really do."

THE END.

ABOUT THE AUTHOR

A 7-time Readers' Favorite Medal Winner. USA Today Bestselling Author. Former scientist. Recovering geek. Mom. WOC.

L.B. Gilbert is another name for USA Today Bestselling Author Lucy Leroux. She is an award-winning novelist who spent years getting degrees from the most prestigious universities in America, including a PhD that she is not using at all. She moved to France for work and found love. Her family moved back to California a few years ago after a decade abroad.

Lucy has always enjoyed reading books as far from her reality as possible but eventually the voices in her head told her to write her own. And so far the voices are enjoying them.

And if you like a little more steam with your Fire, check out the author's Lucy Leroux titles...

www.elementalauthor.com

or

www.authorlucyleroux.com

amazon.com/stores/L.B.-Gilbert/author/B015T01IVU

facebook.com/elementalsauthor

twitter.com/elementalauthor

instagram.com/elementalauthor

bookbub.com/profile/l-b-gilbert

tiktok.com/@lucythenovelist